"I can't imagine waking up to this view every morning."

"You can," he says. "I won't stop you."

She swallows hard. He can be so tempting when he wants to be. She looks down at her plate, deciding to bite into her garlic bread before taking another drink.

"Hey, the offer never expires." He picks up his glass, eyeing her deliciously.

Eileen wipes her lips with a napkin. Her heart is beating erratically. Why is he so alluring? When she took the coaching job she never suspected that she would fall for one of them; in fact, she was teased when the idea surfaced that they would be fighting over her. That, of course, wasn't true; she kept her eyes on the job. But Ty just has a way of magically securing her neediness and leaving her wanting more. Is he testing her to see how far she'll go? Did he really have a bet going on to see if she would sleep with him?

Without notice, Ty leans over his chair and gently takes her face in his hand, his lips closer, like they are calling for her. She jumps suddenly, realizing that he is about to kiss her. She is craving his affection, yet scared to lead him on. His hand cups the back of her neck, easing forward.

She closes her eyes, wanting so bad to kiss him back. "I can't," she whispers, anticipating his touch.

"It's only a kiss," he whispers back as his lips find hers . . .

HIS GAME, HER RULES

CHARLENE GROOME

KENSINGTON BOOKS
KENSINGTON PUBLISHING CORP.
http://www.kensingtonbooks.com

ACKNOWLEDGMENTS

I would like to sincerely thank the people who helped me make this book possible.

My husband, Jared, for supporting my dreams and encouraging me to keep writing.

My amazing literary agent, Dawn Dowdle of Blue Ridge Literary Agency, for believing in me. It's a pleasure to work with you.

My wonderful editor at Kensington Books, John Scognamiglio for your support and encouragement. I'm really proud to be working with you.

There are other people to thank for their hard work. Emily Lawrence, for your helpful suggestions and keen eye; my copyeditor, Erin Barker, for your attention to detail; production editor Ross Plotkin; and the design team for making such an attractive cover.

Thank you!

Chapter 1

Eileen Francis parallel parks her car on a side street at downtown's most popular ice rink: the Dome, home of the Vancouver Warriors Hockey Club. She steps out of her car, trying to get her balance from her black Nine West sling-back sandals and digs into her oversized purse for change to feed the parking meter. She is sure she has quarters at the bottom of her purse, remembering that she tossed in a bunch of change this morning.

Eileen glances at her pearl-faced watch. "Come on, come on," she mutters to herself as she continues to dig, shuffling her wallet around and sifting through scattered Tic Tacs and old receipts, hoping to find a quarter or two beneath the garbage.

She scrapes through the nickels and dimes and finds four quarters, which will only give her forty minutes. Surely the interview won't take that long, will it? They know who she is and what she does. She brought along her skates and a change of clothes in case they ask to see her perform. She knows the interview in the boardroom won't be as important as the interview on the ice, but that may have to be on another day, if she gets through the first round. Eileen inserts the last of her four quarters, and digs for more, hoping to make an hour. She was positive she had enough, but should have been more prepared for a once-in-a-lifetime opportunity. Forty minutes will have to do. She turns quickly, steps to the side without looking up, and her shoulder makes contact with another person. The edge of her heel wobbles, throwing her off balance and causing her to fall backwards and hit the parking meter before a hand reaches out to grab her arm and keep her from falling to the ground.

"Are you okay?" the man asks.

She gasps a breath and moves her feet around to feel solid ground. "Yeah," she answers in a daze, meeting the man's blue eyes.

It's a recognizable face; she's seen this winsome grin before, although she can't recall his name at the moment. He is wearing long beach shorts and T-shirt. His blond hair is messy, yet stylish. Flustered that she is short on time, and not as prepared as she should be for an interview—like making sure she has quarters for the meter—she uses her index finger to slide her thick-rimmed sunglasses up, waiting for the familiar-looking guy to walk past. However, to her surprise, he stops and asks, "Do you need some change?"

He reaches into his side pocket. His voice is warm and subtle, putting her more at ease. "How much do you need?" He pulls out some change and holds it toward her.

A little taken aback, Eileen smiles and says, "Thank you. My mom always told me not to take money from strangers."

He laughs. "Money? I thought it was candy. Don't take candy from strangers," he says, still grinning, showing off a dimple on his left cheek.

"Candy, money—to a child it's all the same, isn't it?" she asks, trying hard not to get stuck at staring into his deep blue eyes. They are so bright and light that they remind her of glass marbles.

"I guess, eh?" he says. He picks out coins from his hand and feeds the meter. "How long do you need? You've got an hour and a half."

"That's perfect! Thank you," she says and pulls out a five-dollar bill from her purse. "Here." She gestures for him to take it.

"Ah, don't worry about it." He slides the leftover change into his pocket. "My name's Ty," he says and extends his hand.

Eileen can't help the permanent smile on her face and she gives his hand a firm squeeze. His name comes to mind. "Caldwell," she states. The star hockey player for the Warriors. He looks even better in person than on TV.

He nods.

"Eileen Francis," she says in her businesslike tone. "Nice to meet you." She adjusts her purse on her shoulder and stands tall, looking up slightly to meet his glorious eyes. "Thank you for the change."

"No problem!" He's still standing in front of her as though not yet finished with their conversation.

She glances at her watch and moves her purse strap over her shoulder, trying to distract herself from getting caught gawping at him. "Well, I have to go! I'm going to be late for my interview," she says, not wanting to tell him she could be his new skating coach if all goes well today.

This could be a chance of a lifetime, a rare opportunity that just happened to come her way thanks to her uncle Gary, the senior adviser to the general manager of the Warriors. The phrase, "it's not what you know, it's who you know" enters her mind, but she knows that, to the surprise of most, she is just as talented as the guys who play professionally.

She pushes her sunglasses back as she peeks through the glass window to see a woman with a broom in one hand and a dustpan in the other, listening to her iPod as she cleans the floor. Eileen knocks on the door, hoping to get the woman's attention, but the woman is in her own world, her black ponytail is swaying like a tree branch in the wind as she grooves to the music. Eileen knocks again and waves her arms to get the woman's attention.

"Are you looking for the offices?" a male voice asks from behind her.

Eileen jumps with fright, and her glasses move down her nose. She looks behind her, relaxing her shoulders when she sees Ty Caldwell again. "I am." She smiles back at him. "I can't remember what door I'm supposed to go to."

"I'll show you another way in. Follow me," he says with a wave.

She doesn't remember her uncle telling her about a private entrance. Thankfully, Ty found her and will help her get in and point her to the right direction.

"Great!" She takes quick, small steps, afraid she'll do a face-plant on the sidewalk if she's not watching where she's going. Eileen has never been late for anything; it's one of her personal rules. If she's going to be late, she can kiss this job good-bye.

"Are you interviewing for guest services?"

Eileen smirks.

"What's funny about that?" he asks. "You wouldn't be here for the skating coach position." He laughs to himself.

She tightens her lips. Her eyebrows rise, causing her sunglasses to move.

He laughs again. "You're kidding!" He stops in his tracks. His head tilts slightly and his mouth tugs at the side. "You're kidding, right?"

"Why is it so funny? Your skating coach has taken a leave and they need a replacement until he can come back."

"Are you sure you're not confused with coach's personal assistant?" he asks, beginning to laugh some more. "I know he's looking for one."

She lifts her oversized sunglasses off her face and pulls them back as a headband. "Hmmm, I don't think I have those qualifications," she says. "Or the patience."

"As a skating coach?" he asks, opening the door for her.

She lifts an eyebrow. "I've never known a coach to have a personal assistant. Maybe you were confused with the owner?" she says, trying to offer him a better suggestion as they walk to the elevator and Ty presses the button.

"What qualifications do you have to teach professional hockey players?" he asks, sounding intrigued. "I'm curious. I didn't know the Warriors hired outside . . . talent."

She stands up straighter and looks at him. He sure knows how to rattle one's confidence before an interview. "First off, I'm one of the most skilled female hockey players in the country."

"Yeah, but still—"

"It's because I'm a woman."

"Well, it's just, you know, a guy's league—"

"Uh-huh." She waits patiently for him to recover.

"I know we need a coach, but—" He pauses.

"I just happen to be female." She keeps her head high. Why is she wasting her time convincing him? It's management she needs to sell herself to. "But it's the job I am interested in and a job I do quite well."

They step into the elevator.

He laughs as the door closes. "You could have fooled me."

"I've played nationally, as well as for the Olympics. Twice."

"And that makes you a professional?"

She gives him a fake smile with the intent to kill him with kindness. "Yes. If women were playing in the NHL, I'd be playing."

The elevator doors open. "Well, here we are," Ty announces.

"If you want a skating tip: races are won or lost in the first three strides," she says, gripping her heavy purse.

"Huh." He nods.

"Thanks for the interview warm-up," she says as she takes a step out into the hall. "And for your personal assistance showing me to the right floor."

"I'm glad I could help," Ty says with a forced grin.

She points her finger in the direction of where she thinks she should go.

He nods. "You want the last door down the hall," he says, sticking his head out of the elevator and pointing. "Good luck. I might see you on the ice." The elevator doors begin to close.

"Thanks," she says, getting one last look at him before she's on her own.

Eileen follows the bright blue carpet to the end of the hall, noticing a gallery of framed hockey scenes and players displayed throughout the top floor. Eileen can't help but stop to take a quick look. How great would it be to work here? The thought is enough to weaken her knees. When she was a child, her dad and uncle would talk proudly about Canada's national sport and her uncle, especially, would say he has the best job in the world. She admired him. How could she not want to be part of the greatest sport there is and have the chance to work alongside her uncle? Not that she would work directly with him, because his job is to scout for new talent and evaluate players, but it would be nice to be part of the same profession.

Eileen takes in a deep breath and then slowly opens the door, peeking inside and hoping it's the right entrance and not some joke Ty is playing on her. She isn't sure he can be trusted. There is something about him that doesn't sit right; she knows that men in this league are all selfish and irresponsible because, in this country, they are put on pedestals and the fame goes to their heads. At least that was her experience with her ex-boyfriend.

"Hello. May I help you?" the receptionist asks as Eileen walks up to the desk.

"I'm here to see Gary Williams."

The young woman with shoulder-length hair bats her light brown eyes. "You must be Eileen," she says, her eyes suddenly shining.

Eileen smiles at the warm welcome. "Yes, I am."

"I finally have a face to a name. Nice to meet you. I'll let your uncle know you're here." She speaks softly into her headset. "He'll be right out. You can have a seat while you wait if you'd like."

"Thank you," Eileen says and then walks away from the desk, letting her eyes drift around the room, admiring the memorabilia hanging on the walls. She glances at her watch—two minutes after nine. She's late. She hopes they're too busy to notice. She squeezes her hands together to contain the jitters and clenches her jaw as she thinks about the interview.

"Elle!" a voice yells out.

"Uncle Gary!" she exclaims and walks toward him, holding back from giving him the usual hug, but he makes the first move and wraps his arms around her. A quick squeeze relaxes her, and lets her know she has his support. "How was Arizona?"

"Hot!"

"Looks like you got some sun," she says, eyeing his uneven graying strands, which look white against his leathery, tanned skin. Even his mustache is sprouting gray.

"Got some golf in," he says, extending his arms and taking a pretend swing. "Our place was right beside a golf course. We had a great time. Your aunt is making arrangements to go back."

Although Gary's blue eyes are behind thin-rimmed glasses, their oval shape reminds Eileen of her mother's. She beams at him and remembers her mom. The sweetness of her voice, her kind nature, and the love she had for her children has been irreplaceable. She misses her parents. She sniffs to clear her nose and blinks. This is the last place she would allow herself to be weepy. She throws back her shoulders and stands up straighter.

"You should come with us next time. We'll do a family trip and I'll get Keaton to bring some friends," he says with a wink.

Eileen just smiles. She knows what her uncle is getting at. His son, Keaton Williams, plays for the Kings and he'd probably bring along some of his teammates to hang out with. There is no way Eileen is going to get involved with a hockey player. She did that once before and it was a big mistake.

"I'll take you into the boardroom for our meeting and introduce you to the coach and owner; they'll be sitting in on this meeting as well."

"Okay," she says and lets out a heavy breath. *This is it. Time to impress.* She follows his lead down the hall.

"They can't wait to meet you. I've talked a lot about you. Remember, just be yourself," Gary whispers and pats her on her shoulder. "Don't be nervous. You'll do great."

"Me, nervous? Never." She laughs, trying to hide her unsettled nerves. Do they genuinely want to work with Eileen or are they doing her uncle a favor?

Gary pats her on the shoulder again and swings open the boardroom door. Silence clouds the room as Eileen steps inside. She views their long faces and stern upper lips.

"This is Eileen Francis," Gary says proudly, taking a side step. "Eileen, please have a seat." He closes the door behind her. "I'll introduce you. To my left is Ted Walker, the president and general manager of the Warriors. Rick Bissel, VP of hockey operations. Steve Morrow, the head coach . . . and Joe Smith, the assistant coach."

They each nod in turn.

"Everyone, Eileen Francis," he says with an upbeat demeanor.

"Thank you," she says, making eye contact with each of them.

"Eileen comes to us with years of experience and talent," Gary says, beaming. "I'm not just saying it because she's my niece; Eileen is a very capable young woman and I know she can help our team develop the skills we are looking for."

Eileen clears her throat while trying really hard not to show her excitement of being in the same room as the Warriors' management team. She rubs her sweaty palms on her thighs of her summer dress.

"Her skating ability is above standard and I believe she'd be an excellent choice to replace Ritchie," Gary says and then turns to Eileen with hopeful eyes. "This would only be temporary of course, but I know she can do the job well."

"So you are here for the skills coaching position?" Ted asks, lowering his round, chubby face to meet Eileen's eyes. "The job focuses on skating. It's temporary, but we need someone to fill Ritchie's skates until he comes back. I don't know exactly how long he needs. So this would be a contract position for now. And"—Ted lifts his head, folds his beefy hands on the table, and leans in—"we're heading into training camp. It's critical we get the boys off on a strong footing."

Eileen nods slightly, giving him her full attention.

Steve straightens up and folds his hands together. He's the youngest of the men sitting at the table. His dirty-blond hair is feathery as though it has just been washed and left to dry. When he jots notes on his notepad, he looks sideways at Eileen and his hair slides forward, covering his forehead. "We had a horrible season last year, one we don't ever want to repeat. We have some exceptional players, but we need to practice playing together and build chemistry with some of our new players. That's my job, to shuffle lines, but we have a lot to do this season and we're looking to make changes. I need to make sure we coach these guys with the full ability and dedication."

"No offense, Eileen, but you are a woman," Rick says, his voice husky. He stares her down with squinted brown eyes, the same color as his tailored suit.

"And obviously you've never played in the NHL," Joe says, his mouth twitching into a smirk. He places one hand behind his head, feeling the short strands of his brown hair. He smirks again, releasing his hand to the table.

She relaxes her shoulders. Eileen isn't going to let him make her feel incapable. Joe's cold stare makes his brown eyes seem black. Her body quivers and she has to look away from him before he gets the best of her.

"You're right. I haven't played in the NHL," she says with a devious smile. "But I have equal talent as the men on your team. I've played in the 2010 Olympics in Whistler and 2014 Olympics in Sochi—"

"Congratulations on winning gold," Steve interjects. "That was a huge accomplishment."

"Thank you. It's one of my most prized possessions," she admits.

"And it should be."

"Did you see her on the cover of *Maclean's* magazine?" Gary asks. He turns in her direction and smiles.

"She was also on a cereal box," Rick snaps. "I want to see the skills, not hear about them." He taps his pen on his notepad.

"I've also played for the women's national hockey team," she emphasizes. "And currently I run my own hockey school. I teach all ages how to skate and the fundamentals of hockey."

"But can you teach professional hockey players new skills?" Rick asks with a sarcastic laugh. He runs his fingers through his thinning, coffee-colored hair and stops at the crown of his head. He narrows his eyes, studying her like he's judging her looks.

A professional player is as good as it gets. Isn't she considered a professional?

Eileen steels her gaze at Rick. "Yes. I wouldn't be here if I didn't believe I could do the job."

"She can skate circles around them," Gary interrupts and then bows his head when all eyes are on him.

"I'm sure she can," Rick says.

"It doesn't mean she can teach," Joe snarls, puffing out his chest to make his small frame bigger. "It takes a certain attitude and skill to be able to get through to the guys."

"I'm not an intimidating person, is that it?" Eileen asks jokingly. She notices his stubby nose twitch.

"Look, the boys need coaching while they practice," Gary says. "I know you would much rather have a male teach them, but this girl's got what it takes." He lifts his hand up and motions it toward her as though she's on display at an auction. "Just wait until you see her skate and see what she can do. I'll bet my house she can show the boys some new skills."

Eileen takes a breath. *No pressure, no pressure*, she thinks, trying to calm herself.

"We believe you, Gary," Steve says. "But let's face it, the guys are going to take one look at her and laugh. Sorry, Eileen, but I just don't think this is going to work."

She shakes her head. Maybe they have someone else in mind for the job. Didn't Gary tell them she was female before she arrived? What was the point of her coming here today if she didn't have a chance? She would be at the top of her career if she got the job. Just when she is about to say that they should give her a trial run, Gary interrupts with a sales pitch.

"Look, Ritchie is gone for approximately eight to twelve weeks— we know that. There's no obligation to have Eileen fill in."

The men study Eileen as if she were some foreign object.

Gary breaks the silence. "Who will you find in a short time that has this much experience and will be willing to take the job not knowing how long it will be for?"

Rick bites his lower lip.

"I brought some lesson plans." She reaches into her purse and pulls out a folder. "Obviously nothing can compare to being on the ice, but this will give you an idea of what I teach."

The men pass around the handouts. Their eyes skim the stapled pages.

She would just have to fight back without words. That is, if they gave her the opportunity.

Rick ignores the question and turns his attention on Eileen in a sharp but direct tone. "Do you honestly believe you have what it takes to teach these men performance skating?"

Eileen is so tired of men making her feel like she is not worthy of the game.

"Why can't I?" Eileen snaps. She isn't going to let these men make her feel incapable. She doesn't need this job; she *wants* it. For the accomplishment, for the bragging rights, to top her resume.

Rick pushes in his face as though caught off guard. "You may think that you can—"

"Oh, I can," she retorts, knowing she has nothing to lose. "I'm sure you think because I'm female I can't do the job."

"I didn't think that at all," Rick defends. "What I'm getting at is, can you handle it? It has nothing to do with you being a woman." He moves his chest in closer to the table and folds his hands on his notepad. "Some players may have a hard time accepting a woman instructing them," he says, lowering his voice and making eye contact with a cold stare. "Especially when it comes to hockey. Are you going to take it personally? Or are you going to give up after a week? It won't be easy."

She wouldn't let anyone push her around and tell her she can't do this job. No one's stood in her way before.

"When I'm on the ice, I give a hundred and ten percent. It's a job that I'm passionate about." She pauses. "I won't be easy on them."

"I appreciate your effort," Rick says with a chuckle. "But I can tell you there are at least five guys on the team who will give you a hard time. How will you handle it? I mean if you're giving an instruction and a guy heckles you because he says he was taught the exercise when he played Bantam, how will you respond? Will you give up?"

"Of course not!" Eileen says, resting her arms on the arm rests, trying to appear calm in front of the panel of judges. "First off, I respect—"

"Respect is earned." Ted lingers on the word as though giving valuable advice.

"Yes," Eileen agrees. "I know at first it will be hard for the guys to take, but I can assure you that once I show them how they will benefit from my instruction, I'll earn respect."

"You think so?" Ted says. "It won't be easy."

"I don't expect it to be," she answers.

The men are once again silent, scribbling notes and staring at Eileen until the owner pipes up, "Can we see you skate? Show us what you've got?"

"I brought my skates!"

Ted glances at his watch. "We practice in an hour. It should give us enough time to see you skate, and for you to show us a few lessons."

"Let's go to the rink," Rick says. "See what you can do." He slaps his hands down on the table before standing up.

Eileen is determined to nail this. "I'll get ready." She picks up her purse.

"We'll be right down," Steve says.

Chapter 2

Eileen opens the bench door, breathes in the cool air, and steps onto the clean, smooth ice surface. A surge of adrenaline rushes through her body as she glides on her skates, warming up before launching into instruction with Steve and Joe.

She stretches out one leg at a time, making sure every joint feels flexed and every muscle is limber. She doesn't want to disappoint her male judges or her worst critic: herself. She came prepared to show the Warriors she can do the job as well as any man.

Steve, the head coach, joins her on the ice. "Hockey must run in the family," he says as he strides alongside her.

"It does," Eileen replies, focusing on stretching out her quadriceps and hamstrings. She had time to run to her car to grab her hockey stick.

"How long have you been playing?"

"For as long as I can remember. My cousin Keaton Williams plays for L.A. and my dad and brother played hockey, too—not professionally, although they both always dreamed of it. And, of course, my uncle Gary."

"Very good," he says. "You've had a lot of exposure."

"I guess."

"Well, good luck today," Steve says, making a turn for the bench to grab a bag of pucks.

Joe skates up to her. "Let's get started, shall we? Show us what's on the agenda, Ms. Francis. The guys will be on the ice in under an hour."

Steve dumps the pucks on the ice.

"Okay, I'm ready," Eileen says, skating with her stick in hand and scooping up a puck as the two men trail behind, watching her every move. She stops at the goal line.

"One exercise I teach in many of my classes is a simple passing drill called 'follow the leader,' " she says.

"They're not amateurs." Joe smirks.

She ignores him and continues explaining. "This drill works for every skill level. The trick to this practice involves more than two players, making you keep your eye on where the man with the puck is," she explains. "Wherever the player with the puck is, you need to make sure they can receive the pass as you skate toward the net. I'll show you. Joe, follow me," she tells him and he watches her carefully. "I'll pass the puck to you and you do a drop pass so that Steve picks it up and skates along the boards.

"When we have more players on the ice, they will act as the opposing team and will try to intercept the pass. Got it?"

She skates hard and pushes Joe to make a mistake. With a few fumbles of his stick, they make it through the first drill. Eileen runs through some of her most challenging drills, hoping to win them over. When her instruction is over, she skates to the bench and grabs her water bottle for a quick drink. The two men follow.

"Where did you learn to skate like that?" Steve asks. His grin gives her a boost of confidence.

She gulps down some more water before replying. "What do you mean?"

"You're good."

"Thanks." She smiles. "I'm a professional, remember?" she tells them modestly, but can't help the grin that creeps on her lips. She eyes Joe and he gives her a cold stare.

"And the drills? I don't think I've seen those before."

She keeps her attention on Steve. "They're my own." She swallows some water. "I've tried something similar in one of my skating classes, but it's less complicated, of course."

"Oh, that's right," Steve says. "You run a hockey school. Well, I think your strong skills may have an impact on our team."

"I hope so," she agrees. "Or I wouldn't be here."

Joe pipes up, "The job will probably only be for a few weeks. Hardly worth your time."

"Oh, it's worth it. Are you kidding?" She meets his dark stare again, and a shiver runs down her spine.

"Before we make a decision, it's up to Ted and Rick. They're watching from the box seat." He looks up to the near corner of the arena.

Eileen doesn't want to follow his eyes, afraid to find the men peering down.

"What's there to think about?" Eileen asks. "Either I have the job or I don't."

There is a brief moment of silence, and she relaxes her stick to her side. "I can't see what there is to think about except the fact that I'm female and that it could cause conflict for the team," she says. "Once the guys see what I can do, I'm sure they'll change their minds."

"I'll be honest with you, Eileen," Joe says with a straight face. "You're right. I'm not sexist, but the competition here—"

"There's no competition, Joe. I'm all you have right now," Eileen shoots back. She isn't sure if they interviewed other people for the job, but why not be overconfident rather than mousy? All she has to do is demonstrate she has what it takes. "Give me a chance and I will prove to you that by the time this team plays their exhibition games, they will have developed new skills and—"

Joe cuts her off. "That's a big promise."

"I am confident I can do my job."

Steve grins and says, "Ultimately, the decision is up to Rick and Ted, but if I can give you some advice. When and if you get the job, at the next couple of practices, work the guys hard and use your skills to show them new practice drills. It will only increase your chances of keeping this job."

"Okay, but I hope your boys are used to hard work," she says.

"They know what hard work is," Joe snaps. "They're professional athletes."

"Good! So do I! We'll work perfectly together then," she says, driven by his lack of interest in her.

"Hey, Coach!" a man calls out to Steve as he walks closer to the bench.

"Caldwell!" Steve answers with a lift of his chin. His parted dirty-blond hair slides along his temples.

Ty approaches the group; he smiles at Eileen and announces to his coaches, "Lenny phoned me, says he's sick, maybe food poisoning? Says he couldn't get a hold of you but would call you later."

"Thanks," Steve says. "I got the message already." He looks up at the box and gives a thumbs-up.

"Oh, okay," Ty says, and his blue eyes meet Eileen's gaze before leaving. "I see you're back for more."

"You two have met?" Steve asks.

"I let her into the building," Ty answers. "Good to see you again." His eyes are sucking her in like a sponge, and she can't seem to free herself from his magnetic gaze. "Well, I've got to get ready. See ya!" Ty disappears down the hall, leaving her feeling warm like melted butter.

"He'll be one of your hardest critics," Joe warns.

Steve hollers, "Tell the guys I want them on the ice right away. I want to introduce Eileen to the team." He gives her a nod and wink. "I can't see why you don't have the job."

"Seriously?" she asks.

"Ted's not usually this quiet. If he objects hiring you, he would have said something by now."

Eileen smiles. "Thanks."

"Don't forget, work the guys hard during practice if you want to keep the job."

Ty walks into the locker room, where his teammates are tying up their skates and taping their chin guards, talking amongst themselves. "Steve wants us on the ice! Right away!" His sounds both cool and irritated.

"What's the rush?" Bret Thompson asks, looking up from securing his laces.

"I don't know," one player says. "Probably the new skating coach."

"I don't know if they hired her yet," Ty says.

"Her?" Bret asks.

Ty grabs his helmet from his cubbyhole. "Yeah. Eileen Francis."

"What's this organization coming to?" Bret asks, rolling clear tape around his socks.

"I know. It blows."

"How do you know her name?"

"I ran into her."

"Oh, yeah, she must be a killer if you talked to her," Bret says. "What's she like?"

"Are you sure you talked to the right woman?" Mark Buckley asks.

"Yeah, is she butchy and talks like a guy?" Another player mimicked a deep female voice.

The team joins in, laughing.

Ty snaps on his helmet. "You would think so, but not what you'd expect."

"What do you mean?"

"She's good looking!" Ty says. "I'm not kidding. She's hot! I don't know how she plans to teach us anything—we'll be too distracted."

"Looks don't mean anything," Mark yells out from across the room.

"Just wait until you meet her," Ty urges. All he needs is to have the guys tease him about sleeping with the coach, but judging by her professionalism, it will take more than a simple request to make her want to have sex with him. "You'll know what I mean."

"I'm sure they hired her based on her performance," Mark yells out. "How couldn't they?"

"I wonder how good she can perform." Bret smirks, as he laces up his hockey shorts. "Does anyone want to bet how long it will take before Caldwell gets her into bed? You've probably made the moves on her already, haven't you, Slick?"

Ty concentrates on lacing his skate. "I don't know. . . . She's cute, no doubt about that, but who knows if she'll be able to keep up."

"How did she get the job anyways? You can't tell me that there wasn't a guy that had experience!" Bret asks.

"I don't know," Ty says, walking to the door with his stick. "I was just watching her skate and she's pretty good."

"She's got to know someone in the league. How else does a woman get hired or know about the position?" Bret asks, throwing his roll of tape into his bag and walks toward the door.

"That's all we need, a woman telling us what to do," Bret added.

Another player called, "She won't last long—one or two shifts and she'll call it quits."

"It depends on her attitude. If she has one, she may stick around for a while, just like you, Slick," says a player. "Just like you."

"Hey, what does having an attitude have to do with it?" Ty asks.

"It means a lot. If she doesn't take crap from anyone, she'll stick around," Mark says. "But I haven't yet met a woman like that."

"I've spoken to her," Ty says casually. "She definitely has an edge to her."

"Then she'll be staying for sure."

Ty shakes his head as he heads out of the locker room. "Not if I can help it."

Chapter 3

"Do you ever see Cathy?" Eileen asks jokingly, sipping her water and enjoying dinner with her brother at the golf course he manages.

"She doesn't complain," Nick says. "She knows it's temporary. My assistant quit and I haven't been able to replace her."

"And the kids? I haven't seen them recently," she says, feeling guilty about not stopping by for her weekly visit.

"You're busy," he says, scooping a bite of rice into his mouth. "Max seems to be growing every day. He sure reminds me of Dad."

"Oh, yeah?"

"The way he talks himself out of punishment. He tries making deals with me," he says, shaking his head with a small sideways grin. "I'll wash your car, Dad. Or, I'll cut the grass. Even though he doesn't do those things, being five years old, he sure knows how to throw out the charm."

Eileen laughs. "Always thinking like Dad did."

He nods. "I caught Max and his friend climbing the neighbor's fence to get to the apple trees. I told him the fence was there for a reason, and Max's explanation was he wanted to help pick up the fallen apples. He knew he wasn't supposed to trespass, but he puts a spin on it so that he won't get into trouble."

"Smart kid."

"It's hard to get mad at him. He looks so much like Dad. Sometimes when I'm talking to him, I get flashbacks—a certain look he gives. It's very eerie."

"At least you get a glimpse of Dad every now and then. I miss them so much, especially now that I'm working with the Warriors. Dad would have been excited," she says, feeling the tears prick the back of her eyes. "He loved the game."

"Yes, he did. You know he would be proud."

She grins, then asks, her voice quiet, "Nick, do you ever think that if Mom and Dad had left the party later that night, they would have been alive today?" They've had the same discussion many times over and it doesn't matter how many what-ifs they ask, it can't bring their parents back.

"It was black ice, Elle," Nick says tiredly. "Had they left later, I'm sure the accident would've still happened. The car lost control. Flipped over into a ditch. Even if they did survive, they wouldn't have been the same. You know that."

"I know." Eileen pouts. "I just think that if they drove home at a different time, it wouldn't have happened."

Nick picks up his ice water. "Dad had an early bedtime, always had. He got up at the crack of dawn. They wouldn't have stayed past nine o'clock." He takes a sip and sets down his glass in front of him.

"I don't know where the five years have gone," she says, playing with her fork, rolling it between her thumb and finger.

"Wait until you have kids. You'll miss Mom and Dad even more."

Eileen swallows a bite. "Is that even possible?"

"Every day is a reminder of what they are missing out on," he says somberly.

"One day, maybe kids will be in my future."

"Just don't go hooking up with another hockey player."

"Don't worry. I don't want a repeat of what happened with Mario."

"That was a big lesson, huh?"

Eileen falls quiet. Her brother wouldn't understand her relationship with Mario.

She loved him. And just like any relationship when one was on the road half the year, they had their difficulties. Mario was exciting to be around and she hasn't found that spark with anyone else.

"Now that you're working with jocks, your choices are unlimited."

She smirks. "I'm not falling for any of them. Not like I have an interest . . ." she says, thinking that some of the guys on the team do have the looks to sway a woman's mind. But she has better things to do with her time than fall for a guy who she knows would eventually break her heart.

"Did you see your poster I stapled to the bulletin board at the entrance?"

"How could I miss it? You put it front and center," she says. "Thank you. Every bit of advertising helps."

"Cathy posted one at the rec center where Max takes his swimming lessons."

"Thank you. I appreciate it," Eileen says. "I've had inquiries for my co-ed program starting in September. I already have two full classes! Normally that doesn't happen until weeks before the class starts."

"That's good then."

"My new website seems to be working for me. People can call me direct or email me."

"Excuse me, Nick," says a woman employee dressed in a black skirt, with shoulder-length hair. "A guest would like to know if he could reserve a day for a tournament at the end of this month."

"August is completely booked up," he says.

"That's what I told him, but he doesn't believe me," she says.

Nick glances at Eileen. "I'll have to speak to him." He wipes his face with the cloth napkin and stands up. "I'll be a few minutes."

"Take your time," Eileen says, scooping up a veggie with her fork. "I'm almost done and then I should get going."

"Don't worry about the bill. I'll take care of it," Nick says as he leaves with the hostess.

She finishes her meal and takes a sip of water.

"Eileen?"

She looks up to meet those glorious blue eyes that have her mystified.

"Caldwell!"

"Alone tonight?"

"Uh, no, no." She shakes her head, noticing his striped polo shirt and tanned arms. "I was just leaving." She stands up from her seat and picks up her small purse.

"How's your shoulder?"

"My shoulder?"

"Hope you didn't crash into the parking meter too hard."

"Oh, yeah, no, I'm fine. Not even a scratch!" she says and laughs.

"Good thing the meter was there. You came pretty close to falling to the ground."

But you saved me.

"I had my balance," she says.

"Just finished a round of golf. Some friends of mine are in the dining room. Did you want to join us for a drink?"

"Thanks. I'm going to head home."

"Are you sure? It's just a few of the guys from the team. Come on," he urges. "You're one of the guys now." He laughs. "Come have a beer!"

"I guess I could stay for a few minutes."

She follows Ty to the dining room and spots the table with familiar faces, all of whom have a drink in their hands.

"Look who I found!" Ty announces as he pulls up a chair beside his spot. The guys say hi and a server approaches the table.

"Rum and Diet Coke, please," Eileen orders.

"We have a hard ball!" one player says.

"I know what I like," she says, flashing him a raised eyebrow. "Why change?"

"I'll drink to that," he says and swigs his frothy dark ale.

"What are you doing here by your lonesome?" Ty asks, throwing his leg over his opposite knee, half covered by his long shorts. He sits back, relaxed in his chair.

"I came by to see my brother. He runs this place."

"Your brother?" Ty asks, leaning forward.

"Yeah, you seem shocked."

Ty lifts a shoulder. "I guess I am."

The server sets down her drink and takes the guys' dinner orders.

"So, it's been two practices. How do you think we're doing so far?" Ty asks, bringing his lips to his glass. She tries to look away, but can't. She has to answer his question. He pulls his glass away from his mouth, his top lip plump, and she can only imagine what it would be like to have those planted on hers. She has to stop thinking about him this way. It will only get her into trouble.

"I think it will take a good month for us to gel as a team, with new players . . ." Her voice trails off. "Give it time. We just need to get our goalies comfortable with the D and vice versa."

"Funny, that's what Steve was saying."

"Is that right?" she asks, her eyes wide, for she hadn't spoken to Steve or Joe about the team's positioning yet. "It's a good thing we're on the same page, then."

"So tell us. How did you get the job?" Ty asks.

"I'm qualified," she answers.

"I gather that, but how did you get the job? It's not known for the league to hire a random person."

"Wait a minute! I have a pretty solid resume to be teaching this caliber of hockey. If I were a guy, I wouldn't be questioned."

"No, it's not that—"

"Sure, it is!"

"You have to admit, it's unheard of."

"Times are changing," she says. "I just happen to love what I do and it shows."

The guys exchange glances. Eileen doesn't let it bother her though. For the next couple of months or how long she will be their skating coach for, they'll see she's an asset to the team and forget that she is female.

"How did you find out about it?" Ty asks, shaking his elevated foot.

Eileen holds the straw to her mouth. She didn't think about this question after the interview. Of course guys would pry.

"It wasn't like the job was posted. You must have known about it through the organization," he says.

"I know someone," she says modestly, keeping a hand around her glass.

"Who?" Ty asks.

The men at the table stop their conversations among themselves and listen in.

She is tempted to lie, but then if the truth comes out, she'll lose respect and respect is what will allow her to keep her job.

"Gary Williams," she answers.

"Oh, you know Gary?"

She nods her head. "He's my uncle."

"I knew it!" Ty says, smiling and throwing a weak punch in the air. "I knew you couldn't be just anybody."

She shrugs. "What does it matter how I got the job? I still had to be interviewed."

"We're all just surprised. Some guys would kill for your job and I wonder how easy it came for you."

"I'm sure they interviewed other candidates. I have nothing holding me back. I could start right away, something they needed."

"I'm sure we would have been fine until Ritchie came back."

"It was obviously a concern—otherwise they would have made do until he came back. You guys are professionals. You take your job seriously, so why would you want to jeopardize your practice time when you want to start off the season strong?"

"If I were in your position, I'd take all the advice and ice time possible to improve."

Ty laughs. "You think I need improvement?"

"Just saying. Last season you ended with only forty-five points, down from the season before."

The guys sit numbly.

"You can do better, Caldwell," she says, grabbing her glass. Thankfully, she read the team's stats the first night she got the job.

"I . . . uh . . ."

Eileen takes a drink from her straw, finishing it by the time the food arrives. She slaps down money for her drink and stands up. "I'll see you at practice," she says and turns on her heel.

She leaves the room and walks through the hall to the main doors. Her phone rings. Unknown number. Reluctantly, she picks up.

With a swing of her neck to wave away her long hair, she taps her phone and answers, "Eileen Francis."

The voice is smoky and deep. "If you're smart, you'll decline the opportunity with the Warriors."

"Who is this?"

"Think again about your career. You'll regret it later."

The line goes dead and Eileen's stomach sinks. Who would call to threaten her? Has word gotten out that she's the new coach?

Eileen can't move. For a second, she feels scared, and then she feels powerful and confident. Nobody is going to stand in her way of getting this job.

I will not be defeated! If this job weren't so important, no one would bother to make that kind of phone call. *I will prove I am capable. I will prove that not only can I do the job, but I can do the job better.*

Chapter 4

Eileen skates around the rink, stretching out her legs before leaving the ice. It has already been a week and a half since she became a member of the Vancouver Warriors coaching staff. She even has her own blue and white skating uniform to match the other coaches'. Although it's a temporary position, and she's working without a contract, she is taking the new job seriously and working tirelessly to prove herself. The team isn't big on change, and she's asked daily how long she is there for and when Ritchie will be coming back. Maybe that's why she hasn't been presented with a contract—because it's pointless to draft one up if Ritchie is due to return back to work any day.

It will take some time for the team to get used to the idea of a female on the ice and so far, she hasn't had any other phone threats. Eileen remembers the voice and it's not one she recognizes. Even now she can still hear the words "you'll regret it" ringing in her head, but can't seem to place the voice. Who is it and how did they get her work number? Although she's hung posters in different facilities and placed an ad in a parents' magazine to attract new business, so it could be anyone.

The cold air tingles her nostrils. The familiar smell of the rink is distinct—cold, sweaty, and stale. Eileen takes her mind away from the thought and skates around the rink, looking around at the empty seats, imagining her father there, wearing his winter jacket and toboggan like he always did, giving her a heartfelt smile as she skated by. She tries to keep the memories of her parents alive, but with every memory she feels an ache in her heart.

Her mother and father would have been proud, especially her father, a man who loved hockey and inspired her to play. She remembers five-in-the-morning practices. Her father would make coffee to go and wake her up to leave, and they would be home by the time her mother woke. It was a bond they shared, every weekend the same routine. Even when she made it on the national women's team, her father was at all her games, cheering her on; he was always her number-one fan. Her parents may be gone, but her father's love and devotion to playing the game lives on. What she wouldn't give to see her parents now.

The sound of skates cutting into the ice, smoothly and carelessly gliding closer and closer, snaps her back to reality. Eileen turns her head to meet Ty's friendly smile—a change in attitude maybe or he has an idea for a drill. She can't seem to figure him out and wonders what he wants from her.

"I thought practice was over?" Ty asks as he skates in pace with her, holding his hockey stick loosely to one side.

"Sometimes it feels good to just skate," she says simply, looking down at her stick and moving it around with one hand as though not sure what to do with it.

Ty looks at her as they skate in unison. "I've never met a woman who enjoys the game as much as I do."

"In this city? I find that hard to believe." Eileen stares ahead at the rough ice patches, marked from the challenging skating lesson.

"I'm serious."

She glances his way, only to be met by startling blue eyes. His wet, sweaty hair is sticking to his ears, and his facial hair is rough around his chin. It's hard to miss his solid upper body. It's also hard to stop herself from wondering how those muscular arms would feel wrapped around her, but that's not going to happen. He is too much of a playboy for her even to consider the chances.

Besides, most of the guys on the team aren't interested in a relationship. She knows that from experience, and never again will she get involved with a professional athlete. They are too unstable in the relationship department and unpredictable when it came to commitment.

"Are you trying to stay in my good books?" she asks.

"Hoping."

"I guess that's more than what your teammates are thinking and probably saying."

"They're not saying much."

"I'm not sure that's a good thing either."

He cocks his head to one side. "Why not?"

"I don't think you and your team are happy that I'm sharing the ice," she says, wishing she didn't bring it up since she isn't in the mood to play defense. It will take time for the guys to see that being a woman shouldn't have anything to do with her hockey skills.

"Face it, you're a woman in a man's league. It isn't right."

She shoots him a dirty look. She knows they are all thinking it, but hasn't heard it until now. "Oh, really? That's pretty sexist, isn't it?"

He shrugs. "It is what it is. Hey, most of the guys feel that way. You can't be surprised. Can you blame us?"

"So is that the team consensus? They really don't want me here?"

"Well, you know how it is. Not all the guys like taking instruction from a woman," he says, looking at her with an honest gaze.

"So, you think I should quit?" She gives him a slight pout, not that she cares what Ty Caldwell thinks or what the other guys think for that matter. It would be interesting to hear what is said in the locker room when she's not around though.

He exhales a slow puff. "If that's what you want to do, but yeah, some of the guys are hoping Ritchie will be back in a few weeks."

Eileen gives him a sharp look. "Just to be clear, I'm not going to let you or the others dictate my career. I'll be here for as long as I need to be. If the guys don't like it, that's too bad. I'm here to do a job and I plan on finishing what I started."

"Okay, okay, I just thought you'd like to know." He throws out his hand to stop her.

Her eyes narrow. Why is she drawn to another overconfident male?

"Why are you telling me this?" she asks.

He stops to face her, shrugs, and says, "I thought you might be curious how you are perceived by the guys. Women are always concerned about people liking them, aren't they?"

"Not me! I could care less," she says. It's only half true. She only cares about performance and not so much about personality.

"You're the exception, I guess."

Her uncle Gary warned her how the guys would feel about her if she got hired, and she had a feeling it wouldn't be easy, but it would be nice if they kept their opinions to themselves and let her do her job.

Eileen skates to the bench. "I know what you're after and I'm not going to let you or your teammates bully me into leaving," she says with precision. "I'm here to do a job and I plan to finish what I started."

Her look is tense, but she keeps her head up and a calm composure. She can't help but stare at him, studying a faint scar on his jawline and wondering why some men are blessed with long eyelashes.

When Ty doesn't respond, she looks into his eyes. "What?" she asks, suddenly feeling self-conscious.

"I've seen that look before," he says.

She steps off the ice, stomping her skates on the rubber floor to shake off the excess ice. "What look?" she asks, puzzled.

Ty grins. "It's the 'you want to go out to dinner with me tonight, but are afraid to ask' kind of look."

Is he kidding? Is he always this full of himself? He acts like women should be falling for him all the time.

Eileen shakes her head in disbelief. "Really? That's what you think?"

"Go ahead, ask," he encourages with a slight nod of his chin. "I won't make an embarrassing statement, I promise. You have my word." He brings his hand to his chest.

"You're serious! I don't believe it!"

Eileen looks at him blankly, trying to comprehend his sudden desire. She can't go out with him. They work together, and she's already been down this road. Besides, she doesn't want to date Ty—he's too much of a player.

"Thanks, but no thanks," she responds, taking a seat on the bench and unlacing her skates. She keeps her head down so she doesn't have to look at him staring at her from the ice. Who knows what he'll say next.

Ty leans over the ledge. "Okay, so maybe tonight's not a good night. How about tomorrow night?" he pushes. "Closer to the weekend. Friday night? Hold on, that won't work. . . . Maybe Saturday night? What kind of food do you like? Italian? Greek? Chinese?"

Did he not hear me?

"So, what'd ya say?"

Can't he take no for an answer?

"Well? What do ya say?" he asks again with a little more assertiveness.

"I can't," she says, drying off her blades with a hand towel and securing her skate guards before placing them into her duffel bag.

Ty scratches his head as though trying to solve a puzzle. "I know you want to go out with me. I don't know why you don't just ask me out instead of playing these games."

Her eyebrows furrow and she looks at him in disbelief. "I'm not playing any games," she retorts. "I can't believe you would even think I would want to go out with you."

He laughs. "I know you do. Come on, I know you want to, and that's why you're acting the way you are around me."

She slips on her running shoes and looks up at his smirk, his pink lips curling as he waits for her reply. "And how am I acting?" she asks, tying her laces.

Hasn't he ever been turned down before?

"I see how you've been giving me the 'come on over here, baby' look," he says, keeping one hand on the bench as though it's an anchor. "It's pretty obvious."

She laughs. "That's hilarious!"

He's crazy!

"I think you're confused with the 'pay attention to my class' look and the 'stop annoying me' look, oh, and don't forget about the 'leave me alone' look." She gives him a sharp eye as she stands up and grabs her bag.

Two can play this game. That'll keep him quiet!

"I'm trying to read you now," he says, closing his eyes for a couple of seconds. "You're hard to read."

"Oh, yeah?" she asks. "Trying to be funny?"

"You're trying to tell me that you want to go out on a date and have some alone time. You, me, and—"

Her mouth drops and anger flares from her frozen toes to her face. Her cheeks grow red as though they were just pinched, and all she can think about is leaving the arena and getting away from Ty Caldwell. Far away until the next practice.

She throws her bag over her shoulder. "There is no way I would go out with you," she says, shaking her head and taking a step forward.

"And why not?" Ty asks, flashing puppy-dog eyes as he rests his chin on the end of his hockey stick.

"I don't date men I work with," she says firmly and begins to walk away. *And I won't date you!*

There is no question of how attractive Ty Caldwell is, but Eileen won't give in to his flirtatious ways if she wants to keep her job. What would management say if she went out with him? What would the public say? Not like she's planning on it. She couldn't. The media would be all over it. A woman gets hired by the Vancouver Warriors and goes out with the city's most famous bachelor—surely her credentials would go down the drain and people would think she took the job just to get a date.

"Wait!" Ty calls as he steps off the ice.

She stops briefly, wondering what he wants now. Ty's messy, wet blond hair, baby-soft skin, and flirty smile are a cocktail for a sleepover and she will have nothing to do with him.

"You don't date guys you work with? How else do you meet your dates?" he asks, his face turning from cheery to concerned. "Don't tell me you don't date."

She gives him a disapproving look, trying hard not to smile. "Of course I date. I choose not to get involved with guys I work with."

"I've never heard that before."

"No?" She laughs. "It's a good rule to live by." She throws her chin in the air like she's outsmarting him with philosophy and continues to walk away.

It takes him a moment to respond, but he follows her anyway. "We don't work together every day. Can you even consider this a working relationship?"

She stops and turns to face him. "Yes!"

"Okay, well, maybe a little . . ."

"I don't get it. Is there a bet going on that I should know about?"

"No, no," he says, one hand on his stick.

"Of course you would say that. You want to win a bet. You have a hard time losing a game and probably have never heard the word no from a woman."

Ty's forehead wrinkles; his eyes squint with wonder.

"I should have known," Eileen says. "There's bound to be another game being played here besides hockey."

"I don't know what you are talking about. There is no bet going on," he says, taking a step in front of her.

She grimaces and folds her arms, trying to believe him, but something in the look he's giving her makes it hard.

"No, really, there isn't," he says. "I think you're interested in a night out with me, but don't know how to ask. And if you're worried about the team finding out, it can be our secret. I can keep a secret."

She can't help the laughter. "Yeah, right. Okay, well, it doesn't matter because it's not going to happen. This is a job and I don't let my personal life interfere with business," Eileen says firmly, taking one step forward, unable to move another step without walking straight into his arms.

"It will only interfere if you let it," he says. "Besides, your work is done for the day and I'm only asking you to join me for dinner. What's the big deal? We both have to eat."

"Yes, but I'll be here next week and the week after that. I can't sacrifice my job for anything," she says, as she looks him eye to eye. "And I won't! Not this job anyway. Besides, I'm not interested." Why is it so hard for him to understand?

Ty looks away every few seconds and rolls the top of his hockey stick around in his hand. "I don't see how a dinner will affect a career."

"I don't want rumors to start and cause media attention when everyone's attention should clearly be on the team practices."

"Rumors are just rumors."

"How can the team trust me if I'm going out with you?"

"It's just one date. Who said it would be multiple dates?" he asks.

Her face flushes again. "Still, one date would mean talk in the locker room and besides, what would Steve, Rick, or Ted think? It's unprofessional."

"I think you're overanalyzing."

"I'm being realistic. I know how it works. It's the same in any job."

"It can be our secret," he says without worry. "What time works for you?"

"No time is a good time," she says, arching an eyebrow for a look she's been told intimidates people. "I already told you I'm not interested."

"You don't mean that."

"Yes, I do!" she says. "What makes you think that I want to go out with you, anyway?"

"I can tell by your eyes—you're always looking at me."

She looks away. Surely he is misreading her. What would he want with his skating coach, anyway? It's not like going out with her would win him gold stars or get him a day off or give him extra media attention. He already has enough of all that.

Eileen takes a deep breath, feeling pressured. "Okay." She sighs, regretting her words before they're even fully out of her mouth. "I'll meet you for coffee." She watches his face change shape.

His head drops. "Coffee?"

"What's wrong with that? Don't you like coffee?" she asks, trying to be serious.

He shrugs. "Yes, I like coffee, but I was thinking of getting a cold beverage and dinner. Who likes to eat alone?"

She thinks about what he's saying. "I see," she says, gripping her bag. "So this is really about eating and not getting together—"

He cuts her off. "We both need to go somewhere to talk and relax. How about I pick you up at six," he suggests, as though he already has a plan, "and we'll go from there?"

She chooses her words carefully. "Sorry if I've disappointed you, but that's not going to work out." She ducks out of his way.

"You've dumped me already?" He laughs and takes a couple of quick steps ahead, still wearing his skates.

"Okay, well, if today doesn't work, how about Saturday?"

What excuse does she have? Clearly he doesn't take no for an answer.

She steps backward. "Ah, I can't Saturday," she replies quickly.

"What's going on Saturday?" he challenges.

"I . . . uh . . . have to . . . help a friend move," Eileen lies. "My friend, uh, doesn't really have anyone to help her so I told her I would . . ." Her voice trails off.

"Where does she live?"

"Downtown."

"House?"

"No, condo."

"And she doesn't have anyone to help her?"

"Well, no, not really," Eileen says, trying to sound disappointed.

"Well, I'm free. I can help."

"Why would you want to do that? You don't even know her and you don't even know me."

"Look, I'm a nice guy," he says. "Give me a chance. Let me help and you'll see."

"You probably say that to all the girls. I'm not buying it," Eileen says. "But thanks anyway, we can handle it."

"You know, Eileen," he shouts. "You think you're an independent woman and you don't need a guy around, but I hate to break it to you, sometimes you need a man to do the physical stuff."

She stops in her tracks, her blood boiling at how arrogant he is. She turns around and yells, "I can handle my own, thank you very much."

"We'll see about that," he calls after her and watches a well-known sports reporter walk toward her.

The reporter nods at Ty and then stops in front of Eileen to get her attention.

"Excuse me, are you Eileen Francis? The new skating coach?" the reporter asks, holding a notepad and pen in one hand, ready to interview.

Eileen flinches. She's tried hard to avoid the media since she got hired, afraid of how she'll be received by the public, but this reporter shuffles closer and it's not so easy to step away from him. She looks at him suspiciously and doesn't answer him right away.

Ty does his best to sprint toward them in his untied skates and answers, "Yes, she is!"

Eileen shoots Ty a disapproving look and then looks down at his loose laces and wonders how he didn't just fall in them. It just goes to show how strong his ankles are.

"He's okay, Eileen," Ty soothes. "This is Bill Braxton, the sports reporter for the *Vancouver Daily*. Bill, this is Eileen Francis, or she goes by Elle." He passes her a sly look and her eyes are disapproving.

"Hi," Eileen says as though too shy to respond. "Actually, my friends call me Elle. You can call me Eileen."

"Okay, then. How do you spell it?" he asks, folding over a piece of paper from his notepad and gripping his pen.

"E-I-L-E-E-N."

"Great, thanks. And your last name?"

"F-R-A-N-C-I-S. What would you like to know?" she asks with skepticism. That there's a reporter around doesn't surprise her; however, she is surprised that she doesn't know what to tell him.

"So how did practice go today?" he asks innocently.

She tries to select her words carefully, but she still can't think of anything to tell him, probably because Ty is practically breathing down her neck. It's hard to concentrate when a popular, outspoken guy is watching her every move and hasn't taken his eyes off her since practice. "It went okay," she finally says.

"That's not what Bill wants to hear," Ty intervenes, giving the reporter a confident nod. "Practice went very well. There are a few things we need to work on, but it's good for us. We're getting the job done, focusing on what we need to do . . . and how we're going to do it. . . ."

Eileen shoots him a look. *What is he, my agent?* She grits her teeth.

"And what do you think your team needs to work on?" Bill asks genuinely, his oval-shaped brown eyes shifting from Ty to Eileen, waiting for one of them to answer the question.

"You know," Ty says, "when you're reminded of the little things, you begin to rethink your game strategy."

"Are you saying your team will start off the new season strong because of your new skating coach?"

"Well . . ." Ty says with a chuckle, again revealing his dimple on his left cheek. He shifts his body weight to one side and puts a hand on his hip. "I think there are a lot of factors involved here. . . . Practice makes perfect, and if we can keep focused, I think we'll have a stronger game."

"Kind of hard to stay focused when you have a female teaching you, don't you agree?"

Eileen looks at Ty and then at Bill and makes a quick response. "Being female has nothing to do with it; it's all about playing the game well. I'm helping them reach their full potential."

"So is there anything between the two of you?" the reporter asks with a straight face.

"Excuse me?" Eileen asks, taken aback by his question. "Between us? You're kidding, right?" she asks and laughs, looking at Ty again and then at Bill. "Just because I'm a woman doesn't mean—"

"You're single, then?" Bill asks, forcing the question.

"What does that have to do with hockey?" she asks, incredulous.

"Nothing," Bill admits. "Just curious."

"That's why you're a reporter, right," Ty says with a nod. "Just getting the goods?"

"Thanks, Ty," Bill says. "Nice to meet you, Eileen." He lifts his head in a quick nod. "We'll see you again, soon." And with that, the reporter walks into the building.

"See?" Ty says. "You just have to tell them what they want to hear and they go away happy."

Eileen shakes her head. "Why do you care if he's happy or not? You're not selling him anything." She pivots on her toes. "I've got to go."

"If you change your mind, you know where to find me," he yells after her.

Eileen walks to her car and glances back to see if he's gone. He is already heading back into the building. What will it take for him to understand that she is strictly business? She opens her door and notices a piece of paper on her windshield held by a window wiper.

"What's this?" she asks herself and snatches the paper from her car.

You are playing with fire. Look out. You are taking chances.

Her stomach tightens. She swallows hard, holding the note in her hand, and looks around her. Who is leaving these threats? She tells herself she can handle this. *It's probably just a threat, nothing more*, she thinks, getting into her car and locking it before turning the ignition. Nothing is going to stop her from pursuing her dreams, not even a threat.

Chapter 5

Eileen throws herself down at the table, late to dinner with her girl-friends. She lets out a big sigh.

"Tough day?" Brooke asks as she takes a sip of her martini.

"Not really," she answers and looks up at the waitress. "I'll get a rum and Diet Coke."

"You look tired," Kelly says, batting her blue eyes.

"I am. This morning I spent an hour and a half with twenty grown men who can't handle having a woman instruct them. I think my six-year-olds are better behaved." She takes a breath. "It's been challenging and exhausting." Eileen rubs her forehead. "If my jobs were easy, I probably wouldn't feel so tired, but there is a lot on my plate right now. I'm already talking with the rink coordinator about planning hockey schools for winter."

"You need a holiday," Brooke says. "We should plan a girls' trip! Forget about responsibilities—we could lie on a beach somewhere and drink mimosas."

"Yeah, like next year," Eileen says.

The waitress sets the drink on the table and walks away.

"I still don't know how long this hockey job will last." Eileen pulls her glass in closer and holds her straw with two fingers. "Uncle Gary says that it could be three months. It all depends on how much time Ritchie needs."

"What's wrong with him?" Brooke asks.

"I'm told he had some family issues to work out. Nobody's told me the details and I didn't want to pry."

"You have what it takes! Don't let the guys get to you. If you let them see you're bothered, they'll discover how to push your buttons," Kelly says, tucking her red strands behind her ear.

"Yeah, and then it will be hard to stay focused, never mind their good looks," Brooke adds.

"Hmmm," Eileen says and takes a sip from her straw. "Somebody doesn't want me working there. I've had a disturbing phone call, and a threatening note left on my car after practice. It's kind of freaking me out."

"That's scary," Brooke says, alarmed. "Did you tell anyone at the rink?"

Eileen shakes her head. "I don't want to come across a wimpy girl, you know?"

"Yeah, but this is serious!" Kelly says. "You need to tell someone. How about your uncle? At least you can trust him."

"Then he'll get all worried and report it. I can't take any chances."

"Your safety is more important than the job," Brooke says. Her small oval face is powdery and her hazel eyes are outlined in liner, making them appear bigger than they are. She is a petite woman with a big heart.

"You're right," Eileen says, thinking what her mom would have said. "But I'm not going to let some jerk dictate my career. I've worked really hard to get here; I don't want it to be over yet. I just started."

"I still think you should say something to your uncle, at least let him know what's going on, or better, call the police," Brooke says.

"Always watch your back," Kelly adds. "Do you have any idea who it could be?"

"No idea. I can't even guess."

The waitress comes by again. "Are you ladies ready to order?"

"I think so," Eileen says, looking at the menu. "I'll have the grilled chicken salad, no croutons, and dressing on the side with lemon slices, please."

"Must you be so healthy?" Kelly snarls. "Go on and order a burger and fries. We won't tell anyone. Promise."

Eileen smirks and hands the waitress her menu.

"And I'll have the rice bowl with two chilies, please," Brooke says, looking radiant in a summer dress, her hair left down falling past her shoulders.

"Make that two," Kelly says and hands the waitress the menus.

"Elle, have you made any dates with the guys yet?" Brooke asks, changing the topic to something lighter.

"Are you kidding? No!" she says. "I'm not interested in any of them. They're all a bunch of big egos. They only care about hockey and getting laid. I'm not into that. I have better things to do with my time."

"They are men." Kelly cocks an eyebrow. "And you're stuck with all twenty of them, lucky girl."

Brooke finishes her drink and pushes it aside. "I bet you've been hit on already."

Eileen fiddles with her drink, running her finger along the wet glass, watching the bubbles come to the surface.

"You have! I knew it. Tell! I want to hear!" Brooke says, sitting up straighter.

"It's nothing to brag about."

"Come on," Brooke encourages her, slapping her hand down on the table. "Of course it is! Tell us! We want to know."

"There's nothing to tell."

"I heard the Warriors' Brandon Keller is a real flirt," Kelly says, putting down her drink.

"How do you know?" Eileen asks.

"One of my clients ran into him at a club, and apparently he had a swarm of women around him and went home with two of them."

"You can't believe everything," Eileen says.

"So, what's the story?" Brooke pushes. "Do tell!" She looks around at the full tables of people surrounding them, all in conversation. Nobody would be able to hear them, not with the background music and serving staff clanging plates and chitchatting.

"Okay, well, one of the guys doesn't take no for an answer. I don't think he takes me seriously, even though I've told him I'm not interested. He doesn't get it."

"Who is it?" Kelly asks. "Is it Brandon Keller? Mark Buckley? Although, I heard he's married, not like that means anything these days."

Eileen makes a face. "No." She shudders and then mutters his name. "Ty Caldwell." She takes a sip of her drink trying to hide a faint grin.

"Oh! Really? I've seen him in a Toyota commercial," Brooke says with excitement.

Kelly pipes up, "I've seen him in an interview once. He's got an ego. Good player, but he's a little high on himself."

"You're not kidding," Eileen agrees, rolling her eyes. "You should meet him in person."

"What's he like?" Brooke asks.

"A little pushy. Can't take no for an answer."

"He might be good for you, Elle," Brooke says.

"I don't see how that's possible."

"You need a guy who can push you a bit, someone who can stand up to you. Ty could be the guy." Brooke shrugs and exchanges a sly smile with Kelly.

"I'm not that hard to be around, am I? You two put up with me."

"We've known you for a long time," Kelly says. "Sometimes you come across a little abrasive."

"I do?"

"Well, yeah, and some guys might find it . . . well . . . they might not be used to a girl who has a mind of her own," Kelly says. "Especially one that doesn't take crap from anyone."

"Funny, I've been told that a lot lately."

"It happens when you're stressed." Brooke sits up straighter. "Anyway, you're not looking for serious, are you? Just a date here and there? Who knows where it will lead."

Eileen sips her straw and smiles at her friend. "I don't mix pleasure with business. That's just the way I work. Even if I did go out with him for one night, if someone found out I'd probably never live it down—and be fired, I'm sure."

"You don't have to tell anyone—except for us, of course, and we wouldn't tell a soul," Brooke says, motioning that her lips are zipped shut.

"Yeah," Kelly agrees. "Our secret."

"Uh-huh." Eileen pushes her lips together studying her friends' faces.

Brooke nods her head. "Honest! We wouldn't."

"I don't trust Ty. He probably would brag just like a rich kid with a new toy. They have to tell everyone their life stories," she says.

"If you tell him to keep it a secret and go out with him for one date, he might do it. It's not going to kill you. Besides, it might help you understand the other guys on the team. You can look at it as a business dinner," Kelly says. "Maybe he'll even give you more respect if you talk with him one-on-one."

Eileen chuckles. "That's what I need, more respect from the guys. Is that even possible?"

"You knew you wouldn't get much respect when you took this assignment. Face it, what guy wants a woman telling him what to do or giving instructions on how to do his job?" Kelly sips her drink. "None. Guys would rather get lost than ask a chick directions."

Dinner arrives and Brooke orders another martini.

"I'll have another drink, too," Kelly says and then turns her attention to her friends. "Well, I think Ty is pretty cute and, if you ask me, he looks harmless."

"I'm not denying it. He's a good-looking man, but that doesn't mean he's right for me."

"He would definitely be good for you. That's what you need in a guy," Kelly says, holding her glass up to her mouth. "Just 'cause your ex was a disappointment doesn't mean all jocks are like that."

"You're right. Mario was different, but I loved him," Eileen reflects and without thinking clearly, she says, "If you want me to set you up with Ty, I can."

"No!" Kelly cries. "Absolutely not!"

"Why?"

"Because I think you should go out with him. He's obviously interested in you."

"How do you know that?" Eileen asks. "You haven't even met him."

"Look, any guy starving for affection from one woman is obviously interested," Kelly explains. "He could be The One and you don't even know it."

"You never know," Brooke taunts.

The waitress approaches the table. "Another glass?"

"No, thank you," Eileen answers, sliding her empty glass across the table.

"Oh, and I've got some great news," Brooke says with excitement. "I sold a purse! Actually, I sold more than one!"

"Oh, wow! That's great!" Kelly says, and Eileen chimes in, "Congrats!"

"You've got a hit product," Kelly adds.

"Who bought it?" Eileen inquires.

"A woman at my office. She was so impressed that I designed it. She said she had to see my collection, so I brought in a few of them to work for show and the women were all over them. It was insane. I sold all six purses that day."

"Good for you! I told you, you're talented," Eileen says.

"I've been thinking of taking a few to some stores to see if they could sell them on commission."

"There's an idea. Do you want to go shopping after this?" Kelly asks, putting down her glass.

"Not tonight," Brooke says. "I have to finish one of my purses that someone ordered. They're coming by tomorrow to pick it up."

"Elle?"

She swallows her bite of salad and says, "No thanks."

Kelly sighs. "Are you ever up for it?"

"No. You know me. I hate shopping."

"I know, but how else do you buy what you wear?"

"I order online, same brands, same stores. Less choice, less shopping."

Kelly shakes her head in disbelief. "I'm sure you can go one of these days." She puts down her fork. "So, Brooke, have you decided on your business name?"

"I thought of that last night. I was thinking of Chic Purses by Brooke."

"How about Brooke's Bags?" Eileen suggests, then gives a giggle. "Simple. Clear."

"That sounds trendy," Kelly agrees.

"I don't know if I want to use my real name."

"Why not? You have a great name for a label," Eileen encourages her.

"A product is all about branding and I want to make sure that it has the right name," Brooke says. "It's all about the marketing."

"Yes, it is," Eileen agrees. "You should try getting into the women's show happening this fall. You'd have to have a lot of product though; it's a madhouse."

"There's an idea," Kelly says.

"That would be so good for me. How many purses do you think I'd need?"

"A couple hundred for sure. There are a lot of women there. It's a great way to get your name out, good advertising."

"I'll definitely think about it," Brooke says. "And you should think about going on a date one of these days before it's too late."

"Too late for what?"

"Too late for having a variety of men at your fingertips before the job is done."

Chapter 6

"Eileen!" Ty shouts as he walks down the long hallway from the dressing room door.

She stops and turns around to face the hockey superstar. Sweat glistens from his hairline, his face moist from exercise, a pink glow radiating from his complexion. He is wearing shorts and a fitted, black Under Armour short-sleeved shirt that reveals his toned biceps.

Eileen closes her mouth. Why is he such a distraction? Ty walks toward her assertively. "Look, did I do something to piss you off?" he asks, putting a hand on his hip.

"No." Although she thinks the cold shoulder she gave him during practice might be enough to bother his ego.

"It seems that way," he pushes.

"I'm here to do a job. Sorry you're taking me the wrong way. I'm professional and expect the same in return."

"I have a simple question," he says.

"And what's that?"

"I want to take you out to dinner."

Her face flushes. Did he always have to be this forward? She simply isn't interested in his playboy behavior, even though his riveting good looks make it hard to resist the invitation.

"Not going to happen," she says coolly.

"What will make you change your mind?"

"Nothing," she answers. Although it's a lie. She would go out with him but not as long as she is a Warriors employee.

He combs his fingers through his damp hair and scratches the back of his head. "You're a tough sell."

"It's not going to happen," she assures him. A slight grin creeps to her lips and she tries hard to bring them together. The last thing Eileen wants is for Ty to think she enjoys being flirted with. "Besides, it's not up to you how I make my decisions."

That ought to shut him up.

Ty lets out a sigh. "Okay then, I have another question for you," he says and takes another step closer.

Eileen looks around her as though waiting for a top-secret request. "Oh, yeah? And what's that?"

"Do you always play these games? I know you love a good hockey game, but how about your life? I can't imagine it being very fun if you're not looking for a good time."

Eileen shakes her head and looks away. *How dare he assume that I'm lonely and afraid of getting into a relationship! Who does he think he is?*

"I'm making things easier for you," he says in a calm voice. "Let's have dinner tonight. Nothing serious, if that's what you're afraid of."

What does he want from me? There are plenty of women who would love to go out with Ty Caldwell and would jump at the chance. Am I crazy not to?

"I'm not afraid," she says. "I thought I told you my reason why."

Ty scratches his head and wipes his eyebrow with a finger. "No, no, you didn't," he says. "I don't recall."

"I did so!"

"No, I believe you said you would think about it."

"Okay, well, I have thought about it."

"And?"

"And the answer is still no," she says, gripping her duffel bag over her shoulder.

"No?" he asks in disbelief.

"Yes."

"Well, which one is it? Yes or no?" Ty says playfully.

Does he realize how annoying he can be?

Furious, she takes in a breath. How does he think going out with her will change how she feels? If she is reluctant to go out with him now, what would make her change her mind?

"I told you," she says, but she can't help that her lips widen into a grin every time their eyes meet. Why does he appeal to her? Is it because he keeps her on her toes? Always making her guess what he's going to say next? Besides the good looks and killer smile, is it because he knows how to get to her?

"It sounds like you aren't sure," he says.

"Oh, I'm sure," she retorts. "You always seem to catch me at a bad time. I've got to get ready for work."

"Okay, now really, what is a good time?" he asks, placing one hand on his hip. "I don't think there's ever a good time, do you? You're always running to the rink and running out to your other job."

"You're right," she says. "There really isn't a good time. I've got to go home and get ready." She turns around.

"Wait! Do you have a piece of paper and a pen?"

She rolls her eyes. "What for?"

"Well, do you?" he asks.

"No, I don't," she says without looking in her bag.

"Let's see your phone," he says, motioning his fingers to give him the device.

"No."

"Why not?"

"What are you going to do?" She eyes him skeptically and then opens her bag and pulls out her BlackBerry. She hesitates. "What do you want it for?"

He gestures for her to bring it to him and she hands over her phone.

He clicks at her phone and hands it back to her. "Here's my number," he says.

"What for?" she asks, taking her phone back. Her hand touches his warm, moist skin. A tingle runs down her spine. "I don't need it," she says, trying not to laugh at his persistence and her attraction to him. This is getting ridiculous.

"Yes, you do," he argues. "What happens if your car breaks down and you can't make it to practice, huh? Who are ya gonna call? Or you're stuck home one night and want to go out, but have no one to go with? There's gonna be a night when you're not working and wish you had called. You'll thank me." He gives his head a quick shake to move the strand of hair off his temple.

She can't help but smile at his efforts. "You're acting like you're desperate for a date, you know that? And I know you're not desperate," she says with an honest face. "You're far from it."

"Oh, yeah? What have you heard?"

"Uh, well, that you're no stranger to women." Eileen clears her throat. "It's not me you want—"

"We would make a good couple, wouldn't we?"

"You think so?" Why is he putting so much work into convincing her that she needs to go out with him? Eileen doesn't think of herself as a model beauty or the type of woman who gets her fingernails painted. She is an athlete with good posture. Her hair is usually tied back in a ponytail, and she wears little makeup except for mascara and lip gloss. Would she even fit perfectly in Ty's arms?

"Yeah, I really do." He smirks.

"That's too bad," she says. "If you're waiting for me to call you, you'll be waiting a very long time."

Ty lifts his chin up. "Then give me your number."

"I can't do that—you'll be phoning me asking me the same question," she says. "Besides, I hope you don't have bets going in the locker room because someone has just made a few bucks off of you."

He hangs his head as though ashamed, "Oh, you caught me. . . . It's a huge bet, too," he says. "It's really going to cost me if you don't at least call me and make one date."

"Date?" she asks as though hearing the word for the first time. "Oh, no, no, no. Absolutely not." *Why is he making this so hard?*

"Come on. What's one date?" he begs.

"Hey, Slick!" a voice yells out. "There are groupie girls out back waiting for you. Nice looking too." Theo rounds the corner.

Eileen's eyebrows narrow and she looks at Ty for an explanation.

"Easy pickin's," Defenseman, Theo Anderson says and he disappears down the hall toward the exit.

Ty ignores the interruption and faces Eileen. "Come on, what's there to think about?"

She clenches her jaw, not wanting to give in. "We can meet, but it's not a date," she finally says. "No wine-and-dine procedure, just a meet and greet."

"You really are all business, aren't you?" he asks. "So I guess, how 'bout a meeting then?"

"I'm free tonight at six," she says, reminding him that she has other important commitments.

"Okay then. Tell me the place and time and I will be there."

Eileen says good-bye to Ty and walks to her car, anticipating another note. Her heart races as she stares ahead, looking for paper under the windshield wiper. Getting closer, she squints, her eyes focused on her windshield. Eileen takes her keys out of her purse just as she reaches her car. There's no note. Relieved the threats have stopped at least for today, she lets out a breath. As she opens the car door, something catches her eye. There are wave-like scratches all over the metallic blue paint. It's been keyed. She throws her head back in frustration. A cold tingle runs down her spine and her heart races. She looks around the parking lot and can't see anybody suspicious. Why is this happening? Who would do this? Is this a coincidence or does someone really hate her?

Chapter 7

Eileen leaves the rink angry. Who is doing this? What's the big deal that she's a woman coaching the guys? Is this what it's about? She's a good teacher and a good supporter of athletes. The past three weeks have been tough and it seems things will only get tougher. How long will she put up with this for? Should she go to the police? Should she tell Uncle Gary? Tell Ty? What will happen? Will she lose her job because she's causing too much grief for the team?

Eileen drives home to have a quick shower and then she's off to the local ice rink to teach six-year-olds their skating lesson and to have a brief meeting with Oliver, the rink coordinator. By the end of the day, she's tired. It's no wonder she feels like staying at home; she has a lot on her mind, especially adding Ty Caldwell to the mix. Does she actually believe he wants a harmless date with her? There has to be more to it than that, like bragging rights to his teammates. She won't allow him to get close to her. Not even a good-night kiss. Nope. This meeting is strictly business.

Eileen stands up from the spare desk, organizing loose papers and placing them into the appropriate folders when she sees Robyn, the receptionist, staring down at her.

"Hi," Robyn says and takes a sideways step toward the desk uneasily, standing beside a framed picture of Jarome Iginla and Sidney Crosby. "I haven't chatted with you in a while."

"Yeah, well, I've been busy."

"How are you?" Robyn asks, holding a rolled-up newspaper in one hand.

"Okay . . ." Eileen says casually, hoping she will get to the point and be on her way. Unfortunately, Robyn loves to talk, even when one is obviously busy.

"Finnne," Robyn answers and then hesitates. "Haven't seen you much these days. You don't stop in as often as you used to. I know you're busy with your other job." She bobs her head. "It must be hard trying to keep up with work and teaching the Warriors. . . . I'm sure you must be on a natural high all the time. . . . I mean who wouldn't want your job, right? Even if it is for a short time," she says enthusiastically. "You must love it. . . . It must be a dream come true."

Eileen shrugs it off as though it were no big deal. "Yeah, I guess."

"Really?" Robyn asks, her green eyes wide with amazement, the same color and brightness as Eileen's the day she got her dream job. "What woman wouldn't want to be in your shoes, working with all those men—hot men, might I add? Have you gone into the locker room, yet? You have to tell me," she shrieks. "Do the guys walk around in their underwear and without their shirts?" She fans her face with the newspaper. "They're all attractive."

Eileen looks at her. "Really? Some have missing teeth."

"It's for the love of the game," she says. "Is Brandon Keller single? Or how about Theo Anderson?"

"Robyn?" Eileen asks, annoyed. She has better things to do than answer Robyn's lame questions. But she knows these guys are celebrities in Vancouver and she is fortunate enough to skate with them twice a week. "Anderson is married, and anyway, is this really what you came to talk to me about?"

"No, but I'd love to meet Brandon. Do you think you could introduce me to him if it's not too much trouble?"

"I don't talk to all the guys on a personal level, you know. I coach them when they're on the ice and I leave the rink to come here," she says.

Robyn swallows and asks, "Did you see today's newspaper?"

"No, I haven't. Anything I should know?"

"There's a small article about you working with the Warriors and it has your picture too!" she exclaims. "Do you wanna see?" She walks over to her desk, unrolls the newspaper, and hands over the crumpled pages.

Eileen briefly skims the article and studies the picture of her instructing with players standing in a semicircle, listening. *Impressive picture*, she thinks, handing the newspaper back to Robyn. The team looks serious and into what she's telling them. If only they were like that all of the time.

"That is so cool to have a write-up about you! Isn't it cool?"

"It's just for a short time," Eileen says softly, studying the picture again.

"Yeah, but still . . . it's pretty neat."

Eileen nods her head. "Yeah, I guess. Do you mind if I keep this?"

"Yeah, go ahead."

Eileen closes the pages.

Robyn sucks in a breath. "Right. Well . . ." She fiddles with her fingers. "I haven't seen you in a while. I figured you'd have some juicy stories to tell."

"I don't have any stories to tell," Eileen says. "I've got some paperwork to do and then Oliver wants to meet with me."

Robyn swings her dark hair around her neck. "Is everything okay with you? I mean, you've been preoccupied lately."

"Busy," she assures Robyn with a couple of quick nods. "I've been working mostly from home."

"You just don't seem yourself."

Eileen looks at her and softens her eyes. "Everything is fine," she says. "I've been busy, that's all. . . . You know how it is." She isn't about to tell her how difficult it's been juggling her career and stressing about which instruction to go over with the guys and how Ty Caldwell is pressuring her for a date.

"You're burning yourself out!" Robyn says. "Look at you. . . ."

Eileen's bottom lip curls up, and she looks down at herself, trying to figure out what is so wrong with the outfit she has on. "What about me?"

"Your hair is all over the place. You have bags under your eyes—"

"I just taught a class!" Eileen corrects.

"I'm not used to seeing you this way."

"I'm having a bit of an off day," Eileen admits.

"I can tell, but I think it's more like an off month. People are noticing."

"Like who?"

"Oliver, Laura . . . they've all asked me what's wrong with you."

"They're just nosey."

"They're concerned."

"They are not concerned! Believe me, they just want gossip and there's no gossip to tell." Eileen shuffles a folder to another pile. "Speaking of Oliver, where is he?"

Robyn takes a step back. "I'll go get him for you."

"Thanks," Eileen says and opens the desk drawer in search for a fluorescent pen.

"If you're up for wings and three-fifty pints, a few of us are going out tonight."

"Thanks, maybe another time?"

"Sure." Robyn pauses before leaving. "Any chance of getting an autograph?"

"From who?"

"Brandon or Ty? Any of them really." She grits her teeth like she's asking for a lot.

"I can see what I can do," Eileen says, and Robyn turns on her toes, at the same time Oliver walks in.

"Hi, Elle! Sorry I'm late. I got cornered by a mom who didn't agree with the refs call on her son." He shakes his head. "So! I have some good news!"

She folds her elbows on the desk, watching him swivel a chair over to sit in front of her.

"I spoke to our rink managers up north and they want to open a hockey school with your name on it for next year. They can use a branded name to attract business."

"Wow, like a franchise?"

Oliver nods. His full head of orangey-red hair doesn't move. "I'll send you the guys' contact info. You'll have to talk to them and hire someone to teach, but they can go through that with you. The main thing is, it's up to you how you want to run your lessons."

"That's great," she says, surprised. "Thanks. Really, this means a lot."

"I've had a couple of inquiries asking if you taught private lessons."

Eileen shakes her head and bites her bottom lip. "I wish I had the time."

"I told them to email you and ask."

"I appreciate all the new business you're bringing in. It's funny—you work for the NHL and everyone wants you."

Oliver pats the desk with his hands. "That's how it goes, especially in this city." His crow's feet are evident when he smiles. "How is it going?"

"Great!"

"Well, if there's any woman who can teach guys, it's you, Elle."

"Aw, thanks."

"You have a mind of your own and you know your stuff." He swings a pointed finger at her.

"I'm glad it's working out," she says, softening her voice. "I better get going." She pushes herself away from the desk and stands up.

"Before you go," Oliver says, getting to his feet, "I've got an idea for your classes. Any chance you can talk a player into dropping by? We could do some promotion to get new sign-ups for our fall programs."

"I don't know. I'm still the newbie." She laughs.

"If there is a chance, keep it in mind."

Caldwell comes to mind, but there's no way she would ask him to please Oliver.

Eileen rushes home to freshen up, deciding on a cute light pink top she wore once for a dinner date and a pair of jean capris.

"I'm glad you agreed to a date," Ty says, watching her slide into the seat in front of him.

"This is hardly a date—it's more like a meeting," Eileen reminds him, making herself comfortable in the large booth.

"Oh yeah?" Ty asks in disbelief. "So, if this is not a date, what are we meeting about?"

She relaxes her shoulders. Her chin pops up and her eyes adjust to his. They stare at each other, transfixed in wonder. Did he have more on his mind than just dinner? Maybe he wants to tell her in person who her biggest threat is and will give her an idea who is causing trouble.

"I don't know. You called it."

"All right," he says, taking a sip of his drink. His hair is gelled in place, his face is clean-shaven, and he's wearing a polo shirt that accentuates his broad shoulders. "It's about you, then."

"Me?" she asks with surprise, and out comes a small laugh.

"I want to know more about you."

"You do? Like what?" She's not sure if she should be flattered or skeptical.

"Like why you have to act standoffish and sometimes rude. I get that your job is a hard sell to the guys, but being cold doesn't change the fact that you're a woman."

"Well, that's one way to start a conversation."

"It's a man's career."

She nods. "I get that. I take this job seriously. I'm not trying to make friends."

"Okay. I want to start off being honest with you." His tone is apologetic. "It's important in a relationship. Trust is huge, besides communication, of course."

"A relationship? Look, you think I'm acting this way because I'm not letting you get your way, but in this business I need to be firm. I'd have people walk all over me if I didn't."

"It's like you don't know how to relax."

It's been a long time since she unwound with the opposite sex. Has she gotten so hung up with work that she has forgotten what it's like to just relax?

"I don't think I'm as harsh as you make me sound, but I am definitely strong minded," she says. "I have to be."

The waiter approaches the table and takes their drink order.

Ty flips over his hand and flicks, pointing his finger to signal Eileen to place her order.

"I'll have a rum and Diet Coke."

"And I'll have another pint. So where were we?" he asks when the waiter leaves the table. "Oh, we were talking about you being strong-willed and not relaxing."

Eileen shoots him a look. "I do what I think is best for me, and right now I'm doing what I think is best."

"Not dating?"

"No," she says. "I'm talking about life in general."

"Sometimes you need to take chances or you will miss out on opportunities and it can mean missed happiness."

"You think so?" she asks. "And you're an expert?"

The waiter gently sets down a pint of beer in front of Ty, takes the empty glass, and sets down Eileen's drink.

"Maybe," Ty says, taking his cold glass of beer in hand. "You're missing out, that's all."

"Just so you know, I am not missing out on anything. In fact, I am quite content with myself and with my life, thank you very much," she says, grabbing hold of her tall glass and taking a sip from the straw.

"I guess if this is a meeting about you, tell me—what's holding you back from relationships?" He takes another sip of his beer.

Eileen cocks her head to one side. "What do you mean? I have good relationships."

"You're not seeing anyone or you wouldn't be out for dinner with me—or I assume so, as you don't seem like a two-timing kind of girl."

Why does he have to challenge her all the time? Can't he be happy that he has her company?

"Why do you have to keep pushing me?" she asks with a touch of annoyance in her voice. "I just need to know—"

The waiter walks up to their table before Eileen can finish her sentence and asks to take their meal order.

"I'll have the grilled salmon with wild rice."

Ty makes a face. "And I'll try the steak dinner with baked potato, loaded."

The waiter collects the menus and walks away, and Ty turns back to her. "You were saying?"

Eileen takes a breath. "It doesn't matter."

Ty nods his head, still gripping his frothy beer. "Yes, it does matter."

A smile keeps creeping to her lips and she's trying her hardest not to crack, but the way he is looking at her, studying her face and watching her every move, it's like he's trying to photograph the moment. No one's ever made her feel this way.

In a gentle voice, she responds, "I forgot. It's okay."

"I'm curious about your love life," he says with excitement.

"You are?" she asks, surprised and intrigued that he'd care. Still, she isn't buying it. "Why?"

"Tell me about your relationships with guys, not that you have supportive parents because I know that you probably do by the way you are, confident in what you do and secure with yourself," he says. "And you also have an uncle you're close to."

Eileen takes in a deep breath before answering. "My parents passed away five years ago." She holds back the sudden emotion that rises up every time she thinks of them. "I have supportive friends though," she says softly and looks down at her table settings.

"I'm sorry," Ty says gently, leaning back against the booth so his head is against the rest and he fingers the cardboard coaster. "That wasn't fair of me—I shouldn't have assumed."

"That's okay, you didn't know. Yes, I had very supportive parents," she emphasizes. "In fact my dad encouraged my hockey career and drove me to early-morning practices every Saturday morning."

Eileen looks at him, trying to hold back tears. She shouldn't let him see the soft side of her—this is the one reason she doesn't mix business with pleasure. She doesn't want to show this delicate side when she has to be strong.

Ty smiles sympathetically and says, "My dad did the same. Those were some early mornings. He would tell me"—Ty lowered his voice—" 'When you get to be sixteen you're on your own' and hand me the keys and say, 'Son, drive yourself.' "

Eileen grins, happy that he can lighten the mood.

"He told me he hated waking up early and how he was going to sleep in Saturdays," Ty says.

"My uncle Gary has been my cheerleader and I'm thankful I have him."

"Yeah, he's a good guy," he says. "I'm really sorry for being a jerk. I shouldn't have pressured you about your personal life—that was really unfair of me to say."

Eileen nods. Does Ty really care about her personal life or is he buttering her up for a nightcap? Not that she's interested. She won't let herself come that close. He'd never let her live it down.

"Can you accept my apology?" he asks and reaches for her hand.

Why did he have to be so attractive? And why did he know what to say at the right moment? As much as he ticks her off, there is something about him that she's drawn to, making her come back for more.

Ty's hand is warm and soothing, erasing the sorrow she felt moments before.

"Elle?" says a voice, startling her thoughts. She pulls her hand from under Ty's as though reacting to a hot stove and looks up to see Robyn. Of all people to run into, how can she hide the fact that she is sitting with Ty Caldwell?

"Hi," she answers sheepishly.

"I thought it was you!" Robyn exclaims in her loud, energized voice. "You're trying to hide from us aren't you?" She giggles. "You're really good at keeping a secret," she says with a wink. "Hello, there!" Robyn extends her hand. "You're Ty Caldwell! A pleasure to meet you. You can't fool me anymore. But don't worry, if you want it to be a secret, I won't say anything."

"We don't want everyone to know," Ty says. "We wouldn't want the press to get hold of the story and blow it up to something it isn't." He clenches his teeth. "Would we, Elle?"

Eileen taps her foot against his leg, giving him a wide-eyed look. What's in it for him?

Robyn makes eye contact with both of them. "You make an adorable couple, by the way. Picture perfect if you ask me. Well, I'll see you later. Bye." She waves at Eileen and walks away from their table with a spring in her step.

Eileen responds with a forced smile. How can she cover up being spotted with Ty? She cringes at the thought of going to the rink and having Robyn press her for more questions, insisting on juicy gossip.

Ty looks at Eileen. "You don't need it to be a secret."

"There's no secret," she says, squeezing her straw to her mouth.

"Good, I'm glad you feel the same way," he says. "When's our next date?"

"Date? There is no date."

"Come on now, we're on a date."

"This is a meeting," she reminds him, putting down her glass and scooping her rice. She can't let his blue eyes talk her into something she may regret, so she looks away for a second to snap back into reality.

"Yeah, whatever."

"We can't do this. . . . We're not dating. It wouldn't be right."

Ty sits up straighter, takes his glass in his hand, and washes down a bite. "What would you consider right? 'Cause this isn't wrong, Elle. I don't see why we can't call this a date." He takes another bite.

"It's not. Can we please move on?" Eileen asks, scooping a bite into her mouth.

"Ty Caldwell? I'm a huge fan," a girl shrieks, leaning forward to reveal her cleavage under her tight V-neck T-shirt.

"Oh, yeah?" he asks, sitting back in the booth, looking more relaxed by the hour.

"Yeah!" She giggles. "I usually sit behind the penalty box. I've waved to you a few times."

Ty laughs. "When I'm playing, my head's in the game."

"I've noticed! Are you able to sign this card?" she asks, handing him his hockey card.

"Oh, wow, look at this," Ty says, flashing the card at Eileen. "Haven't seen this one before."

"It's the best one!" the girl gushes, bouncing side to side.

Eileen rolls her eyes at the girl's breasts popping up from her shirt.

Ty picks up the pen. "Do you always carry hockey cards in your purse?"

"Not always. I knew I'd see you one day," she coos. "Besides, I've waited for you after a game, but I never see you."

Ty just nods and is relieved when she says, "Oh, no! I've got a Sharpie!" She hands him a mini marker.

"Thanks! So who do I make it out to?" Ty asks.

"Baby."

Ty chuckles. "Baby? Really? Come on, what's your name?" He taps the marker against the table waiting for an answer.

"Everyone calls me Baby."

"Oh, yeah? All right then." Ty takes one last look at the card before penning his name.

Baby leans into the table and says, "You're so lucky."

Eileen tries not to laugh at the girl's flirtatious way. She watches him hand over the O-Pee-Chee card as though it's something he will miss.

Is she lucky because she's with Ty? Or is she lucky because she's working with the Warriors?

"Can I give you something else to sign?" Baby asks.

"Sure. What is it?" Ty asks.

"My shirt."

"Okay, where?"

Eileen's eyes widen. Baby's white T-shirt has a print on the front and thankfully for that, the placement is limited.

"Right here." She points to her boob. Ty does what's requested of him.

The waiter picks up their dishes. When they are left alone for a mere thirty seconds, Ty asks, "So do you think Baby loves the game as much as you do?"

Eileen bursts out laughing and picks up her drink. "She loves you more than the game."

He's quick to reply. "She thinks she does." He holds a smirk and then takes the last sip from his glass. "So, Elle, where do you stand in all of this?"

"What do you mean?" Eileen asks.

"Us," he states as though she is supposed to know what he's talking about.

After a brief moment of their eyes holding a stare, Ty continues, "I don't want to keep pressuring you, but I feel something about us . . . you . . ." He pauses and then sadly asks, "Is there someone else you're interested in on the team?"

The waiter drops off the bill.

Eileen holds her fingers to her forehead, her elbow resting on the table. "What are you talking about? There is no one. I'm not interested in any one of them, or you for that matter. I'm strictly business." She puts her hand down, cupping the edge of the table. "Don't be getting all obsessed now."

"I'm not!"

"Good. Don't you have anything better to do than to pester me about my life?"

He stares at her for what feels like a long time. When he doesn't respond, Eileen pulls out her wallet and throws down enough cash to pay for her meal, a tip, and a little extra to cover Ty's. "Are we done here? I have to get up early."

He puts down a couple of bills, shoos her money back to her. "There's enough there," he says.

"It's not a date," she mutters as they scoot out of the booth, heading for the exit. He walks her to the parking lot to find her car.

"This your car?" Ty asks as she stops in front of her Mini. The sky has turned to dusk, making the keyed marks vanish—thankfully, since she doesn't feel like sharing the threats with him tonight. If anyone is going to know about it, it will be her uncle. She's going to have to deal with this on her own.

Eileen nods and unlocks her car.

"It's a small car for someone with a big attitude."

"You are not impressing me, Caldwell," she says, opening her door.

"You want me to impress you?" he asks, leaning into her. His nose skims the side of her mouth. A sudden heat flushes her cheeks, and all she can think about are his wide, kissable lips on her mouth. She closes her eyes as she feels the gentle brush of his lips open to hers. The motion of his kiss takes her breath away. She wants to pull him closer, maybe even feel her arms around his broad shoulders, the indents of his biceps. She holds back from returning the kiss, afraid to lead him on.

Ty pulls away, and as their lips part, she inhales his sweet, uplifting cologne. Her heart thumps heavy in her chest. *What just happened?*

"Is that a start?" he asks, taking a step back.

She doesn't dare say what's on her mind, afraid that she'll fumble her words. Her head is foggy from the kiss. Damn! Why does he get to her this way?

Her body like jelly, she keeps a straight face. The last thing she wants him to think is she likes him. That would just go to his head and he would put more pressure on her to date.

"Good night," she says as she gets into her car, happy that their meeting is over and she can safely walk away.

Chapter 8

It's Friday, another practice, which means having a conversation with Ty. Did he kiss her for reaction? He didn't really want to start something with her, did he? What would people say if it ever got out? This job is too important for her to risk a relationship—not that she is considering a date with the superstar; he is only after one thing. She has to think of an excuse not to see him again. And it's not like she has any plans of her own, something that's starting to become a common theme in her life. Has she gotten herself into a rut? While her girlfriends are out nearly every weekend, she's putting together instructions for one of her skating classes. After her parents died, she kept herself busy, hoping it would help take her mind off of what she lost. Now, it seems she's too tired to want to do anything else. Maybe Ty's right—maybe she needs to get out more or at least start spending more time with the only family she has.

Eileen walks through the Warriors' building as though she been doing this job for years. She says hello to a familiar face and makes her way to the bench, where she laces up her skates, puts on her hockey gloves, grabs her stick, and heads out onto the clean ice surface. The players are due on the ice in a few minutes, enough time for her to set up the practice.

"Good morning," she says as she watches Steve skate toward her.

"How are things?"

"Fine," she says.

"Any issues?"

Her eyebrow arches. "Issues?"

One by one, the players make it onto the ice.

"Are the guys behaving?"

"So far, so good," she says.

"Good to hear. Let's hope it stays that way." He skates away.

"Me too," she mutters and watches the players step on the ice and skate around to warm up. Some are wearing blue jerseys, others white. "Twice around the rink and meet me back at center ice!" she shouts, noting that Ty isn't at practice. Late night with the ladies? Too good for practice? At least he won't be pestering her for a date. Maybe he is done with her. After their *meeting*, he saw that she wasn't interested in him, which is a relief.

Oh, well, he'll be on to someone else who's easier, more into his games.

She stands and waits for the players at center ice with her whistle hanging around her neck and a portable white board and marker in her hands. "We're going to start with the cut cross drill leading into a breakaway," she announces as she draws a diagram of the play. "Wingers, one on each side. You'll skate wide to the net, defense in the middle. It will be a two-on-one. Defense will take the trailer—"

"We know how to play hockey," Bret Thompson chirps. "Show us something we don't know."

Eileen glances at him and carries on as if she didn't hear him. "It will be a two-on-one. Once the man with the puck takes the shot, D picks up the puck and wingers chase to the other side, creating a breakaway. Got it?"

Thompson stands with a gloved hand on his hip. "Yeah, we got it," he says bitterly. "You can call out instructions, but you can't do them." He smirks, looks at the player beside him, who gives him a grin of encouragement. "Why don't you be D? I'd like to see you give this a try."

"Sure," Eileen says with a shrug. "I'm always up for a challenge." What does she have to do to prove to them that she is capable and skilled?

"I need two wingers!" she yells, watching Thompson skate to the side without the puck. *Great*, she thinks, *I've got to take him to the boards*. He's a big guy, tall and known for his attitude on and off the ice. The public calls him the Enforcer. Every team has one, but they are usually nice guys off the ice, or so she's told. Thompson isn't like that. She can tell by his comments and brazen demeanor.

Eileen blows her whistle, and the guy with the puck starts skating toward the net. The play is on. She is using her speed to make level with Thompson, although she can't physically remove him from the play so when she skates for him, she leads into the boards, hunched over and using her shoulder as her weapon to show how she would stop him at the boards without making body contact with him. He has to stop so that their bodies won't collide. As Eileen lowers her shoulder, Thompson lifts his elbow with such force and determination that he pushes her body, throwing her off balance. Eileen hits the boards hard and falls to the ice. Instantly she grits her teeth and closes her eyes as she takes in a deep breath feeling the pain in her right hand. Wondering whether or not she has broken a bone or two, she tells herself she won't cry, not in front of these men.

She doesn't want to show weakness. That's what they want to see—a woman who can't play the game. A woman who is trying to fit in with men but can't take a hit.

Thompson's intentions prove different. He doesn't stop to check on the damage he's caused; instead, he continues to skate towards the net, finishing the drill as though nothing happened.

Eileen can't move; the pain is too much. Her whole body hurts. *It will be okay*, she tells herself. She'll get up in a moment as soon as the pain isn't so sharp.

"She's hurt!" yells a player who skates over to her.

The pain is still there. She can't move, but she tries. She has to get up off the cold surface; she's only wearing coaching gear, including a pair of un-insulated workout pants.

As she lies on the ice, she can hear someone yelling at Thompson. "What the hell was that? Are you for real? Were you trying to knock her unconscious? You did that on purpose, you moron!"

"She did it herself!" Thompson yells back. "She wants to be one of the guys, she has to learn how to take a hit!"

"She's still a woman, you idiot! And she weighs a quarter of you! She doesn't even have equipment on!"

"Are you banging her, Caldwell? Is that why you're so defensive?" And with that, a fight breaks out and two players are throwing punches until Steve intervenes.

"Should we call an ambulance?" someone yells.

Ty bends down to her. "How do you feel?" he asks softly, touching her hand. "You didn't knock your head, did you?"

"No, but I'm really sore." Sore wasn't the right word; pain was more like it. Pain in her leg, her shoulder, her neck, her hand—it was like being in a car crash and afterwards wondering what happened and figuring out what limitations her body has.

"No kidding, I'm sure you're sore. How are your legs? Can you move them?"

Eileen moves her legs slowly, gritting her teeth.

"How about your arms? Can you lift them up?"

She lifts her left arm up with no problem.

"Easy. You don't want to force it. How about the other one?"

She can tell by the pain in her right shoulder that this is going to give her trouble. Eileen slowly lifts her arm and she closes her eyes in fear that the discomfort will show.

"It hurts, doesn't it?" Brandon asks, joining them. He nods as though he can feel what she feels.

"Yes," she mutters.

Steve skates over and leans over Ty's shoulder. "I'll call an ambulance."

"No, I can take her to a clinic."

That's all she needs, to be out on the injured list and possibly lose her job with the Warriors. Is it Thompson who's been threatening her? She couldn't think of anyone else on the team with such anger and hostility toward her.

"I'm going to help you up," says Brandon, putting his hand around her waist. "Is this okay?"

Eileen lets out a weak yes.

"Here! I'll help her." Ty's voice is loud and direct.

"You grab her left arm and I'll hold onto her right side," Ty instructs, gently wrapping his arm around her waist. Her right arm is lying on her body; she doesn't want to move it.

They ease her up carefully. "Put your arm around me," Brandon says. "For support."

"I'll take you to the clinic," Ty says, lifting her up. From the strength of his arm, she knows she'll be okay. He won't let her fall. Is this the real Ty? Or is he trying to score bonus points for another night out?

Eileen glances up at him, only moving her neck slightly to meet his eyes. They are warm, and just like she remembers from their first embrace, her heart picks up and his sweet cologne brings her back to that night. As her eyes take in his comfort, she also is startled by his injury. "You're bleeding!" she shouts.

"I'll be okay," Ty says, calmly.

"But you're bleeding! Thompson is such a jerk. He thinks he can bully his way around—"

"Just a small cut. Don't worry," Ty reassures her. "I'll be fine."

"Don't worry? What's next? Is he going to run me down in the parking lot?"

"He wouldn't do that," Ty says. "He has anger issues and unfortunately he took them out on you. Come on. Let's get you to the doctor. We need to get you checked out. Let's hope nothing's broken."

Ty and Brandon take her to the bench so they can take off her skates.

"Well, maybe he should get some help," Eileen manages to say.

Brandon chuckles. "It comes in handy in a game."

"Other teams don't like him either," Ty says, placing her on the bench for support.

"Do you have her?" he asks Brandon. When he gets the nod, Ty continues. "Coaches get stressed when they know he's playing." Eileen watches Ty unlace her skates, gently removing them from her feet, giving the blades a quick wipe with a hand towel and placing them in her gym bag.

"Has he seriously hurt other players?" She doesn't really care about having a conversation about Thompson, but it's the only thing that she can keep her mind focused on as she tries not to think about the pain.

"Oh, sure, he has, in a game. . . ."

"No one from his own team," adds Brandon. "I'll grab my shoes and give you a hand," he tells Ty.

Ty gives him a nod and slips Eileen's running shoes on her feet. "I don't know what his problem is."

"He has a problem with a woman being on the team," Eileen mutters.

"He doesn't realize his strength," Ty says, holding her, waiting for his teammate to return.

"He knows his strength. He wants me off the team."

"Maybe we should call an ambulance."

"No, I'll be okay," Eileen says, not wanting to cause more of a disturbance than she already has.

Brandon comes back and walks on the other side of her for support.

"I'm going to grab my wallet and shoes," Ty says. "I'll be right back. Will you be okay? I'll be quick."

She nods slightly, bracing herself on the bench with her left hand. She closes her eyes and takes some deep breaths.

"Ty will look after you," Brandon says. "He's a good guy."

Eileen responds with a small smile.

Ty returns fully dressed and grabs her bag. She slowly makes her way to the parking garage elevator with a guy on each side.

When they reach the secured parking lot, Ty says, "I'll go get my truck. Wait here." She watches him run off.

Eileen leans against the building, supporting herself against Brandon.

"Is Ty always this accommodating?" she asks, barely lifting her chin to look at him.

"Oh, yeah. Ty's a good guy. You and him together?"

"Are you wondering if I'm sleeping with him? No." She feels like laughing, but her upper body is sore and every time she speaks it hurts. "We're not together."

"I think he cares about you. I haven't seen him like this. He doesn't normally help out this much unless you're his best friend."

Ty pulls up in his Toyota FJ and jumps out, rushing over to help her into the passenger seat.

Ty picks her up and places her on the seat.

"Thanks," he tells Brandon, as if she's Ty's responsibility.

She rests her head back, feeling numb from all that is going on as they head out of the parking lot and drive to the closest clinic.

"Thanks for this," Eileen mutters. "For taking me."

He has both hands on the steering wheel, his hat worn backwards and wisps of hair curling out at the sides. "No problem," he says with a quick glance and then his eyes are back on the road.

They drive in silence most of the way. Eileen is too sore to talk, and she tries to close her eyes, feeling the pulsation of her head.

Ty pulls up to the clinic, parks, and hops out. "I'll go put your name down," he says and shuts his door.

All Eileen can think about is she needs to get better. She needs to get back out there before the media gets a hold of the story and she's thrown from the team because of all the attention.

A few minutes later, Ty opens the driver's-side door and hops in. "It's an hour wait. Are you going to be okay, or should I drive you to your own doctor?"

"I'll be okay. This is probably easier. I don't want to move."

"They said it could be longer, hard to say."

"I'm okay," she whispers. "Tell me, does Thompson push his way around all the time?"

Ty smoothed the steering wheel with his hand, taking a second to answer. "I've never seen him do what he did. But he does have a big attitude."

Eileen smirks.

"What?" he asks playfully, glancing her way.

"Attitude? All you guys have attitudes." Eileen tries to look at him, but her neck is tender and she'd much rather look straight ahead at all the traffic going by than feel more discomfort. "It's not a bad thing . . ." she says, thinking that sometimes she also has an attitude. "Depends how you use it. . . . Thompson doesn't like me. He's trying to get rid of me."

"He's bitter." Ty shrugs his right shoulder. "He's not all that bright either."

They enter the clinic building very slowly; Ty helps her to the counter, where she gives them her personal information. The medical office assistant talks to Eileen but keeps eyeing Ty, knowing he looks familiar but not quite able to place him. She saw the same look from the waiter at the restaurant.

"Have a seat," she tells them and they wander over to a corner of the room, where they won't be exposed.

"How are you feeling?" Ty whispers. "Better? Worse?"

"The same," she answers. Not long after, Eileen hears her name called.

Ty jumps up to help her.

The woman leads the way to a room, shuts the door behind her, and says, staring at Ty's cut and then at Eileen's hunch, "So were you two in a fight?"

"We were playing hockey and I fell into the boards," Ty says, relaxed, as he helps Eileen stand against the examining bed. "Do you want to sit?"

She lets out a sharp no.

"Dangerous sport." The nurse shakes her head as though disappointed. "That's why I don't let my son play. Scary what can happen."

"Same with skateboarding, or any sport," Ty says. "It's one of those things."

She writes something down on the board and says, "Dr. Martin will be with you in a few minutes."

The door shuts behind her and Ty asks Eileen if she's okay. He suddenly places his hands around her waist, lifting her off the ground and toward the examining bed. "I'll help you up."

"What are you doing?" she asks as though aggravated, but she's shocked that he feels the need to help her all the time. "I can do it." She softens her voice, not wanting to sound ungrateful. She lets him hold her. Her eyes find his and instantly her throat is dry. She is brought back to the kiss they shared outside the restaurant. Her heart is beating wildly again. Why does he make her body react?

"Are you kidding? It will take you ten minutes if I let you," he says.

"Very funny," she says, placing an arm around his neck. Her insides go to mush as she realizes holding on to him comforts her. Ty leans closer, and their noses touch. She freezes, seeing his lips part to hers as he lifts her onto the table. It would be so easy to move an inch closer and taste his kiss again.

The door opens. Ty flinches, plunking her down on the table. He stands beside her, watching a bearded man wearing a buttoned-up shirt and a stethoscope around his neck come in and close the door behind him. "How are you two today?" the doctor asks. Then something hits him and he stops, looks at Ty. "Wait a minute! Are you Ty Caldwell?" He flips through his information sheet.

Ty nods his head and the doctor extends his hand.

"Good to meet you. I'm Dr. Martin."

"Good to meet you, too," Ty says politely.

"Looks like you need a Band-Aid for that cut." Dr. Martin digs in a cupboard and grabs a Band-Aid. "What happened?" he asks as he tends to Ty's face, first cleaning it with a tissue and applying ointment, then placing the bandage.

"We were at practice and one of my teammates accidentally fell into Eileen and she went into the boards, hard."

Eileen scowls.

The doctor puts his hand on Eileen's leg. "Where does it hurt?"

"Everywhere," she says. "Mostly my hand."

"Can you open your fingers?"

Slowly, she extends her hand.

"Yeah, it's swollen and looks bruised. Okay. We'll need to do an X-ray to be certain nothing's broken. What else hurts?"

Eileen feels as if she's at the deli counter, telling the clerk what else she needs to make a hoagie. Can't he tell she is hurting? Shouldn't he prescribe medicine, T3s? Something to take away the throbbing.

"My right side and thigh."

"I'll take a look," the doctor says, pulling her shirt up halfway. Eileen looks at Ty and he slowly turns away. "There is some bruising. What kind of pain is in your leg?"

"I can barely walk on it."

"My guess is you pulled a muscle. It will be swollen for a few days and you will see some deep bruising in the next day. Depending how bad the strain is, it could be two weeks before it heals. Take Advil, ice your leg and elevate it. Keep off your feet for a day or two to help with the swelling. In the meantime, you'll need an X-ray on your wrist." He hands her a referral.

"Thanks," Eileen says as Ty helps her off the table.

"Good luck this season," the doctor says. "I'll be rooting for you."

"Thanks, Doc."

They walk out of the clinic. "I'll drive you to get X-rays," Ty says. "It's not far from here."

"Thanks, but I can go myself. You've done enough for me."

"Might as well get looked after now. The quicker we tend to you, the sooner you'll be back on your feet."

"Why did you lie to the doctor?" Eileen asks, miffed about this being an accident.

"I didn't lie."

"Yeah, you did. You said Thompson accidentally pushed me into the boards. It wasn't an accident."

"I know that. What does it matter what the doctor knows? I didn't lie about how you got hurt."

"You're protecting him." Is this what the team does? Even if someone is in the wrong they cover for each other?

"No, I'm not. I just think it's in the best interest of the team if I kept it innocent. Can you imagine if that got out? Jeez, what would

Braxton say if he heard? Gotta keep the team positive. We're heading into a new season—we don't want that on our backs."

"You mean the truth?"

"Yeah. You'd be gone because the last thing they want is conflict on the team."

"So you were protecting me?" she says with humor.

"I was," Ty says firmly. Not what Eileen was expecting to hear.

His answer keeps her quiet until they walk into the X-ray clinic. They're expecting to wait a long time, but it's only a few minutes before the technician calls her over. Ty waits for her, and when she is finished, he again helps her to his truck.

"Well, this sucks," she says. "What can I do with a sprained wrist?"

"You're lucky nothing's broken and lucky it's Friday so you can rest until Monday."

"I don't feel lucky. I'm supposed to teach a class tomorrow morning."

Ty hops into the driver seat and starts his truck up. "Not tomorrow. You'll have to call in a backup."

"I don't have a backup," she says with worry. "It's my class! I don't have a replacement."

"You should."

"This doesn't happen. It wasn't supposed to happen," she complains.

"It happened and now you need to call whoever you call and tell them you can't teach tomorrow."

"I can't do that." She bites her lower lip thinking of her options.

He drives out of the parking lot.

"You can't teach. You heard the doctor. He said you need to rest."

She pouts for a moment. "Can you teach my class?" she asks in a small voice.

He laughs out loud as though she told the most hilarious joke.

"I guess that's a no," she says crossly, staring ahead.

"You're not serious."

She knew his answer before she asked, but she hoped he'd consider it.

"They're just six- and seven-year-olds. They probably won't even know who you are," she lies. "It's an hour class. I'm sure you can spare an hour out of your busy day, can't you?"

"Elle, it's not that I don't want to. Wouldn't it be weird? I mean, you're the one who doesn't want to go on a date with me, afraid of what people will say, and you're suggesting that I teach one of your skating classes? What happens if the media finds out? You know they will. Word will get around pretty quickly."

"You're right." She sighs with disappointment. "I shouldn't have asked. I wasn't thinking. I just thought it wouldn't hurt."

"Under different circumstances, I would . . ."

"It's okay, really." She tries looking his way. "I shouldn't have asked."

"All right, then. I'll take you home."

"What about my car?"

"You can't drive," he says, looking at her hand and then at her. "You have a severely pulled muscle and a sprained wrist. We'll pick it up tomorrow."

"It won't be safe there overnight."

"We can get someone else to drive it," he suggests.

"Like who?"

"Keller. I'll give him a quick call."

"We can't ask him to do that. I barely know him! Why would he do me a favor?"

"I didn't ask you to make out with him. I'm asking him to drive your car home."

"I'll call Brooke." Eileen unzips her purse with her left hand and grabs her cell phone.

"Who's Brooke?"

"My friend." Eileen dials her number. After a quick chat, Brooke agrees to come and pick up the car. Eileen throws her cell back into her purse.

"Is your friend going to meet us?"

Eileen nods her head slightly, feeling the tightness and a strain below her ear. "She's on her way. She'll drive my car home."

Ty pulls in front of the arena and shuts off the engine. "We'll wait for her here. You'll be able to see her when she pulls in."

"She'll be here in a few minutes."

Ty turns to look at her, his right hand holding on to the steering wheel. "How do you feel?"

"Okay. Still pretty sore. I'll heal. I seem to be a fast healer," she tells him. "It's not the first time I've pulled a muscle."

"Good. You can get back on the ice and show Thompson that you're made of steel."

She smirks. "Yeah, right." Eileen makes eye contact with Ty. "I hope he doesn't come to any more practices."

"He will, so just ignore him."

"Kinda hard to when he doesn't have a problem physically removing me. I can't say anything to the coaching staff. They warned me about some players."

"Like who?"

"They told me that not all the guys will feel equally privileged to have me on the team. So this was like a test, I guess."

"I'm sure it won't happen again."

"I hope not. I don't understand why the guys make such a big deal that a woman is sharing the ice with you. Why is that?"

"You want me to answer that?" Ty says, resting his head back staring out the windshield.

"Amuse me."

"It doesn't matter what I say. You'll find a way to argue it."

"No, I won't!" Eileen says, offended.

"See? There you go, disagreeing with me—again!"

"It's easy to." There's a moment of silence. "So you're not going to explain?"

"Nah, you know the answer," Ty says, his eyes find hers.

She studies him for a second, realizing that he's serious. It doesn't matter what is said in the locker room, and who's on her side; it doesn't change the fact that men have egos and having a woman instruct them only adds salt to the wound.

"Okay," she says, giving in.

Brooke pulls in. "That's her, over there," Eileen says, pointing, and she very carefully slides out of the truck, feeling the tender muscles spasm with every movement.

Her friend jumps out of her car. "You look like you're in pain."

"I am. I'm sore all over."

"I'm sure Ty can help you out in that department." She snickers.

Ignoring her friend's comment, she pulls her keys out of her bag and takes her car key off her ring. "Here," she tells Brooke, who is busy looking over her shoulder trying to spot the hockey player. "I'll keep the set so I can get into my apartment."

"He is really cute." Her eyes widen as she studies his looks.

"I'll meet you back at my place," Eileen says, ignoring her friend's comment.

"I don't see why you don't date him. He's really into you. What guy does this for a woman he knows he isn't going to get far with?" she whispers. "He wants you!"

Eileen tilts her head to the side. "It's not what it looks like."

Ty gets out of the truck.

"Sure, Elle. You're just blind." Brooke gets into Eileen's car while Ty helps Eileen back in the truck.

"I shouldn't have gotten out," she says.

"You'll rest when you get home."

When they arrive, they park next to Brooke in the underground parking garage, and Ty walks over to help Eileen out of the passenger seat.

"I can do this," Eileen says, frustrated that she needs his help and mad that she's in pain.

"I know. I'm helping," Ty says.

"Ty? This is my friend Brooke. Brooke, Ty."

They both exchange a "Nice to meet you."

"Did you always have key marks?" he asks, looking at her car.

"No, that happened at the rink," she tells him.

"Really? When?" he asks.

"Last week."

"After practice? Did you report it?"

"No."

"Why not? You should!" he says, examining the paint and running his hand along the marks. "They did a good job."

"That's what insurance is for," she says. "Look, you don't have to help me. I can do this."

Ty lets her lean on him walking inside to the elevator. "I can carry you. Here," he says, bending down and picking her up.

"What are you doing?" she demands, embarrassed.

"This is easier than watching you in pain with every step," Ty says.

She shrieks, and when he doesn't let her down, she surrenders to his embrace, resting her head on his shoulder until they're inside the elevator. He smells like spring air, not what she expected him to smell like after the confrontation with Thompson and carrying her from the truck.

"You can put me down," she tells him. When he doesn't answer, she encourages him. "I'm okay, really. I can stand."

"Don't argue with him," Brooke says.

"I'm not, but I can hold myself up."

For a moment, she thinks he's going to lock his lips on hers. He is close enough for her to smell his minty mouth. Her hand is resting on his broad shoulder. She wants so badly to touch the strands of hair that are coming out of his hat and covering his neck.

Ty gently sets her down, cautiously, attentively, balancing her on her feet.

The door opens and Eileen slowly takes a step out. "Do you want me to carry you?" Ty asks.

"No." She hesitates. "I should be okay." Her neck feels like she has whiplash and her thigh is like jelly. She can barely walk.

"Here," Ty says, throwing her left arm under his and steadily putting his right arm around her waist. "Lean on me to take the pressure off."

She does what she's told and again is thankful he's there. How would she have managed on her own? She wouldn't even be able to crawl down the hall, let alone slither against the wall with Brooke's support. Maybe Ty isn't so bad after all. Then again, he wants something from her and she's not sure she can help him with his requests.

"This is it," she says, reaching for her keys.

"Here, let me," he says, watching her fiddle with the ring. "Which key is it?"

"The silver one." She points.

He opens the door wide. "Nice place."

"Thanks."

"I feel like I'm walking into a hotel room."

"Oh. Yeah? Well, don't get any ideas."

He chuckles and leads her with her left arm to the couch. Brooke shuts the door behind them. "You'll need to put your feet up," he tells her.

The pain in her shoulder makes her clench her teeth. Slowly, she sticks out her behind to embrace the couch. She lets out a yelp.

"I got you!" he says, bringing her gently to the cushion, Brooke standing helplessly in front of them. Ty helps her swing her legs onto the couch and unties her shoes, throwing them to the ground.

"I'm using the bathroom," Brooke tells them and leaves the room.

"Even my foot is sore," she says, trying to flex her foot forward and backward.

"I'm sure your whole body will be for a few days. Do you need anything? Something to drink? Are you hungry?"

"Wow, Caldwell, what's up with the special treatment? Do you treat all the girls like that?"

"Of course I do. What kind of guy do you think I am?"

"What's in this for you?"

He shakes his head. "Nothing. I'm here to help you so you might as well take advantage of me."

"Come on, now, seriously." Her eyes narrow.

"I am serious. I'm not the type to walk away when someone needs me."

"Really? So you are doing this because you want to?" she asks.

"Yes. Why do you look so surprised?"

"Because I am."

"You shouldn't be," he says, adjusting his hat. "What do you feel like for dinner?"

"I can figure that out. You've helped me out enough. Thank you. I'm sure you have plans so don't let me take up your time."

There is a brief moment when they take in each other's gaze. Eileen's heart beats dramatically as she realizes he hasn't looked away. The intensity wraps around her and she can't seem to take her mind off of his beautiful face, marred only by a hockey slash to his jaw. She looks at the line.

"Hockey's a rough sport," he says, bringing his finger to his scar.

Brooke walks into the room and breaks the moment. Eileen feels a chill pass over her.

"If I didn't want to be here, I wouldn't be. I'll order pizza, with the works?" he asks.

"None for me," Brooke says, setting down a bottle of Advil on the coffee table. "But thanks."

"Are you sure?" Eileen asks.

"Yeah. I'll get you some water."

Brooke comes back with a glass and dishes out two tablets. Eileen takes the pills and washes them down. Her friend takes the glass from her and sets it down.

"Is she the friend you helped move?" Ty asks Eileen.

"Move?" Brooke asks.

"Ah, yeah, the move," Eileen stammers. "Yes! Yes it was! The move went well. We had enough help and it went smoothly . . ."

"Okay," Brooke says, looking at her friend with confusion. "Yeah, I should probably get going. I have plans tonight."

"That's right. You have a purse party. Sorry," Eileen says.

Brooke waves her hand in midair. "Ah, you've seen everything I've made."

Ty takes out his keys from his pocket. "I'll drive Brooke back to the arena to get her car. We'll go and I'll be back with dinner. I'll lock up behind me."

"Take my keys then," Eileen says. "That way you can just come on in."

Eileen lies on her couch, aching. What did Thompson think he was going to do to her? Why did he want to physically hurt her? Could he be that disgruntled about the whole arrangement? Maybe she could just close her eyes for a little bit. . . .

Eileen's eyes flash open as she hears the door shut and she jolts upright, eyes wide open. She doesn't know how long she slept for, but it felt like hours.

"Sorry, did I scare you?" he asks, holding a pizza box, a bag dangling from his arm.

"I'm not used to someone else in my apartment. I must have fallen asleep."

"Hope you're hungry. I bought us some Diet Coke and root beer. I need some sugar," he says as he unloads the plastic bag onto her kitchen counter. She watches him from the open floor plan. "And no one likes drinking alone."

"Just make sure you leave with the beer. Don't get any ideas," she says, her head a little foggy.

"I bought root beer," he says loudly, "not beer. Where are your glasses?"

"Cupboard by the fridge," she says, scratching the side of her head as she watches him make himself at home. "And thank you. You didn't have to stop to buy me anything."

"I don't like eating alone either, if I can help it." He grabs the ice cube tray from the freezer and pops two cubes into her glass. "Besides, what else are we going to do on a Friday night?"

"We're not dating," she reminds him with a smile as he walks over to her with a tall glass of Diet Coke. He hands it to her. "Just pop. The meds should be kicking in."

Ty cracks open a bottle of root beer and takes a sip, then puts it down to retrieve the pizza. "Where are your plates?"

"The cupboard beside the glasses."

"Right." He comes back with plates and paper towels stacked on top of the cardboard box and places them on the coffee table. Ty dishes out pizza on a plate and hands it to her.

"Don't take this the wrong way," she says. "But seriously"—her eyebrows furrow—"why are you being so nice to me? What do you want?"

"Why do you think I want something? I mean, I'd like to go on a real date with you and give you the Ty Caldwell treatment, but I can't see that happening anytime soon, not until you get over your panic attacks."

Her mouth drops. "I don't have panic attacks."

"You do when I mention the word date."

She bites her bottom lip.

"You must have had some bad dates if you have such a fear of them."

"That's not true," she says, thinking of one of her exes, who was not a bad guy. He just suffocated her and wouldn't leave her alone. And Mario, well, he was a different breed altogether. After him, she hasn't trusted anyone else. He's cocky and a smooth talker. He's also good looking, and has lots of money, favoring women who only want one-night stands. Eileen is different from those women; she wants a real relationship, one that can be trusted and can grow. At the time, Mario made her a promise that she was everything to him, but that ended when he had an affair and broke her heart. Since then, Eileen hasn't found a relationship in which she feels like a priority or a lasting romantic connection.

"What's wrong with me?" he asks. "Tell me. Be honest. I can take it from you."

She thinks for a moment. There is nothing wrong with Ty. He

seems like a fun and happy guy. It's her. She is set against dating a guy from work.

Eileen looks up at him and says, "There's nothing wrong with you." She takes a bite of pizza and wipes her mouth with a paper towel. It's been so long since she's had a greasy meal. It tastes so good.

"Then why do I get the feeling that there is?"

"There's a big difference between going out and dating."

"There is?" he asks, laughing. "Okay." He shakes his head. "Let me take you out next week when you're feeling better and after that you can decide. At least give me a chance. I like you, Eileen. I want to get to know you. Is that too much to ask?"

"It is if you want something out of it."

"Your friend Brooke was right. She warned me you would say something to that effect."

"She did? What else did she say?"

"A lot of things."

"Like what?" Eileen urges. She wouldn't have told him about Mario, would she?

"You are actually a very sensitive person, which surprises me, and I'd like to see that for myself, but she warned me that once you're close to someone you have a hard time letting go."

Eileen's face flushes. "That's not true!"

"Then why do you spend more time with work than with your friends? And why can't you relax and enjoy yourself instead of being confrontational and hard to read? Is it because you're scared to have a good time?"

Eileen doesn't know what to say. She knows what to tell Brooke, but Ty? Why can't he understand that she doesn't want his friendship or relationship? She's happy with the way things are, or she thinks she is.

"I'm taking you out next Saturday whether you like it or not, and if after the date," he lingers on the forbidden word, "you don't want to have anything to do with me, then I'll respect that, but until then you don't know what you're missing."

"Oh, no?" she asks, finishing her pizza.

"You'll see," he says, adjusting his backward hat.

Eileen reaches for another piece of pizza and a napkin to wipe her fingers.

"Don't move!" Ty says and jumps up to help her readjust her body on the couch. He leans over her, scooping his arms underneath her to position her comfortably. Eileen freezes, and her heart begins to race again when his lips are close to her ear. The vibration of his voice sends a shiver of neediness throughout her body.

"I can do this!" she shouts nervously, and Ty backs off with a chuckle.

"You need to rest—that means don't move off the couch. I'll clean up!" Ty stands up and collects their plates and takes them to the kitchen. He comes back for the pizza box. "I'll throw this in the fridge. Do you need anything? I should go."

Go? Where does he have to be? Of course, it's Friday night and he would rather hang out at a club or with his buddies than sit here in an apartment listening to a woman whine.

"I'm fine," she says, getting herself to her feet. Ty rushes to her side to help.

"I'm okay!" she says, putting out a hand to stop him. "Thanks for all your help. I really appreciate everything you've done. I'll lock up behind you."

"No problem. Still got my number?"

"On my phone." She watches him throw on his shoes and opens the door. He gives her a genuine smile before leaving.

"Okay, I'm sure I'll be better tomorrow," she says, trying to put on a brave face.

"What time is your skating class?"

"Eleven."

"I'll be there."

Eileen closes the door behind him and for the first time in a long time she doesn't want to be alone.

Chapter 9

Eileen pulls her shirt over her head, managing to poke her sore hand through the sleeve, careful not to bump it. She isn't sure how she's going to sit on the bench and watch Ty instruct her skating class without jumping in and adding her advice. It will be the first session in her four-week program and she'll be unable to introduce herself to the class.

Her phone rings and she picks it up, saying her name as she tries to slip on a pair of shorts, leaning against the wall for support.

"You don't take a hint, do you?"

"Who is this?" Eileen tilts her head trying to place the voice.

"Give it up. Don't think you're equal to Ritchie—you're not. Quit the Warriors, or else."

"Or else what?" She tries to keep her tone fearless.

The line goes dead.

It's just a bunch of threats that won't turn into anything, she tells herself. Her chest is tight and she gasps for a breath. It takes her a few minutes of standing there and clearing her mind to slow her heart. *Ritchie will return soon*, she thinks and closes her eyes until she feels stronger and wipes the phone call out of her mind. Whoever it is, she won't let him get to her. She definitely needs to do something about it though. She's just not sure what.

Eileen sits on the couch trying to piece together the conversation she just had with the other threats. She can't begin to guess who the person is. Could it be a player? Or someone from management?

The phone rings again. She sits up to answer it, her heart in her throat. It won't be another threat; they are always spread out over weeks. She looks at call display this time and recognizes Ty's number. She falls back onto the couch, blinking her eyes and changing her tone of voice.

"Elle! It's Ty."

Her heart skips a beat and she is overcome with a warm sensation throughout her body. His voice is like a break in the clouds after the rain. He has her full attention. Her world stops, she is so happy to hear his voice.

"How are you feeling? Did you manage to get some sleep?" he asks.

She leans her head into the cushion. "I was up a few times trying to get comfortable. I'm still sore, but other than that, I'm doing okay. I can walk with just a small limp!" She laughs.

"That's improvement."

"Yeah, it is." Eileen stands up and goes to get a pair of socks from her dresser drawer. "So are you on your way to pick me up?"

"I want you to take it easy. I got this."

"I can come. Show you where to go and who to talk to—"

"I can handle it."

"I'm sure you can, but I should be there."

"It's your first class, right? The kids won't have any expectations."

"They will the second class when I show up without you."

Ty chuckles. "I'll tell them you'll be back, what, next week?"

"Tuesday."

"Okay, then. We're covered. I have your notes."

"I didn't see you take them."

"It's pretty self-explanatory," he says.

"Simple is best."

"I'll call you if I have any questions, but I'll be fine."

"Are you sure? I can come and sit on the bench." Eileen is secretly begging. She should be there—the rink counts on her.

"I don't want you judging my teaching skills."

"Why would I do that?"

"I'm getting to know you, and I get the feeling you don't let someone who screws up off the hook too easy."

"I forgive."

"How do you feel about Bret?"

"Thompson's an idiot! He meant what he did to me. There is no forgiving. You can't tell me he didn't do it on purpose."

Ty's breath is like a whisper in her ear. "I don't think he meant to hurt you."

"You're just taking his side because he's your friend."

"We're not friends—we're teammates."

She wishes now she didn't ask him to do her a favor. This could turn out to be a disaster. When it's done, he'll be telling her how to run her school.

"Get some rest," he says. "We'll talk later and I'll tell you how it went."

Could she possibly stay at home, wondering how he's doing on the first day? What does Ty know about teaching children? Thankfully there is only one class today. Some days there are three, but those busy days aren't until next week when all her classes are running.

"If you're free tonight, why don't I pick you up? You can come here and we can order takeout?"

It did sound appealing. She hadn't seen his place yet and it would break up her day. She didn't have any other plans.

"I can drive," she says. "My car is an automatic. I should be able to manage."

She hangs up her phone, but not before getting his address and directions to his place. Is she doing the right thing by having a dinner with a coworker? *We're not dating. It could be a business meeting*, she tells herself. He'll tell her all about the class he taught for her today. She calls Oliver to tell him why she's not teaching today. He isn't bothered when she mentions Ty's name; in fact, she knows that, being a hockey fan, he'll be like the other kids probably wanting an autograph or pictures.

Surprisingly, she sleeps part of the day, which helps her nerves. All she can think about is Ty and how her class is going. Her mind runs wild thinking about the parents doing double takes on who the instructor is. Several times she picks up her phone to call Ty to find out how it went and if there were any problems. She knows there won't be, but the idea of her not being there causes her much anxiety.

She needs to let go and not worry so much about how others affect her job.

By five o'clock she leaves to go to the store to pick up lasagna, garlic toast, and frozen yogurt for dessert. If Ty wants to have a relationship with her, then he'll have to wait until Ritchie comes back to work, but for now, they can be friends. It's turning out to be a comfortable relationship, and as much as she denies herself from the feelings that arise, she misses Ty when he's not around.

"What's this?" Ty asks, greeting her at the door. "Here, let me take it." He grabs the plastic bag from her hand and shuts the door. Eileen gets a whiff of his fresh soap scent. He is wearing a hat backwards to hide his damp hair and his shirtsleeves are tight around his biceps, revealing his toned body. Eileen looks away so she's not caught staring and envisioning him wrapping her up in his arms.

"Dinner." Eileen takes her flats off and walks barefoot across to the open kitchen. "Ready-made lasagna."

"Surprise dinners. Gotta love them. I thought for sure we would be ordering in."

"I thought I'd save us the trouble."

Their eyes lock for a second before Eileen blinks and turns her attention to his home. "Very nice," she says, looking around, admiring the artwork and carefully thought-out mementos. His place is stunning. It looks like a page out of *House & Home* magazine.

The windows are tall, perfect for staring out into the evening summer sky. The brown and beige couch and recliner chair look like they've never been sat on. The fabrics are firm and lint-free. The solid wood coffee table displays a hardcover book on the history of hockey.

Eileen looks around at her surroundings. "I have to say, I didn't expect your place to be so . . . so . . . spectacular. I mean, the details! You sure know how to decorate."

He grimaces. "I can't take all the credit. I had help," he admits, popping their dinner in the oven to warm. "Something to drink? A glass of merlot?"

She hesitates, knowing that one glass has its disadvantages. She is firm about not spending the night and doesn't want to unwind too much. She tries hard not to get too comfortable; that will only lead to trouble.

"Come on," he says, sensing her hesitation. "You have to have a glass with lasagna." He slips two glasses off the metal rack under the counter and reaches for a bottle from his wine rack.

"Those are generously sized glasses," she says, watching him uncork the bottle with one easy lift of the corkscrew.

"Do you want a glass of wine or a sip of wine?" he teases as he pours.

She lifts her glass with her left hand. She's gotten used to using her left hand, even though her right hand is feeling better.

"Cheers." Ty clinks her glass, takes a sip. "Here, let me show you around."

"It's the biggest apartment I've ever been in," she admits, taking in the luxuries of his penthouse overlooking English Bay.

He shrugs. "It's not bad."

"Not bad?" she balks. "It's beautiful! Jeez, it puts my place to shame."

"Come on, Elle. You have a decent apartment."

She knows she does for a modest person. However, this is breathtaking. It's hard to wrap her head around something this grand. It's like having a choice of owning a Volkswagen or a Porsche. They're both well made, but one is more desirable.

"Yeah, but you have a built-in Miele coffee machine!"

"You may have noticed when you got here; the bathroom is on your right, just through those doors," he says, lifting his glass in that direction. "And over here, is what the Realtor called the study. Some study, huh? It's more like a closet without a door." He laughs.

"It serves its purpose," she says, as though she's doing a walk-through as a buyer. "Big enough for a computer and a bookshelf."

Ty opens the French doors. "And here is my bedroom," he says proudly. "Not much in here, but really, what does a guy need? I've got a walk-in closet that's only a quarter full, a bed, a dresser, and a bathroom."

"I like it!" she says, impressed by the well-appointed space.

"There's another bathroom down the hall beside the spare room." He swings open the door to reveal the empty space. "I never did need the extra room. I guess with just me, I don't have too many possessions. Especially when I don't know how long I'll be here."

"I guess so," Eileen says, realizing that Ty could be living here until the end of the season or for a few years. "Do you think you'll be traded?"

"I don't know," he says. "There's speculation, but my agent thinks it's just talk."

"I guess you don't know," Eileen says.

"Sometimes it's a surprise." He leads her to the living room.

"You've got quite the view," Eileen says, gazing out the window. "I could stand here all night."

Ty turns around to appreciate the ambiance and catches Eileen's eye.

"I'm dying to know about my class," she says, gritting her teeth.

"It was easy."

"It was? You didn't have people chasing you down in the parking lot?"

He takes a sip from his glass and says, "Actually, the class was a breeze. It was the parents who had to be told to relax. That Oliver guy was a big help. You must have told him I was coming. He was standing outside waiting for me."

"He was?"

"He gave me a rundown on where to go and what to do."

"Your own assistant!"

"I could have figured it out on my own, but he insisted on helping. He also had an idea. Asked me to show up one Saturday to sign autographs."

"Yeah, I told him it probably wouldn't work."

"Oh! I said I'd be happy to."

"You did?"

"Yeah, why not?"

"You know," Eileen begins, shrugging a shoulder. "You're busy. It's not for charity."

"Yeah, but fans like that sort of thing, showing up, talking to them. I told Oliver we would be in touch."

"I'm glad it went okay," she says.

Ty looks out the large window and then glances back at her. "I can see why you like working with kids. They were a lot of fun. You can tell them to skate to one end and back and they don't complain."

"They complain, just not to you!" she says, spotting Ty from the corner of her eye as she looks out onto the water. His relaxed demeanor puts her at ease and she sips from her glass, relieved that her class went well and that, by the sound of it, Oliver was pleased.

Just then the oven timer beeps. "Dinner's ready!" he says, stepping away.

Eileen follows him into the kitchen. "Where do you want to sit?" She spots his staged dinner table. Hardly used—she is sure it's all for looks, though it would be foolish not to think he entertained women at this table. Eileen finishes her wine and places her empty glass on the counter.

"How about outside?" he suggests. "It's a nice night."

"I'd like that," she says, watching him fill her wineglass. She hears her cell phone ring and takes it out of her purse to check the number before answering. Eileen hesitates.

"Go ahead," he urges, topping up his glass.

"I'll be quick," she says and brings her phone to her ear.

"Hi, Eileen. It's Bill Braxton calling from the *Vancouver Daily*. I hope this is a good time."

"I was just sitting down for dinner."

"I'll make it quick then. Since your accident at practice, how are the guys treating you, now?"

"They seem to be accepting me," she says. "I can't let one guy ruin it for me."

"What challenges have you had recently?"

"I don't think I've had any. I'm trying to meet the team's expectations and I think I've done that."

"Do you have anything to say about Bret Thompson?"

"No, I don't," she says, biting her tongue. *It's not worth it,* she thinks and hangs up.

They portion out their dinner and take a seat side-by-side, facing the water. The breeze is light and warm.

"I can't imagine waking up to this view every morning." She takes a bite of her dinner.

"You can," he says. "I won't stop you."

She swallows hard. He can be so tempting when he wants to be. She looks down at her plate and decides to bite into her garlic bread before taking another drink.

"Hey, the offer never expires." He picks up his glass, eyeing her deliciously.

Eileen wipes her lips with a napkin. Her heart is beating erratically. Why is he so alluring? When she took the coaching job, she never suspected that she would fall for one of the players, though she was teased that they would be fighting over her. That of course wasn't true. She kept her eyes on the job, but Ty just has a way of magically securing her neediness and leaving her wanting more. Is he testing her to see how far she'll go? Did he really have a bet going on to see if she would sleep with him?

Without notice, Ty leans over his chair and gently takes her face in his hand, his lips closer, like they are calling for her. She jumps suddenly, realizing that he is about to kiss her. She is craving his affection, yet scared to lead him on. His hand cups the back of her neck, easing forward.

She closes her eyes, wanting so bad to kiss him back. "I can't," she whispers, anticipating his touch.

"It's only a kiss," he whispers back and his lips find hers. She can taste his sweet cologne. His tongue moves inside her mouth and skims her bottom lip like a feather flittering. *He's such a good kisser*, she thinks as he plays with strands of her hair. She has to stop him before they lose control. Eileen puts her hand to his chest, tapping him and pushing him away.

"I really like this. . . . I don't want to start something that has a short shelf life," she admits. And although it sounds silly and untrue, she has to tell herself nothing will become of them. It's safe that way. Her heart won't break.

"I'm not asking for anything. It was just a kiss."

"That's not what I want," she says, hating herself for ending it so soon.

"What *do* you want, Elle?" His blue eyes are eager for something more.

She doesn't know how to answer such a big question. "I don't know," she says, lying back in her seat and wondering why she's here in the first place.

"I'll tell you what. If we're still on for next Saturday night, I have tickets to a concert. We'll have a bite to eat beforehand and I can give you the Ty Caldwell treatment." He sits back and picks up his glass, taking a long sip.

Eileen likes the sound of that.

"I'll drop you off at home after the concert, okay?"

She gives him a smile.

"I want you to get to know me." His upper lip curls as though his statement is an afterthought.

"I'd like that," she says. "But it's not really a date, is it?"

He shakes his head. "Whatever you want to call it is fine by me," he says, taking a sip from his glass.

Eileen can see why he is so successful with women. He's a smooth talker, he's attractive, and he knows how to make a woman relax. Fortunately, she won't ever know what it's like to fall in love with him because this is as far as it goes if she can help it.

Chapter 10

A week later, Eileen walks into the restaurant with a slight limp, looking casual in jeans, a black top, gold hoop earrings, and a gold ring on her right index finger, a treasure from her parents on her sixteenth birthday.

She looks around for Ty, but doesn't see him.

A waitress interrupts Eileen's concentration. "Are you looking for somebody?"

"I'm supposed to be meeting someone here . . . a guy . . . tall, dirty-blond hair—"

"Is that him over there?" The waitress points, and Eileen tries to focus in on the table he's sitting at. He's not alone.

"I'm not sure. It looks like him," Eileen says, staring, trying to get a better look. "I'll go over and see. Thanks."

"Two girls just joined him."

"Yeah, that would be him," Eileen says and approaches the table. There are indeed two beautiful women sitting with Ty and talking his ear off, laughing as though they're all old friends.

Do I go over and talk to him? After all, he's the one who wanted to go out with me tonight and I did remind him that this isn't a date, so if I turn and leave it's not like I stood him up.

Eileen eyes the two women as she walks toward them.

Either they are both trying to pick him up or they know him. Judging by his deep laugh, he is enjoying the company. What made me agree to dinner? Can't I say no to a blue-eyed, overly attractive hockey player?

Eileen makes eye contact with Ty and he jumps up as though caught in the act and motions her over to the table. The two women look over as he says something to them and smiles.

"Hi, Elle!" Ty greets her, homing in on her with a pleasing eye.

"Have a seat," he says and pulls up a chair from another table.

"Thank you," she says as she takes a seat, feeling a little awkward sitting with two other women and one sexy bachelor. Are there going to be questions asked and the best answers will win?

"What a gentleman," the woman with tight black curls says. "Mark needs to take tips from you."

Eileen looks at Ty and is impressed by his outfit, loose-fitting jeans and a golf shirt. His blue eyes are what gives him away though; they're bright, happy, kind.

"This is Jen and Ali—they're the wives of Buckley and Anderson," he says by way of introduction.

That's a relief.

"And this is Eileen," he says to the wives. They both look like models: tall with fresh faces and skinny arms. "She's our skating coach," he adds proudly. "She's a heck of a skater, too." He takes a gulp of his beer.

"I've heard," Jen says with a lasting smile.

"Oh, yeah?" Eileen says with amazement, pushing her chair closer to the table.

"Uh-huh. Stealing the attention from the boys," Ali says.

"Hardly!" Eileen says. "I'm there to coach."

Jen glances at Ty and then back at her. "Right."

Her doubtfulness stings. "I'm all business—you have nothing to worry about."

"That's why you're out with Ty?" Ali asks. "Business meeting?" She laughs.

"Nothing's going on here," Eileen says.

"I know what you're doing. I said the same thing four years ago and married him."

"We need to go," the other woman says, and they both stand up at the same time. "We're off to the movies."

"Girls' night!" whispers Jen, grabbing her light knit sweater and giving a quick wave before turning on her toes.

"Have fun," Ty says with a quick nod.

"Enjoy your night," Ali says. And the two women walk off in laughter.

"What's with them? Jealous because I skate with their husbands?"

"Nah, they don't care. They're teasing," Ty says, clutching his half glass of beer.

Eileen drops her shoulders. "That was not teasing."

"Ignore her. Ali can get worked up at times."

"Did you see how she was looking at me?" Eileen asks as she takes a seat. "It's as though I'm a threat."

"I told you before, not everyone likes the idea of a woman on the team."

"I'm not on the team. I'm the temporary skating coach, remember?"

"You have to expect it," Ty says soothingly. "Ali's harmless."

"Well, someone really doesn't want me working with you guys and has been threatening me."

"Threatening?"

"Yeah. I told you about my car getting keyed—well, that's part of it. I'm sure. I have had notes left on my car and phone calls. It happened again the day you covered my skating class. I had a phone call saying to quit the Warriors or else."

"Or else what?"

"The person hung up."

"Did you tell the police?"

She shakes her head.

"Maybe you should."

"How does someone I don't know, know where to reach me? How does he know where I work?"

"Media?" Ty leans back in his chair. "You have posters hung at various places."

Her eyes squint and she turns her head slightly.

"I saw your poster at the golf course."

Her mouth widens into a smile. "Glad they're getting noticed."

"It has your name and number on it. Maybe that's too much information."

She blows out a breath. "It's just my name."

"You have a name for yourself, and anyone who has been following the league knows who you are and what you do."

"I suppose. But the first threat was the same day I had my on-ice interview and then again the other day, except this time the guy asked me to simply 'give it up' and said 'don't think you're equal to Ritchie because you're not.' It was so strange. The call caught me off guard. I mean, who does that? Someone really doesn't like me working for the Warriors and it's not just Thompson. At least I don't think the calls are from him. It's kind of hard to tell."

"I don't know what to say."

"It has to be someone from the team." She exhales and rubs her forehead. "I can't think of who it could be."

"Maybe someone from your other job doesn't like the idea of you splitting up your time."

"No, I can't think of anyone. And I don't know anyone who cares what I do for a living."

"Someone could be jealous or it could be someone you don't know. You need to get the police involved so they have a record. This has been going on now for a month."

Eileen chews on her bottom lip.

"You're safe. I'll take your mind off it. I'll order you a drink! You obviously need one."

The same waitress comes by their table. "Did you decide on something to drink?"

Eileen replies, "I'll have a rum and Diet Coke, please."

The waitress looks at Ty and asks, "Another one for you?"

He looks at his half-filled pint of beer. "No, thank you," he answers and the waitress leaves the table. "So what did you do today?" he asks. "Sleep in, go to the gym, have time for a little shopping?"

Eileen smirks. "Yeah, right, sleep in? What's that? And shopping? I like to stay away from the malls. I'm not much of a shopper."

"A woman who doesn't like to shop? I had no idea she existed. I think I just found the woman of my dreams." He laughs.

"Don't get any ideas, Caldwell," she tells him playfully. "I can't be bothered to walk through a mall in search of something I don't really need. I shop when I need something."

"We make the perfect couple then." He takes a sip of beer. His grin is everlasting.

"Couple? I don't know about that."

He swallows hard and then says, "Haven't you heard?"

"What?"

"We're a couple. That's the rumor."

She rolls her eyes. "I think you're trying to start one."

The waitress delivers her drink. Eileen takes her glass in her hand and takes a sip. "What?" she asks, feeling self-conscious. "Why are you looking at me like that?" She takes a drink.

"Okay, I've started a rumor," he says.

She laughs. "Yeah, sure."

"No, really. I hope you're not mad, but some of the guys asked me if we were dating and I couldn't lie."

"You mean you lied," she corrects him, trying to keep her cool. There is no point in throwing a fit now.

"Well, no. I told them that we've been on a couple of dates."

"We met once and it was a meeting."

"Yeah, and we had dinner the other night and again tonight. If I didn't know better, I'd think you were trying to play hard-to-get, Ms. Francis."

Usually she would argue, but something about Ty makes her smile like a lovesick teenager. "You didn't really tell anyone, did you?" she says. When he doesn't respond, she can feel her cheeks flush and panic overcomes her.

"Why would you do that?" she asks in a soft but striking tone.

"It's not a big deal, is it? I thought it would save a lot of confusion."

"No one is supposed to know that I've . . ." She pauses, trying to choose the right word. "I've met up with you tonight. I don't want people to know because they'll start assuming things that aren't true. Besides, I don't want your teammates or management to find out. The guys won't take me seriously. They'll think I took the job to get a date."

"Relax. They don't think it's a *date* date—they think we're hanging out."

"Oh, yeah? And why would they think that? Are you assuming that's what they think? You and I both know that's not how it will be taken."

Ty takes a gulp of beer. "Just a few guys know that we're out tonight."

Eileen fidgets with her straw, thinking hard about how the guys will react to her when they find out that she's spending time tonight with Ty Caldwell. Her gut tells her it's a bad idea, but her mind can't help but think of the possibilities of being with him.

"I want to make something clear," she begins, playing with her straw. "Although this may seem like a date to you, it's not, so I don't want you thinking that I'm coming over to your place tonight for a nightcap. It's not going to happen."

Ty relaxes in his chair. "I didn't have those intentions," he says, playing innocent, but his sneaky grin tells her otherwise.

"You didn't?" She doesn't believe him.

"No. I want to get to know you." He shrugs and leans in to grab his beer.

Why me? He can have any woman and he wants to get to know me?
"Really?"

"You seem disappointed."

"I'm not! No, just surprised."

Ty takes a drink and then says, "You have that look on your face."

"I'm just happy we got that out of the way," she says and takes her glass in her hand. "I feel so much better. Except when you look at me like that."

"I'm trying to figure you out."

The waitress comes by the table. "Would you like to order?" she asks.

Ty glances from the waitress to Eileen. They both grab the menu off the table and their eyes skim the page.

Eileen looks up at the waitress. "I'll have the turkey club on multi-grain ciabatta bread, no mayo, please, with a tossed salad and your light Italian dressing on the side."

"Make that two," Ty says. "Except I'll have mine the way it comes, on white is fine, and we'll both have another drink." He looks at Eileen for reassurance before the waitress leaves the table.

Eileen nods. "So you trust my decisions."

"It's helping me in practice."

There's a moment of silence, and then Ty says, "You look really good."

She smiles at his comment.

"I need to ask you something." He pauses. "What brings a woman like you to the NHL? I know you have the experience, and it shows, but really, it's gotta be a tough job to take on."

"It's what I do," she says without hesitation. She flattens her lips. "What better way to enhance my skills than by working with other professionals?"

He nods as though he understands. "Tell me about your other jobs."

"Is this an interview?" she asks with a slight tease in her voice.

"Are all your skating classes with rambunctious children?"

Eileen laughs. "So the truth comes out. I thought the kids were a breeze?"

"They're kids, but they were excited about skating."

"Well, I teach kids the basic skills and really anyone learning how to skate and to play hockey," she says. "I enjoy teaching kids the most." She smiles. "They are so eager to learn and they get excited when they've mastered a skill."

Ty's eyes find hers. His eyebrows lift. "I remember those days," he says. "It was hard then, trying to beat the other guys in a scrimmage."

"It's a great feeling, isn't it?" she recalls.

"Yeah," Ty says with a partial grin. "It makes you strive harder the next time. When I was a kid, I hated power skating, hated it, but I knew I had to do it if I wanted to succeed. And I had a vision."

"I don't think anyone enjoys power skating," she says with a chuckle. "You do it because you want to be better."

"Yeah, you're right."

"The adult classes I teach are fun too, but there's something special about teaching children."

The waitress wanders to their table with their food and sets it down.

"Did you always want to play hockey?"

"I did." He nods his head. "Yeah, but it wasn't in the plan." He moves his chair in closer to the table.

She takes a bite of her sandwich as she waits for him to continue. When she swallows her food, she finishes her first drink and sets down the glass in front of her.

"You see the plan was I would go to university, just like my brother did, and become a doctor."

Eileen smiles and can't hold back her laugh. "Seriously?" she asks. "A doctor? You're joking!"

"No, I'm not," Ty says, his lips curving into a grin. "Why do you find that so funny?"

Eileen tries to regain her composure. "I'm sorry, but I just can't picture you as a doctor."

"You're not the only one," he admits with a smile and takes a drink. "My father is a doctor, so is my brother, and all I wanted to do was play hockey, so you can imagine my dad's fear when I didn't want to go to university. All my life I worked hard in school because I thought I was going to join the family practice, and before I graduated I was off to play junior in Moose Jaw and from there, I never looked back. . . . I was thankful."

"Nothing wrong with that. You have to do what you're good at, right?" Eileen says. "You're successful in your profession."

Ty nods, accepting the compliment, and wipes his mouth with a napkin. "My dad doesn't understand that I wasn't cut out to be a doctor. I respect him for what he does and I think he's okay now with what I'm doing, but at the time it was a real struggle."

"Well, you're in the NHL," Eileen says happily. "And that right there is a career accomplishment."

"Yeah, I guess so."

"Was your father ever supportive when you played junior?"

"Not really. I think he thought hockey was just a sport I played. Don't get me wrong—he loves the game too. He was the one who drove me to my five o'clock morning practices before I could drive, but he really wanted me to succeed in school. Education means a lot to him."

Ty takes another bite of his club sandwich.

"Do you see your parents often?" she asks, intrigued by his family and wanting to know more.

"Sure, we talk and I see my brother once in a while. We get along, always have."

"And your mom? Has she always been supportive?" Eileen inquires.

"Oh, sure. My mom and I talk. She's been a wife and a mother her whole life and doesn't care what we do as long as we're happy."

"That counts for something, doesn't it?"

Ty nods his head. "My mom encouraged me to continue to play, and that of course would set my father off. He would say, 'Son, you'll go to university, I don't care if you play hockey while you're there, as long as you go. Make me proud,' " Ty says, trying to imitate a deeper voice like his father's.

"Look at you now!" Eileen reminds him. "I'm sure he's really proud of you."

Ty shrugs. "I remember the fear I had, telling my father that I wanted to stay in Saskatchewan and play hockey. I pleaded with him that if I was there for more than two years, I would come home and register for university. I prayed that didn't happen."

"I bet that wasn't an easy conversation."

"No, and the first thing I thought of was, what will my father's reaction be? I asked the coach in Moose Jaw if I could play and go to university, and he laughed at me," Ty says, breaking into a light chuckle. "I didn't know any better. He said I needed to stay where I was and play professional hockey because playing in the minors *is* professional. I wanted to explore my options. I knew I wasn't cut out to be a doctor, but my father wouldn't believe it."

"So what happened when you told your father?"

"At first, I couldn't tell him. I was scared to hear what he was going to say. I knew his reaction—I just didn't know his answer."

"Naturally."

"I knew if I was going to continue playing, I had to figure out where I would live because my father would tell me to go live somewhere else, that was a given. I ended up talking to the coach, and he told me not to worry, that I would billet, stay in a house with another family and another teammate. He even offered to talk to my father for me, but my father is not one to be easily convinced," Ty reflects. "I thought I could handle it best. So I sat my parents down for our big talk. I prepared by practicing on my brother. I knew he would be honest with me. Then, when I told them, my father was mad and he was quiet, and usually my dad always has something to say."

"That's too bad."

"Oh, I don't worry about it anymore," Ty says and takes a drink. "I can't be bothered by it. I'm sure he's over it. I know I am."

"You've been playing for the Warriors for what? Three years?" she guesses.

It takes him a second to respond. "Yes, I guess it will be come this season."

"It's gone by fast," she states and he nods with agreement. "Do you think you'll stay here?" Eileen takes a bite of her sandwich.

"I'm hoping they'll renew my contract—at least then I would feel like I have a permanent home."

"It must be real nerve-wracking, huh?" Eileen asks, curious what it would be like getting paid to play the game she loved. "Not know-ing where you'll end up?" She pushes her empty plate away.

"I guess so," he says and then sighs. "I'm happy to play. It would be nice to play here for another few years though. You never know. Sometimes it works out and other times you're due for a change."

The waitress swings by the table. "Another drink?"

Ty looks at Eileen for an answer. "We probably should go if we want to make the show," he says.

"No, thanks," Eileen agrees.

The waitress leaves and returns with the bill. Ty grabs the paper and looks it over. Eileen unzips her purse, but Ty already has his wallet out and slaps down a fifty.

She takes some cash out of her wallet. "This isn't a date, so I'm putting in my share," she says.

"Don't worry about it," he says and slides the money and bill over to the end of the table for the waitress to pick up. "Ready to go?"

"No way," Eileen says, feeling uneasy about his generosity. "I have to put some money in." She holds two twenties in her hand.

Ty waves his hand and says, "Don't worry about it, I got it."

"This isn't a date," she reminds him with a sharp eye.

"Uh-huh," he mutters.

She finds it hard to keep a straight face. "I don't take money from strangers."

He gives her a playful look. "I'm no stranger." He smiles. "I thought we went through this before."

She smiles back.

"We've got to go," he says and he stands up. "You don't have to be so difficult."

"I'm not trying to be difficult, I'm being fair," she says, standing up and taking her purse in hand, wishing she could just grab hold of his hand as they walk out the door.

They decide to leave her car parked at the pub and take one vehi-cle, as parking is always a challenge downtown. It doesn't take long for Ty to get recognized between parking his truck and walking to the club. They pass people and hear whispers: "Is that Ty Caldwell?" and "I think that's Ty Caldwell—who's he with?"

When they approach the club doors, someone standing in the line announces, "Hey, that's Ty Caldwell! Cool! I wonder who else is here!" Ty is grinning from ear to ear, proudly walking to the doors, where the bouncer nods his head in approval and shakes Ty's hand before they walk inside.

Eileen glances back, feeling privileged that they didn't have to pay a cover charge or wait in the long line. Ty grabs her hand as though it's expected for him to have a woman by his side.

She curls her fingers around his larger hand, her body light as a feather.

"This isn't supposed to be a date," she whispers in his ear.

"Can't we pretend tonight? At least pretend that you like me," he whispers back, his lips touching the top of her ear.

"Caldwell!" a guy shouts from a distance and charges across the room carrying a drink at shoulder height, trying hard not to bump into people and spill his drink.

When the stranger gets closer, he yells, "How are you, buddy? It's been a while," he says and throws a hand on Ty's shoulder.

"Yeah, it has," Ty admits. "How are you?"

"Good, very good. What's new?" the guy asks and looks at Eileen, then at Ty.

"Not a lot, training for the new season," Ty says, still holding on to Eileen's hand.

"And who's this beautiful lady you're attached to?"

"This is Eileen," Ty says smugly, making eye contact with her. "Elle, this is Bernie." They shake hands.

"Nice to meet you," Bernie says, giving Eileen a once-over and then turns to Ty and says, "Maybe we can go for a beer, or something. It's still poker night on Wednesdays—feel free to join us if you wanna."

"Thanks," Ty says. "I just might. We're going to grab our seats. I'll see you around." Still gripping Eileen's hand, Ty leads her past Bernie and right into another group waving their hands to get his attention.

"Who was that?" Eileen asks.

"No one important," he whispers.

"Ty!" another guy shouts.

Ty ignores the man and looks at Eileen. "Would you like something to drink?"

"Please."

"Me too. We'll grab something at the bar," he says.

"Aren't you going to go over and talk to those people who are calling for you?"

"No," he says, stiffening.

She looks at him and his eyes are glued to her, giving his full attention. They approach the bar, and Ty lets go of her hand and places his on the counter. He looks at her. "What would you like?"

"I'll have my usual," she says, wondering if he'll remember.

Ty grins at her and looks at the bartender. "Can I get a rum and Diet Coke and one bottle of Bud?"

"I got it," Eileen says and reaches for her purse.

"No, please, I got it," Ty insists and takes out a twenty.

"It's on me tonight, Caldwell," the bartender says.

Ty holds up the bottle and says, "Thanks," and hands Eileen her drink.

"Thank you," she says to the bartender and then says to Ty, "I'll pay for the next round."

"You need to learn to relax," he whispers in her ear. She feels his nose tickle her skin as though he's going to kiss her. "It's not a big deal."

To Eileen, it is a big deal since she has no intention of it being a real date. She doesn't want him to think of her as wanting a handout; she is more than capable of paying her own way. Yet she feels like it's a formula for a date, and she likes this, likes being with Ty. He keeps her guessing as to what he's going to do next.

"I am relaxed," she tells him.

"Good. Should we go find our seats?" he asks, leading her in that direction.

"Sure," she answers, taking a sip of her drink as she follows. "There're a lot of people here. Where should we sit?"

"Our seats are upstairs."

Why is she so surprised by his royal treatment?

They head to the balcony and scan the room. When Ty's eyes catch the RESERVED sign, he picks it up to read the name on the guest list.

"This is us," he says and sits down on a roomy leather love seat. There are a half dozen of these couches, mostly reserved for the elite or friends of the club's owners.

"Perfect!" she says and takes a seat beside Ty. "What a great view of the stage," she says as she looks ahead and places her drink down on a table in front of them.

"Not bad," Ty agrees, scanning the room.

"Caldwell?" a guy shouts out approaching the table. When Ty looks up, there is a round-bellied guy holding a bottle of beer in one hand and smiling at him. "I'm a big fan," he says, breathless. "The name's Dell." The man extends his chubby hand. "Well, my friends call me Dell. . . . Wow, and they're not going to believe that I met you. Wait 'til I tell them this."

"Hi, Dell," Ty says, shifting in his seat.

"Can I get an autograph? Oh, wait, I don't have anything to write with," he says, frantically searching his front pockets.

"I think I have a pen," Eileen offers and opens her purse. "Here you go." She hands it to Ty, thinking that when she's with him, she should always carry one since this is becoming a usual thing.

"Thank you. That is sure nice of you," Dell says.

"No problem," Eileen says and smiles.

"What would you like me to write on?" Ty asks. "I'm sure we can find a napkin."

Dell fumbles through his back pockets. "Oh, no," he says with a look of fear. "I thought I had a piece of paper on me."

"I'm sure I have that too," Eileen says and pulls a small notepad from her purse. She tears off paper and hands it to him. "Here," she says, handing Ty the paper.

"Thank you again. You're very kind, very kind," Dell says, nodding at Eileen and then hovering over Ty as he writes.

"You must be Eileen," Dell says. "You're the skating coach, right? I've read about you."

"You have?" she asks, taken off guard. "I try not to read those stories."

"They're always saying good things about you. It's never anything bad, but they do seem to mention your relationship quite often," Dell says. "Not like it's any of my business, but you two make a good couple—you know, with playing hockey and all."

"Thank you," Ty says, looking up from signing the piece of paper.

"Just to keep the facts straight," Eileen says and pauses. "There is nothing—"

Ty cuts her off. "It's always nice to be with someone who complements your career. Thank you, Dell," he says, handing him his autograph and passing the pen back to Eileen. "We try to keep our relationship private. The more people know about us, it seems like they just want to know more, and that's not our style."

Dell nods his head. "I understand," he says, holding up his signed paper. "Thank you. You've really made my night. Good luck this season."

"Thanks! Have a good one," Ty says, grabbing his drink in front of him and crashing back into the couch.

"So why didn't you tell him we're not dating?" she asks, holding her drink with both hands.

"It just confuses people."

"Not if you tell them the truth."

"It's easier to go along with it. No harm done, right?"

She takes a sip of her drink. "I don't want people to get the wrong impression."

"What's that guy Dell gonna do? He's happy and he doesn't care who I'm dating. No big deal, is it?"

Is it?

"Well, don't get any ideas," she says.

"Why not?"

"Because—because it can't happen, that's why."

"And why not?"

It takes her a second or two to answer. "I think your intentions are different from mine."

"You think so?" he asks, his eyes capturing hers.

"Yes," she says, feeling his stare warm her body.

"You don't know the new Ty."

The lights dim and the show begins.

"And if my intentions are different from yours, how come you're out with me tonight?" he asks, looking at her and then looking ahead at the stage. The music is loud and the audience is standing and cheering.

Eileen leans to one side so that Ty can hear her over the music. "Can't two adults go out casually and have a drink, see a concert? Get out and have some fun?"

Ty takes a swig of beer. "Isn't that my line? Face it, Elle—we have the same intentions," he says, loudly.

"You think so?"

"I know so," he answers. "You're just playing hard-to-get."

"How do you figure?" she challenges him.

"We're both single, we both love the same sport, we both hate shopping. . . . I guess our jobs are similar in some ways, and both could use the company," he says with ease. "We're perfect for each other."

"Pardon?" she asks, straining herself to hear him.

"We're perfect for each other," he repeats in a louder voice.

"I don't know about that," she yells back.

"You have a hard time admitting when you're wrong, don't you? You also don't like to be told what to do."

"You're right—I don't like to be told what to do. At least I can admit that."

"And for some reason you don't like people to know about your personal life either."

She eyes him and says, "What's wrong with that?"

"Nothing," he says casually. "You're just hard to read some times. It's hard to tell what you like. I mean, I don't even know if you like me." He looks at her and then at his bottle of beer. "I think you do or you wouldn't be out with me tonight, right?" He sounds serious. Eileen thinks he might smile and turn his question into a joke, but to her surprise, he doesn't. "And you wouldn't have had dinner with me at my house."

There is no way around this.

"I like you," she says quietly.

"What?" he shouts.

"I like you," she says, a little louder, bursting into laughter.

Ty cups his ear. "Sorry, what's that?" he asks, and she can tell he's teasing her now.

She looks around them before answering him and sees a set of eyes staring back at her. "I like you," she says, looking into his eyes. "You're right. I wouldn't be out tonight if I didn't."

"Do you really?" he asks with a grin. "I couldn't tell."

"Yeah."

"I'm actually surprised. You don't act like you do."

"I do," she says, trying to sound convincing.

A smile comes across his face. "I never thought I would hear that from you."

"Are you happy now?"

"Yes, I am," he says, slightly amused.

She takes a drink. "Okay then, please don't ask me again." Eileen puts down her glass and sits back on the love seat. "You're putting me in an awkward situation."

"Why? Are you not one to show your feelings either?"

She crosses her arms. "I'm a private person and I'd like to keep it that way."

"I like to think of myself as a private person too, but sometimes there are things that have to be out in the open and if you're true to yourself, you should be fine with people knowing a little bit about you. I'm sure you're dying to tell me more. I know there's more to tell."

"There really isn't."

"I know you're not boring," he says. "I bet you have a lot to tell me. For some reason, you're holding back."

"What do you want to know?" she shouts.

"Where do you hope to be in five years?"

"Married," she responds without thinking it through.

"Kids?"

"Oh, yeah."

"Okay, and do you like cats or dogs? Those seem to come before everything else."

"Dogs," she answers. "I volunteer at the animal shelter some-times, and I wish I could take one home."

"You do have a soft spot." He gazes at her before taking a swig from his bottle. "So, going to the movies or renting?"

"Renting. You can wear your pajamas and order in pizza. And you?"

"Both. And what kind of ice cream do you like, chocolate, vanilla, or strawberry?"

"Haagen-Dazs Sticky Toffee Pudding," she says with a laugh.

"Wow, I guess there's no such thing as just strawberry, is there? You probably like Strawberry Supreme with walnut pieces," he says with a laugh, and she can't help but laugh with him.

"Okay, I'd take chocolate. And you?" she asks.

"Vanilla."

They watch the concert and tap their knees and bob their heads to the music. "I saw these guys play when they released their hit, 'Moonshine.' "

"Love that song!" she says. Her eyes meet his, and at the same time, her stomach leaps with excitement.

"Me too!"

It's like the music has stopped and all she can hear is the beat of her heart. Is she falling for this guy?

After the show, Ty grabs for her hand and they walk to his truck.

"White or red wine?" he asks as they approach his truck.

"Are we still playing this game?" she teases.

"Come on, I want to know more about you," he says as he turns his alarm off with a click of the button on his keychain and opens the passenger door for her. "You won't tell me about yourself unless I ask."

"Red," she answers as she hops into the seat.

Ty starts up his truck, and instead of driving to pick up her car, he drives to her house.

Why did being with Ty feel different from before? And why did she feel a strong desire to hold on to these new growing emotions? She doesn't want to see the night end. For once in her life, she was on a "date" and wasn't in a rush to go home or dreading the thought of a phone call to invite her out again. This was real. Or was it the rum and Diet Coke?

Ty parks his truck and turns off the ignition. "I'll walk you to your door," he says, jumping out of his truck and greeting her at the passenger door.

"You don't have to," she says, walking with him to the front entrance.

"I want to make sure you get to your door safe. I can come by tomorrow to pick you up so that you can get your car."

She uses her key to open the glass door, and they walk inside to take the elevator up to her floor. "Right, my car. I hope it's okay parked there overnight."

"I'm sure it will be. I should have picked you up though," he says. "But then that would make this a date."

She laughs as the elevator doors shut. "But it wasn't a date," she says, suddenly getting a whiff of his sweet scent. A warm sensation comes over her, and she tries to look away from him, breaking his warm stare.

"I don't know why you just can't let loose and have a good time, regardless if it's a date or not," he tells her, following her out of the elevator.

"I think I did pretty well tonight," she says as she unlocks her door. She doesn't want to admit to him that she is scared of a repeat of the relationship she had with her ex, Mario. She wants a guy she can trust and build a relationship with. Could Ty possibly be that type of man?

"Yeah, you did," Ty says, leaning in closer so that his one shoulder is bracing her doorway and they can feel each other's breath. Eileen leans against the door, one hand on the knob. She twists to open it and from her weight, it does. She falls backwards and Ty reaches for her and instantly goose bumps speckle her arms. She sucks in a breath, unable to control the sensations that are coming over her again. As the door opens and they both are inside, Ty closes the door behind him with one hand while his other hand is still on her arm. He holds her gently. She feels blissfully happy, more so than she ever imagined she would feel.

Ty brings his other hand to her face, leaning in and kissing her fully on the mouth. His lips are soft, tender, and full of desire as though satisfying a craving. *Is this really happening?* she asks herself. Why must she enjoy this so much? She is his skating coach, she tells herself over and over. She's breaking the rules, her rules.

He releases her lips and smiles. "Well, looks like you changed your mind about mixing business with pleasure."

Her cheeks grow warm. "It's not supposed to be this way," she murmurs quickly. "And you're right, I'm breaking my rule," she manages to say and takes a sudden deep breath.

He holds her close and looks into her eyes. "Rules can be broken as long as nobody gets hurt," he whispers, reaching for her head. He combs his fingers through her long strands of hair as though fascinated by the length.

"That's why I have rules."

"Is that what you're afraid of? Getting hurt?" he asks, lifting her chin when she tries to look away.

Eileen looks him in the eyes. What was she afraid of?

"I'm not afraid," she stammers. "I'm just unsure."

Ty's lips find hers again. He holds her face lovingly and embraces her body as though keeping her from falling away from him. Eileen finds comfort in his strength and his energy. She can't help but let him care for her at the moment. She lets go.

Being in his arms gives her a sense of security she never thought she'd find—not that she needs it. She is her own person with her own set of rules. She doesn't need a man to make her feel safe and looked after, but she does feel something with Ty that she hasn't experienced before. Is this how his other women feel when they are with him? Eileen tries not to think that she might be just another woman, because right now she feels like the only one.

Ty kisses her neck, his lips trailing down to her collarbone. His hand traces her cheekbone down to her fingertips.

"We shouldn't be doing this," she whispers.

"Why not?" he whispers back.

"I'm your skating coach." Her eyes are shut as she feels his lips kiss her neck and then find hers. Ty feels for her shirt and lifts it up over her head, revealing her sculpted black bra. His hand runs over her padded breasts, and he cups her hips so that his hands are touching her bare skin. Eileen's emotions cloud her brain; it's impossible to think straight. She's dizzy with emotion.

"I am so attracted to you," he says in her ear and kisses her earlobe. "I'm sure you know."

"I had no idea," she murmurs.

"Where's your bedroom?"

Eileen walks backwards as they kiss, leading the way. This is so unlike her. She has never let a boyfriend, or a guy, into her bedroom after just one date. She can't help the feelings that overpower her, at least not tonight. Maybe Ty's intentions are different. Maybe he wants more than just to sleep with her.

"I've wanted you since the day we met," he says before their lips connect again. His tongue circles the inside of her mouth, and she lets him taste her and returns the pleasure.

This moment is too much, she thinks as he kisses her with more intensity. Eileen brings her hand between his shoulder blades, feeling the tightness of his back. Ty's lips have weight to them as they cover her mouth. She is pulled into a trance of fulfillment.

Ty slowly moves her toward her bed. She follows his lead, and he lays her down softly, kissing and holding her, caressed in his arms. She's entwined in his embrace, letting her hands feel the strength in his arms. He is too much. Too attractive. Too sexy. They kiss like two desperate people in need of affection.

She pulls at his shirt, trying to lift it up, and without resistance, Ty does it for her. His generously sculpted abs have her in awe. She can't help but run her hands over his chest in admiration. He is a work of art. No wonder he's featured in magazine ads and television commercials; he is simply gorgeous from head to toe.

Ty runs his hand over her silky black bra and gently kisses the tops of her breasts. He lifts her chin to him for a kiss as he lets his hands run over her skin as though searching for more options to place his lips. He takes his time, caressing her body.

"You're so beautiful," he says, as he stares into her eyes. He kisses her again, and without looking, he unbuttons her jeans, slides them off, and tosses them onto the floor. He runs his hand between her thighs, making her toned legs feel like jelly, and brings his lips to her skin, running his tongue along her smooth legs.

Ty strips off his jeans. His boxers are fitted, revealing a generous package waiting to be opened. He's as ready as she is, she thinks, gazing at his perfection. He grabs for his jeans and pulls out his wallet, taking out a foil square, and lays it on a pillow for when the time is right and slips under the covers. They stare into each other's eyes and she feels the need to be loved. Ty slowly closes himself onto her and she wraps her arms around his neck and loses herself in the moment. He discreetly opens the condom wrapper and puts it on. Once secure, she lets him come inside her. He doesn't take his eyes off her, combing her hair with his fingers. He kisses her neck and she closes her eyes with satisfaction. *This has to be some crazy dream*, she thinks as she breaks her number-one rule.

Chapter 11

Ring! Ring! Ring!

Eileen wakes up feeling a little groggily. She rubs her eyes and realizes it's her telephone ringing, and not her alarm clock going off. She looks to her left at the man lying beside her, verifying that she indeed did something last night that she probably shouldn't have done.

She looks at Ty, who is comfortably sleeping, and reaches for her phone beside her bed. "Hello?" she asks in a sleepy voice.

"Elle!" a tense male voice says. "I wanted to catch you before you left for the rink."

"I don't work Sundays," she says in an annoyed whisper.

"I knew you would be up. You never sleep in."

"I was sleeping, Nick," she says, pulling her hair back from her face.

"Sorry," her brother says. "Have you read today's newspaper?"

"No! I was sleeping," she hisses and scrambles out of bed, almost tripping over her scattered clothes on the floor. Thankfully wearing cotton shorts and a tank top, she scurries her way out of her bedroom to the living room, and doesn't dare look back, afraid of waking him or worse, having to say the first awkward words. Eileen doesn't want to explain to her brother who she invited for a sleepover.

She holds the phone tightly to her ear, closing her bedroom door as quietly as possible behind her.

"It says you and Ty Caldwell are dating."

"What are you talking about?"

"Ty Caldwell? The guy you're supposedly dating? And why are you whispering? Is he there? Don't tell me he's there, Elle," Nick says in a desperate plea. "You don't want it to turn out the way it did with Mario. I thought you learned the first time."

Eileen tries to fake a yawn heavily into the receiver, acting like she is still waking up. "No! Definitely not," she says. "You woke me up and I'm tired."

He ignores her. "Well, it says here—"

"Well, whatever it says, I hope they have my title right. Last time they called me their personal trainer," she says, rubbing her eyes. "I'm not their personal trainer."

"Don't play around, Elle, I told you to watch yourself and to not bother with any of those guys. They'll hurt you and leave you for dead, just like Mario did."

Eileen sits on her couch, pulling her feet behind her. "What are you talking about?" she asks, rubbing her temple to ease the tension of a soon-to-be-pounding headache.

Her brother continues, "They only think of themselves, you know that? They get what they want and then leave you when they've had enough, or in your case, leave you when there's a choice of three other women."

"Thanks for the reminder," she says, coolly. "I can figure that one out for myself, Nick."

"I'm just saying."

"I understand what you're saying, but honestly, it's not serious."

It can't be serious. I'm sure Ty doesn't think last night will lead to anything; it was just sex, no emotions attached, right? Isn't that how it should be with a superstar? He's used to this sort of thing.

"I've heard that one from you before," her brother says. "And the next thing that will happen, he'll sweep you off your feet and it will be serious and it will end with him breaking your heart."

She exhales and then says, "It's not like that, Nick, so you don't have to worry about me. I'm the skating coach, remember?"

"If I don't worry about you, who will? Is this okay with Uncle Gary? Does he know?"

Eileen sits back on her couch and rubs her eyes. "Nothing is going on. Besides, I'm not a teenager."

"It says here, on page twelve." She can hear him flipping the pages to get to the story. "Here it is . . . page twelve. . . . It's not even in the sports section!" he exclaims. "It's in the entertainment section, of all things! It says that you two are a couple."

"What?" she asks, bursting out laughing. "That's crazy and totally not true."

"It says, 'Caldwell Courts Coach. . . . Warriors right winger Ty Caldwell is rumored to be dating skating coach Eileen Francis, ice hockey Olympian and former pro of Canadian Women's Hockey League.'" Nick pauses for a second and then reads, "'Francis, who is taking over for Ritchie Forbes, until he comes back from a leave of absence due to family circumstances, is scheduled to return to the Warriors coaching staff sometime in October.'"

"That's news to me," she says.

"You didn't know you were finished in October?" Nick asks harshly.

Eileen presses her palm to her forehead trying to ease her headache. "No, they told me they weren't certain on a date."

"If I were you, I would find out. What does your contract say?"

Scared to answer his question, she hesitates. "Contract?"

"Yeah, contract. You did sign a contract, didn't you?"

"Ah, not exactly."

"What do you mean?" Nick asks.

"They asked me to work a month or so—"

"They are paying you?"

"Yes!" she snaps. "Yes, they are."

"That still doesn't seem right," Nick says, confused. "Why wouldn't they give you a contract?"

"Look, I don't need the job; I took this job for the experience of teaching the pros. It's not like this comes around all the time. This is a once-in-a-lifetime opportunity."

"If you don't give them rules, they'll walk all over you," Nick warns.

"I know, but this is a dream, Nick. Not every woman pro hockey player gets this chance. In fact, I've never heard of it before."

"Neither have I, but you still have to look out for yourself."

"I know," she says, thinking about last night and knowing that Ty is sleeping in her bed. She could hang up and go back to bed. Maybe he would cuddle her. . . .

"That's not all the article says."

Eileen's perfectly arched eyebrows heighten. "Oh, really? What else?" she asks, intrigued, going into the bathroom and taking out a bottle of Advil.

"It says . . . 'Eileen Francis is in a league of her own. She is the first woman to teach the Warriors, and with vast experience behind her, she deserves the position, says head coach, Steve Morrow. "Even though her position is temporary, it comes with many challenges," he says. "Including meeting the team's expectations and she does that well." And Francis agrees. She says men have a hard time accepting a woman coaching in the National Hockey League, especially giving them tips and suggestions on improving their game. "They seem to be accepting me," says Francis, ex-girlfriend of the legendary Mario Visconti, who is no stranger to the National Hockey League,' " Nick reads and takes a breath. " 'Although a relationship hasn't been confirmed between Francis and Caldwell, a source says they have been spotted together off the ice at different local events.' "

"What?" Eileen shrieks. "It says that?"

"Yes!" Nick says. "You are quoted in the story. I sure hope you did talk to this reporter or this paper is full of lies and you can sue their asses."

"Yes, I did," she moans and pops two pills and washes them down with a glass of water.

"Be careful, Elle. They have a picture of you and Caldwell together."

"At the rink?" *I hope.*

"It doesn't look like it. Looks to me like you two were at a restaurant. It's hard to tell."

Eileen is speechless. Was it someone at the club? She did remember people recognizing Ty. Maybe someone took a shot and she just so happens to be in the picture.

"It looks like you're holding hands."

Eileen can't speak.

"Holding hands?" She has to see the picture for herself. When did she hold his hand? At the club?

"If the article is not true, I think you should call up this reporter and tell him to get the facts straight before writing about your personal life. Where did this guy get his information from anyway?" Nick asks, sounding disgusted.

"I don't know." She sighs. "If the reporter starts writing that I'm pregnant with his child, then I'll call him on it, but until then, I'm not wasting my time."

"That's not like you, Elle. Usually you confront people and stick up for yourself."

"This doesn't bother me." *This doesn't bother me.* "I don't care what people think about me."

"You have changed," Nick comments.

"Not really. There are some things that I wouldn't lose sleep over and this is one of them," she says, remembering last night and what Ty did to her, how he held her and kissed her body while making love.

"I want to set you up with someone I work with," Nick says.

"Hmm . . ." she says, pinching the bridge of her nose and inhaling a breath. Why don't people think a woman can be single and happy?

"He's a good guy, plays one heck of a game of golf, loves dogs, has three of them, and owns his own place."

Eileen tries not to sound ungrateful for her brother's matchmaking ability. "Sounds like a well-put-together guy," she says, plunking herself down on the couch.

"He is a good guy. . . . Can't wait for you to meet him. Let me know when you're out my way and I'll set you two up."

"Thanks, Nick, but I'll have to pass."

"You haven't met him yet!"

"I don't need to."

"If it makes you feel better about it, Cathy says if she weren't with me, she would date him."

Eileen relaxes her free arm to her side. "If I change my mind, I'll let you know. Besides, my schedule is so full right now, I don't have time to date."

"All right, but you should slow down. You don't want to burn yourself out."

Eileen presses her palm to her forehead, trying to ease her headache. "Thanks, but I'll be fine."

"Do me a favor and be careful? You can't forget what Mario was like."

"How can I?" He broke her heart. She was in love with Mario until it was clear he wasn't as serious as Eileen thought. Did Mario think of her now? It's been almost two years and she still thinks of him from time to time, wondering if he ever thinks of her.

"You don't want a repeat of that relationship. . . ." Nick's voice trails off.

"I know. I think I've learned my lesson. I appreciate your concern, I'll be fine," she says, easing him off the phone.

"Okay. I'll talk to you later."

Eileen clicks off the phone, carrying it into her kitchen, where she makes a pot of coffee. Her head feels like it's in a vise. She's hoping the caffeine will ease the tension.

What time does Ty wake up on Sundays? Does he sleep in? What will she say to him when they face each other? Does he think this is a start to something between them?

Don't panic, don't panic.

Maybe he'll know what to say. Maybe if she hops in the shower, he'll get up, leave her a note, and be gone before she gets out so that they don't have to speak.

The phone rings again, and Eileen lets out a huge sigh and reaches for her phone on the kitchen counter.

"Hello?" she answers.

"Good morning, Elle!"

"Mornin', Brooke," she says, trying to sound as energetic as her friend.

"I hope I didn't wake you. I figured you'd be up."

"Yeah, I'm up."

"Good. Just waiting to have coffee with a potential client," she says. "This is the second person this week who wants to meet with me and do business."

"That's an early-morning meeting you planned. And on a Sunday?"

"Yeah, well, weekends seem to work best. Anyways, I got here early and decided to read the newspaper," she says, taking a breath as if she's trying hard to hold in her excitement. "You probably haven't read it yet. . . . I can't believe this! I just about fell off my chair. I don't think you're going to believe this either. But there's an article written about you and Ty!"

"I know, I know. I heard," Eileen mumbles.

"You heard?" Brooke asks, sounding disappointed that she wasn't the first one to break the news. "How?"

"Nick phoned me, and trust me, Ty and I are not dating," Eileen stresses.

"I thought you went out with him last night. Isn't that a date?"

She didn't want to admit to her best friend that Ty spent the night. It's so unlike Eileen, and she wouldn't hear the end of it.

"It wasn't a date." Eileen places a hand to her forehead. How many people would see this article? Let alone read it? She was sure the team would, or worse, Joe! Steve! Of course he'll read the article—he's quoted in it! Ugh! Rick, and Ted would see it too! How can she explain this? They can fire her. Oh, no! It's like a teacher dating a student—it can't happen. It shouldn't happen. And who would they believe? A woman who wants to keep her job or a jock who is known for his rendezvous?

Eileen tries to relax, watching the coffee maker drip and listening for it to percolate. "I'm his skating coach and we went out to discuss business." It's her story and she's sticking to it.

"Come on now, the guy is too hot to just have a business dinner with. There's something more. There's nothing wrong with seeking out a relationship with him," her friend counsels. "Maybe you could learn new talents. You teach him if he teaches you a few things," she teases.

"Brooke!" Eileen exclaims.

"Well?" her friend says playfully.

"I am a professional! I'm not looking for a relationship right now."

"Sure, you're not," Brooke says. "We need to work on your love life."

"Since when did my love life become a task?"

"Since walking dogs became a hobby."

"Very funny."

"Even if there was something going on between the two of you, I don't think you would tell me."

"Of course I would tell you!" Eileen says, a little disappointed that her friend was right.

"I don't know. It's not like I'd tell anyone about you and hottie Ty Caldwell."

"There is nothing going on," she says. "You know, just a few outings here and there. That's all."

Just then, Eileen hears her bedroom door squeak open.

"I think he's better than what you're saying," Brooke says. "I finally saw that Toyota commercial he's in. He's absolutely gorgeous. Well, you know that—who doesn't? Is that why you're lying low and not going after him—because he's already seeing someone?"

Eileen can feel her cheeks warm, and her eyes are stuck on Ty, who is facing her and smiling, shirtless, in his Calvin Klein boxers. She eyes him up and down and has to remember to close her mouth. He is amazing, just how Brooke described him. His abs and thighs are well defined, bringing back memories of last night.

Brooke breaks her concentration. "Are you going to be home later? I'll stop by."

She's trying to give her friend her undivided attention, but is a little distracted by his physique and wide smile. "Uh, um, I don't know," Eileen answers in a daze. "Call me."

"Then you should go for him. What do you have to lose?"

Eileen smiles at Ty and looks back at the coffee maker, trying to snap out of the trance she's in. She grabs two cups from the cupboard, holds up a cup to Ty, and mouths, *Do you want one?*

Ty nods his head in response and walks closer to her. Trying to juggle the phone between her ear and shoulder, she carries the mugs to the coffee maker and pours the coffee. Ty walks closer to her, but instead of grabbing the full cup of coffee like Eileen expects, he wraps one hand around her waist in a strong, secure hold. Eileen smiles when he nestles his lips into her neck and instant tremors of seduction come over her. Wow! Is he amazing!

"A lot. I . . . I have a . . . a lot to lose and I'm trying to be very, uh, careful," she stammers.

"Well, I say go for him. Mario treated you like crap. I'm sure Ty is different. Judging by all the publicity he gets by visiting sick kids, I haven't heard anything bad about him."

"Ah, no, no, I haven't either," Eileen says. She's trying to concentrate on her conversation with her best friend, but Ty doesn't make it easy for her, as he sweeps her long hair over her shoulders and explores the back of her neck with his lips.

"There you go. There's your answer."

Ty's hand is creeping up the back of her tank top, feeling her bare skin and massaging it with nice easy strokes, enough for her to feel like putty and want to crawl back into bed with him. It doesn't seem like a bad idea.

"My answer?" Eileen asks while staring at Ty.

"Are you okay?" Brooke asks. "You seem distracted."

"Oh, no, no. I'm fine. I better go," Eileen says. "I'll call you later."

Eileen hangs up the phone, dropping her hand, tossing the phone to the counter.

"Busy morning?" Ty asks, embracing her in a hug. "Ms. Popular," he teases.

"Sorry about that. I don't usually have phone calls before nine. Did you sleep well?" she asks, breaking away so that she can see his face, getting a sweep of his short stubble that must have grown overnight.

"You have a comfy bed," he says as he reaches for his cup of coffee. "I can get used to sleeping here."

She opens the refrigerator door. "Keep dreaming," she teases. "Cream or milk?"

"This is good." He takes a sip. "I take it black."

Eileen takes out a carton of milk. "Great. Because I don't have cream."

"Is everything okay?" he asks, bringing his mug to his mouth.

She pours milk into her coffee cup and reaches for a spoon in the drawer.

"Apparently there's an article printed in this morning's paper about us," she says, stirring her coffee.

"You're surprised?"

"I was afraid this would happen." She takes a sip, puts her mug down on the kitchen counter, and then says, "I'm very surprised."

"Why?"

"It's not like we go out all the time. I wonder if that Dell guy said something to reporters." She crosses her arms to her chest.

Ty shrugs. "He could have."

"I hope not."

"Even if he did, it's no big deal."

"Nothing's a big deal to you, is it?" she says, eyeing him with a neediness she knows he can fulfill.

"Stuff like that doesn't bother me the way it bothers you."

"I guess I worry about my reputation."

"I don't care what people think of me. I'm human, and I just happen to play this country's most popular sport."

"I guess so," she agrees. "When you put it that way . . ." Eileen picks up her mug and takes a sip of coffee.

"Don't beat yourself up about what other people say about you. You have to do what you think is right for you," he says.

"I don't care what people think about me, but I do care what people say. This could hurt my career."

"No, it can't."

"Yes, it can," she says sternly. "I've worked really hard to get where I am, and it could be over before I know it."

"You shouldn't care so much about other people's opinion. It will get you nowhere, and create negative energy."

"Thanks, Dr. Caldwell."

He laughs. "That's a good one. It does have a nice ring to it, doesn't it?" he teases and takes a gulp of coffee.

"Well, if you want to read the article, apparently it's in the entertainment section."

"You sound insulted."

"I am," she says, cupping the mug with both hands and holding it up to her chin.

"Why?"

"Because it's an untrue story, that's why. And why is it entertainment? Why is it even a story?"

"Is it untrue? They knew something that we didn't, don't you think?" he asks, putting his mug down on the counter, leaning against the wall of the kitchen.

"We can't go on like this. If anyone finds out you spent the night . . ." she says with worry, trying not to be distracted by his almost naked body. "I don't want to know what the newspaper articles say about me," she says, wiping her eyebrow in distress.

"Relax, no one's going to know," he says, reaching his arms out for her, but she isn't quite sure if she can trust him yet. She doesn't even know if she can tell her best friend, afraid more people will find out.

An odd ringing sound is coming from her bedroom. She looks up at him, listening to the ring. "That's my cell phone," Ty says, breaking away from her. He walks into her bedroom, searching for his phone. "Hello?" he says and Eileen can't help but listen in on his conversation.

He stays in her bedroom, and she listens, wondering whom he's talking to. "I'm fine. . . . I'm just out, doing some running around. Where are you?" he asks. "Where? In an hour? I'm not sure I can make it there in an hour. How about noon? Yeah, well, I'm a little busy at the moment or I'd come over right now. . . . Yes . . . uh . . . no . . . okay, see you then."

He disconnects and walks back into the kitchen. "We'll have to get your car," he says, scratching the back of his head.

"Hopefully it's still there," she says, taking another sip of coffee.

"It'll be there," he says, reaching for the mug he left on the kitchen counter. "Are you able to go now?"

"Now?"

"Yeah."

"I need to take a shower. I feel gross," she says, wrinkling her nose. "I can't leave the house without getting cleaned up."

"We're just going to pick up your car. Nobody will see you. You'll hop out of my truck and into your car, unless you need to stop somewhere on the way," he says, gulping down his hot coffee.

"I won't be stopping anywhere if I don't have a shower," she argues. "What's your hurry? Where do you have to be so early on a Sunday?"

"I forgot about my plans today."

"Now I'm curious. Please, do share," she says, not wanting to let go of her coffee mug.

"Are you jealous?"

She spits out a "No. Of course not." Is she? Her stomach feels tight from the thought of Ty kissing another woman or even holding another woman, for that matter.

"Good. There's nothing to be jealous about."

"What would I be jealous about?"

"Me seeing someone else."

"What?" She laughs nervously, feeling her cheeks warm. "I don't care."

"Sure, you do. But don't worry—I'm not the two-timing type."

Well, that's a relief. She smiles.

"We're not really seeing each other."

He combs his fingers through his dirty-blond hair. "Some guys and I are going trail biking."

"Oh," she says, feeling left out. Why should she care what he did without her? It's not as if they're a couple, right?

"I'd invite you, but people would talk and you don't want anyone to know about . . . us," he says, putting his empty mug in the sink.

"Right," she says, feeling disappointed.

"I'll get dressed and then we should go."

"Don't you want me to make breakfast?"

"Maybe another time, sweetheart," he jokes and pecks her on the cheek. "I don't have time. You'll be home in half an hour."

She follows him into her bedroom and grabs a pair of sweats and a faded T-shirt. She feels sheepish about getting undressed in front of him, so she takes her clothes into the bathroom to change, pulls her hair back into a ponytail, sprays a lightly scented body mist, and brushes her teeth, trying to feel a little human.

When she steps out of the bathroom, Ty is standing in the hallway with his shoes on and his keys in hand. "Wow! You look amazing!"

She touches her ponytail to make sure it's secure and says, "You don't waste any time, do you?"

"I don't like keeping people waiting," he says.

"It must be important," she says, putting on her shoes. "I mean they must be important people if you're dropping everything to see them."

"It's not like we had plans. I don't think you even expected us to shack up, did you?"

Eileen feels her face redden and tries to hide her complexion by turning around to pick up her keys. "Uh, no, of course not!"

"Unless you knew this all along and were playing hard-to-get."

"No! I'm not like that," she says, locking the door behind them. "Trust me, this was very unexpected."

Ty cracks a smile. "I don't know. I think you had this in mind all along," he says, laughing. "I think you portray yourself as some hard-ass woman, but really you're a softie."

"Really?" she asks as they leave the building and head for visitor parking. She hops into his truck.

"Uh-huh, I do," he says, turning his key in the ignition. "You obviously couldn't resist my charm."

She rolls her eyes as she clicks her seat belt. "Please, I don't want to hurt your feelings, but it was the alcohol talking. I don't usually drink enough to get tipsy and invite guys back to my place, so don't let this one-nighter get to your head because it won't happen again."

"You sound like you mean it, but I find that hard to believe."

"You shouldn't. This was all just a—"

Eileen can't quite finish her sentence. Was this truly a mistake?

"Go on, this was just a what?" he asks, driving and eyeing her tight lips.

"A mistake," she says softly.

"You think it was?" he asks sadly, bringing his free hand to his chest. "I'm hurt."

"Well, don't you?" is all she can say.

"No. Definitely not."

"I'm surprised."

"You shouldn't be," he says and looks at his gas gauge. "I've got to stop at a gas station and fill up. We should do this again some-time."

This brings a smile to Eileen's face. "I don't know about that."

"Why not? You had a good time. I had a good time. It's all good."

She shakes her head with embarrassment. "The more we see each other, the more people will talk."

He pulls into a Chevron. "You really need to let things go."

Ty hops out of his truck. She glances back at him as he leans against his truck, with one hand on the gas pump. He's wearing last night's clothes, a wrinkled shirt and blue Mavi jeans, but one would never know that he wasn't wearing clean clothes. He looks downright sexy. Eileen can't stop thinking about last night. It wasn't just a make-out session or a close dance at the concert. She slept with him, and it doesn't seem real for some reason, more like a dream. Why he picked her, she'll never know.

She waits patiently in the passenger seat, fidgeting with her hands. She clicks off her seat belt and gets out of the truck and walks over to Ty.

"I'm going to grab a coffee since I didn't have time to finish mine. Do you want one?" she asks.

"Yeah, okay," he answers.

She walks inside the convenience store and pours two coffees. She stirs in milk for hers and puts lids on the cups when she hears her name.

"Elle!" a female voice cries.

Eileen turns around to meet her friend's confused eyes. "Where are you off to?" Brooke asks, stepping away from the counter.

"I . . . uh . . ." Eileen looks down at her coffee cups. "Grabbing drinks."

Brooke glances out the door window. "For who?"

Eileen's face flushes.

Brooke's eyes grow wide with amusement. "Is Ty with you? You spent the night?" She gasps. "You did, didn't you?"

"No, uh, we went out last night and he crashed at my place. It's nothing really. . . ."

"Good for you!" Brooke lowers her voice. "How was it? What's he like?"

Eileen can feel her face getting hotter. "Shhh." She looks around.

"Why are you in denial?"

"I'm not. It's just that I don't want anyone to know."

"Why not? That's amazing! I knew you would hook up with one of them."

"He's not one of them," she corrects. "He's different."

"You need this," Brooke says, giving her a reassuring nod.

"I better go. Ty's dropping me off to get my car."

"Call me later with details. And I want to hear about everything."

Eileen ignores Brooke and pays for the coffees. From the window, she watches her friend wave to Ty as she passes to the pump. So much for keeping a secret.

Chapter 12

Later in the afternoon, Eileen drives over to Ty's apartment holding the *Vancouver Daily* in a tight grip, rattled and aware that hanging out with the hockey player is not helping her career. She had no idea the general public would be interested in her personal life. Eileen needs to put an end to these meetings and get-togethers fast before they move onto a deeper, romantic level in their relationship. Something she can't afford to risk.

Ty opens his front door for her, looking muscular in a T-shirt and shorts. His hair is damp and wavy, curling at the top of his ears. His blue eyes are surprisingly piercing as though he sees something he can't explain.

Eileen slides off her shoes. "What?"

He steps forward to shut the door, turns around, and kisses her fully on the mouth. Her body falls into his arms, leaving her breathless when he releases her. "You look really good," he manages to say.

She takes a quick look at what she is wearing. Apparently he finds a woman in a basic summer dress appealing.

Ty walks into his kitchen and pulls out a jug of milk. "Can I get you something to drink? I'm making a smoothie. Want one?"

"No, thanks. Listen, about last night—"

"Yeah?" he says casually, taking a banana from the fruit bowl on the kitchen counter and peeling it. His shirt is form-fitting, revealing his broad shoulders. He gives her a half smile as though waiting for a compliment. "You enjoyed yourself?" He throws the banana into the blender and takes out a handful of cut strawberries from a bowl in the fridge.

Her shoulders fall. "Ty! I'm talking about us! This is serious!" She unrolls the newspaper and flips to the page. "I had to read the article for myself. It's horrible! I don't get it! Why is there so much hype about our personal life?"

"Did Bill write something he shouldn't have?" Ty scoops protein powder into the blender and turns it on. "What does it say?" he shouts.

"I'll let you read it," she says, throwing it down on the counter.

He turns off the blender, grabs a tall cup, and pours himself a smoothie. "Are you sure you don't want any?"

She shakes her head. "No thanks."

Ty wipes his hand on a tea towel and takes the article in hand. "Hey, that's us! It's a good picture!"

"Never mind the picture—read the article!"

He smirks as he reads.

"I didn't think it was that funny," Eileen says, disturbed.

"This story about the cat that ran up the tree and his owner followed, thinking that he could just climb back down, but he got stuck. . . ."

She shoots him an unimpressed look.

"Are you trying to be funny?"

Ty doesn't answer as his eyes skim the page. When he finishes reading, he looks up.

"So?"

"I don't think it's a big deal." He puts down the newspaper, takes a straw from the cupboard, and puts it in his cup.

"Really? I don't think it's right having articles written every week about you and me. And why don't you think it's a big deal?"

Ty takes a seat in his recliner and sips his frothy drink while Eileen sits down on the couch across from him.

"It is what it is," he says. "Who cares?"

Her eyes narrow. "This is horrible!"

"Come on, Elle. It's a good article."

"It is not! Seriously, this is my reputation. I made it very clear in the beginning that I don't mix business with pleasure and I sure don't date men I work with." She covers her face with her hand.

"We had a date," he mocks.

She tries to be serious, but his playfulness is killing her. Why did he have to be so hot and so much fun? He was supposed to be done with her by now. What was she getting herself into?

She takes her hand away from her face. "I told you it wasn't a date. It was a meeting," she emphasizes. "That's what I'll say. I'm sure I'll hear from Steve, or Joe or Ted. . . ."

"It was fun. You can admit that, Elle."

She can't. It would mean she liked him more than she bargained for. As long as she had a job to do, she would have to end it with Ty.

"People are going to think I took this job to get a date . . . to be close to men! People will forget I have talent. You heard what Ali said. And how about the other wives? This is going to jeopardize my job." She takes a breath. "Ty." She says his name softer than planned, with more feeling than she wanted. Her eyes close to focus on how she is going to tell him that they need to separate and go their own ways, but as she opens her eyes, she feels a tug at her heart. Ty is watching her as though he is really listening to her. Does he really care about her?

She swallows a gulp of air before talking. "I . . . we . . . can't do this. We can't see each other anymore. The team is going to read this and then what?" she asks with a steady voice. "They're going to think that we're dating and we're not." She folds her arms to her chest, thinking of how Ty greeted her and how close they've become. Why is this so hard? Harder than she imagined.

He kicks the leg rest down to stand up. "I disagree."

Her head leans slightly forward as she waits for an explanation.

"I don't know what the big deal is. Who cares what people think?"

"Maybe it's not a big deal to you, because this is another game you play, but I don't play this game, so I would appreciate it if you would talk to this Bill reporter guy and tell him that he needs both sides of the story. Didn't he learn that in journalism school?"

Ty starts to chuckle while trying to keep a straight face. He stands in front of her, hands on his hips.

"Now, what's so funny?"

"You."

She gives him a disapproving look. "I don't think this is funny. I'm concerned."

"Don't be." He sips his drink and puts it down on the coffee table.

"Are you going to speak with Bill or should I?"

"I can talk to him if you want," he says.

"Good. That's what I was hoping for." She walks to the wall-size window and looks out at the view. The water glistens like sequins on a ball gown. Breathtaking.

"Feel better now?" he asks as he walks over to her. The scent of his cologne paralyzes her. "By next week, this story will be forgotten."

"Why isn't this a big deal to you?" She knows he's not some regular guy looking for publicity because Ty has enough of that.

"I don't care what people think of me. I get paid to play hockey," he says, staring out the window. Ty smiles. "Besides, I think it's true. I think the reporter is right."

"Come on," she says with a nervous laugh. "I don't know what you're trying to do and what you want from me. You know you can have any one of those puck bunnies . . ." She catches his stare. "What do you want from me?"

Ty takes a step closer to her and he tilts his head slightly. Eileen is frozen, unsure of what her reaction should be.

He doesn't answer her question. Instead, he stands tall, throws his hands together, and asks, "Hungry?"

Isn't he going to kiss me?

If only he were a horrible kisser, she could turn away. And if only he were boring, she could leave for better company.

"I'll make us something to eat," he says, finishing his smoothie and walking into the kitchen to set his empty glass down in the sink. "I missed lunch. The trails were insane! Brandon flew off after he tried to make a jump."

"Is he okay?"

"Oh, yeah," Ty says, going to the fridge and taking out a package of ham and a block of cheese.

"And the story says a source confirms the relationship. I'd like to know who that person is."

"Do you though? Does it matter?" he asks, making his sandwich.

"I don't know. I guess not." She leans against the granite counter and watches him cut open a bun. "You're known for having a lot of girlfriends."

"I am?"

Her cheeks flush, as she realizes that they haven't talked much about their personal lives. They've kept quiet about their pasts.

"I don't know what you're talking about," he says, adding some mustard and lettuce.

"Yes, you do! From what I heard, you are carefree when it comes to women. Taking them home and trying them on for size, so to speak." She clears her throat.

"Where do you come up with this?" Ty asks as though he's hearing it for the first time. He takes a bite of his sandwich, still standing in front of her.

Eileen's cheeks are warm. "I don't know," she stammers. "It's a known fact that you're a casual-sex kind of guy."

He swallows. "Really? I didn't know."

"Seriously? You're kidding, right?"

"Yeah, I had no idea," he says, filling a glass of water. "And you want to know where you stand? Is that it?"

"No . . . uh . . . I'm just wondering, that's all. Are you still having casual dates with other women?"

"Do I sense jealousy?" He smirks.

"Huh? No! Not at all."

"Then you're okay with me seeing other women?"

She watches him take another bite and wipe his lips with a paper towel.

"Yeah, yeah, of course." Her voice is small, and she feels her chest tighten as she thinks of women hanging off of him, proud of the attention.

"Because you don't want anything between us, is that right, Elle?"

"I . . . I . . ."

"Look, if it makes you feel better, I'm not seeing anyone and I'm not having casual sex."

"You do though, don't you?"

He shakes his head.

"You're just saying that, Ty. Tell me the truth! I need to hear it from you."

"I just told you! I know why you're asking," he says. "And I can tell you, I'm no Mario."

She swallows hard, feeling the overwhelming fear and hurtfulness return.

"Okay, well, what happened at a club two years ago with an eighteen-year-old?" she asks, desperately changing the subject.

Ty's quiet for a moment, running his hand over his scalp and scratching the back of his head. "I thought she was older."

"So I heard."

"If you think I do that all the time, I don't. I've changed, Elle. I'm not like that anymore." He braces his hands on the counter and looks at her endearingly.

She gives him a slow nod, reassured. She wants to believe him. A part of her does.

"Look, do you want to get some fresh air? We can both use a walk."

They stroll down the road, making their way to a nearby trail. The birds are singing and the wildflowers sway from the ocean breeze. The fresh air is indeed what she needed.

Eileen cautions herself against walking too close to him, yet she desperately wants him to pull her close, wrapping a strong arm around her even though she knows she's risking more articles and jeopardizing her career.

"Are you planning a visit with your family before the season starts?" she asks him, taking a long look at the gravel path ahead.

"Yeah, I'll go see them soon," he says, sounding as casual as he looks in his Maui Jims and flip-flops.

They walk over a wooden bridge and Elle stops to watch the ducks quack and bob at every wave. "Ever notice that male and female ducks stick together?" she asks. "Rarely apart."

"I never noticed that before," Ty admits as he leans up beside her, admiring nature.

Elle folds her hands over the railing. "This is so relaxing," she says, letting herself fall back and inhale the fresh air. It's the first time she's been with him that they haven't been stopped and harassed for an autograph or picture. "I needed this."

"Me too." He puts an arm around her waist and brings her close, giving her a little squeeze.

Why does anyone care about them? They're like a normal couple. What does it matter what they do? The focus should be on her coaching the team, not who she spends time with. And as hard as she tries, Eileen puts the thought away for as long as she can to simply enjoy the view until her phone rings and she casually takes it out of her purse.

"Eileen Francis."

"I've warned you," the man says stridently.

The color drains from Eileen's face. She stares at the ground. "What do you want from me?" she asks in a mere whisper, her body feeling weak. Why hasn't this guy stopped calling her? "Who are you?" Her back stiffens.

"You don't belong on the team."

Ty takes the phone from Eileen's ear and yells, "Who is this?" He pauses. "Who is this?"

The line goes dead. Ty takes the phone away from his ear. "Another threat?"

She nods as though her neck muscles are tight and takes a deep breath. "I wish I knew who it was," she whispers. "I can't even guess who would want to threaten me."

"You have to tell the police," Ty says, putting his hands on his hips. "You have to put a stop to it."

"I don't want to lose my job," she pleads. "There is so much attention about me teaching the team—this will only bring on more negativity. Ted won't have it. He'll get rid of me before it becomes an issue."

"He won't," Ty says, shaking his head. "This is about your safety."

Eileen throws her phone into her purse and holds on to the wooden pier railing. Ty wraps his arm around her, pulling her in for a tight squeeze. She lets herself fall into him, breathing in the fresh ocean air. Her head rests on his chest. *Being with Ty doesn't feel so wrong*, she tells herself, relaxing in his arms and letting him hold her.

"Did you hear his voice?" Eileen asks, looking up at Ty to meet his troubled eyes.

"No, but he heard mine. I think he was going to say something and then hung up."

"I don't know the voice."

"We have to get help before something bad happens."

Up until now, she was sure the words were meaningless. What happens if Ty is right? Could her life be in jeopardy?

Her nerves are a ball of tangled mess so she waits until she's home to call the police and to see what can be done.

Chapter 13

Two days later, Eileen still hadn't heard back from the police. She left a message and still there was nothing done to stop the threats. Maybe the police were so busy that non-emergencies were on the bottom of their to-do list.

"Hi, Elle!" Robyn sings and tries stopping her in her place, but Eileen is on a mission. She has work to do. Perhaps showing up at the rink early to call new clients before instructing her class was a bad idea. "So, I guess I was right. You and Ty? Dating?" she asks in a rush.

"No, I'm not dating him."

"But you were with him on the weekend and I read that you two were spotted several times together. I think that's evidence enough that you two are dating," Robyn says, her dangling earrings swaying as she bobs her head. "If I were you, I'd announce it."

"Do you believe everything you read?" she says, taking a step backwards. "I've got some calls to make before my class."

"That's why I'm asking you!" Her voice raises, but Eileen ignores her and keeps walking toward the empty desk she uses. Does Eileen have to answer that? Even if she lies, what excuse does she have that's believable enough?

Eileen finishes up with her six-years-olds and heads out of the lobby when her phone rings. She looks at the unrecognizable number and takes a breath, unsure if she should take the call. Her body freezes, wondering what the threat will be this time. But then, the more she speaks to the harasser, the closer she will get to understand what he really wants from her and who it is.

"Hi, Eileen, it's Constable Dundas."

She exhales, relieved.

"I understand you have been a victim of harassment?"

"That's right," she answers, keeping her phone as close to her mouth as possible so her eavesdropping coworker can't hear her conversation.

"These phone calls you've been getting, do you know the phone number?"

She heads out the main doors, keeping her head up so she's aware of her surroundings. "No, they've been unknown."

"Typical. How about the notes? Are they all the same printing, have you noticed?"

"Looks similar."

"And you said you only get these notes when you're at the Dome?"

"That's right. Same goes for the key marks on my car. It happened at work."

"I'm going to say that it's pretty obvious from what you've told me that it could be someone who knows your schedule. At this point, you don't know who it is."

"No."

"Any indication? A coworker? Ex-boyfriend? Did you have a run-in with someone other than work-related issues?"

"No. None."

"If you can record the phone calls, we'll be able to have evidence of the harassment. However, at this time, I have nothing to go on."

"I was afraid of that," she admits, getting into her car.

"You need to be diligent when alone."

"Do you think I could get hurt?"

"You don't know. I'm saying take extra precautions. We need to know who is making these threats before we can get to the next step. Pay attention to the people around you. I'll give you my number. Call me if you receive another threat or if you can pinpoint who the person is. Or if you think you are in danger. I want to know. In the meantime, be conscious of who's around you. Change up your routine if you can."

"Thank you," Eileen sighs and hangs up. She drives to the Dome feeling a little more settled now that she has made contact with the police. How can she change up her routine when her life is on a schedule?

Eileen sneaks into the rink, hiding from what looks like Ty and Brandon talking to a group of women, smiling, laughing, and being loud and flirtatious. The guys are drawn into the conversation by their long, streaked-blonde hair, big earrings, and tight jeans.

Eileen pushes her sunglasses off her face so she can be certain it's Ty chatting it up. She sucks in a breath, trying not to be distracted, and tells herself that what they shared Saturday night was two lonely people having fun, nothing more, nothing less. Yes, Saturday night was amazing, really amazing. Never has any guy made her feel so beautiful and wanted, special and attractive. Even Mario didn't make her feel so alive and she dated him for a year!

Was what she and Ty shared just a one-time fling? Although it feels like so much more, she has to remember to play it smart with Ty now, pretend nothing happened and maybe, just maybe she can accept that they'll never be a real couple even though her heart tells her different.

Eileen warms up her legs by skating around the rink before the team joins her for an afternoon practice.

"Eileen!"

She hears her name and looks to the bench. It's Ted Walker. His arms are crossed and she can see his bushy white eyebrows before his dark eyes.

She skates over to him, her heart pounding so hard that her hands begin to sweat in her hockey gloves. She's never spoken to the owner one-on-one before. Is he going to tell her this is her last shift as a Warrior?

"Eileen," he says her name with assertiveness.

"Mr. Walker!" She stops at the bench, keeping a little distance between them. She holds her stick with both hands for comfort.

"You're getting a lot of attention these days. I suspected you would. . . . It's good publicity for the team." He undoes his hands. "However, having a relationship with another employee is against company policy. I can't tell you who you can involve yourself with, but if you want respect from this industry, I would advise you to clean it up and make your job here a priority."

"I do, sir. Perhaps I don't know the company's policy because I wasn't given a contract," she says, steadying her voice. The last thing Ted would want is a mousey employee. She's in the big league now; she needs to act as though there's no fear.

He gives her a nod. His eyes squint as though in thought. "I will have one drafted up. Until then, it would be wise to keep your distance from Caldwell or you will be terminated, no questions asked."

Eileen watches him turn around and leave, relieved that she still has her job. He didn't even give her the chance to defend herself, although what could she say?

She has to remember to stay away from Ty before people do take notice. Not like some haven't already, but she needs to be more discreet or people will be talking more about them as a couple rather than about their careers.

The team slowly makes it onto the ice, one by one, like an army of ants. Making long strides, their sticks in hand, they're ready for instruction. "Five hard laps around the rink!" Eileen shouts. "Meet me down in this corner. Whoever is last will have to complete a set of push-ups and a set of sit-ups."

"What do you consider a set?" one player yells out.

"Twenty-five," Eileen says in a firm voice. "Let's go!" she shouts and then blows her whistle. They all take off racing to the finish line while Eileen grabs small cones and sets them up on the ice in a zigzag line for the first drill.

Her hair tied back into a tight ponytail, Eileen sports a blue tracksuit and wears a touch of mascara and a dab of pink lip gloss. She smiles at her team, watching the players complete their hard skate. "Looks like you're the chosen one," she says to one player and he drops to his knees.

"While he's busy, we're going to work on transition skating. I need defense right here," she says, pointing to the spot with the blade of her stick. "And forwards over here," she says. "Forwards, you'll skate with the puck around the cone. Defense, you'll skate backwards around the cones. You'll be slightly in front of the forwards, and once you're around the cone, defense will skate forward and then backwards trying to check your opponent. Does everyone understand?"

"Sure. Why don't you show us?" one player asks and then laughs.

"Okay," Eileen says easily. "Ty," she calls, saying his name naturally and regretfully. She passes him a puck, knowing she's safe with him. "You can help demonstrate."

"Don't they make a cute couple," Thompson mocks, laughing.

Eileen ignores him. She hasn't spoken to Thompson since the incident. She wants to, but can't find the words or the energy to confront him. Besides, what can she say that would make things better? The more she thinks about it, the more she realizes she was giving him the attention he wants.

"Okay, you skate with the puck," she tells Ty as he begins to skate. "I'll be defense," she shouts and glances at Ty, who hasn't taken his eyes off her. "I don't lose sight of the forward with the puck. I stay with him so that he has to eventually make a move. I don't want to give him space"—she waves her hand between them—"because that will allow him to make a play. Let's get into position." She watches the team split up and carefully examines their abilities. She can't help but watch Ty skate and move on the ice with strength and agility. His legs are powerhouses, able to skate hard and fast. He makes every exercise look effortless.

They get to the end of the drill. "Okay, next," she yells out and blows her whistle, watching for Ty's number twenty-two jersey, although she can spot him easily during practice. He leaves his helmet strap undone and tucks in his jersey at his hip.

They stay where they are, watching the rest of the team go through the practice.

"You're pretty good," Ty admits.

"Are you just saying that to butter me up?"

"No, of course not," he says with a mischievous grin. "I really do mean it."

"Then why do you have that look?"

"What look?" he asks.

"I don't know, Caldwell." She can't put her finger on it. "You seem different."

"Well, we did spend practically the whole weekend together," he says. "How am I supposed to act?"

A reminder that she's mixed business with pleasure and this is what she has to expect.

Eileen holds back her answer when his teammates skate in for another instruction. She makes the team practice another drill as Steve and Joe join her on the ice.

She gives them each a nod as she keeps her attention on the team. Because of the talent on the team, it's not easy telling them what to do, but her job's on the line. She has to push their limits. It's the only way she'll get recognized and respected as a pro.

Eileen blows her whistle. "Okay, guys, bring it in," she yells. When the group surrounds her, she explains the next drill. "The next thing we're going to do is a forecheck drill. I want two teams—blues against whites. I'm going to shoot the puck into one of the corners. It will be the same scenario as a game."

"No need to do a scrimmage," Joe points out. His black, short, straw-like strands are evenly cut around his forehead and ears. "These guys need something fresh, something new!"

"It's not a scrimmage," Eileen bellows. She ignores Joe's brown weasel eyes and thinks about the play she wants the men to practice. She continues to ignore Joe, looking at the players as she explains. "Except, defense"—she makes eye contact with the players—"two at a time, one of you loses your stick. You must defend with your body—"

"They're not blocking shots, are they?" Joe asks, all serious. "Don't need an injury before the season starts."

Eileen puts a hand on her hip. "Would you like to instruct, Joe? It sounds like you have another idea for practice."

She hears the guys whisper as she stares at Joe. His face changes from expressionless to hard. He clenches his jaw and puffs out his chest. *Isn't he going to back down?*

"Go ahead, Joe," she presses. "The ice is all yours."

Joe relaxes his mouth, but his beady eyes haven't left her. Eileen's back stiffens. She licks her bottom lip, waiting for him to respond to her. Clearly he wants to take over her instruction. He can't seem to leave her alone.

"Continue, Eileen," Steve says with a tap of his stick on the ice. He stands taller than Joe with a courteous nod.

"Here we go!" She regains her composure. "I'll shoot a puck into one of the corners. Defense, you'll be at the blue line skating back. It's a three-on-two, first to the puck makes the play. You get three tries to score and then we change ends. There's no stopping until I blow the whistle. Got it?" She pauses and waits for any questions. "Joe? Why don't you shoot first?"

He takes a slap shot into the corner of the rink, hitting the boards with a loud bang. She watches the men perform and is enjoying how well they are playing. Her eyes tune in to Ty; his ability to make a play is impressive. It's hard not to watch him skate and easy to ignore the others. Finally, the men change ends and there is a new group to watch as she stands at the boards. The men are skating so hard, she can feel the wind against her face as they pass her. She could get used to this job.

When practice is over, she gets Steve's consent to have the ice to herself so she can practice puck control and slap shots. Some of the guys are stretching on the bench, and Ty is busy talking with a team-mate.

Eileen skates around the ice, taking long strides and stretching out her legs. She picks up a puck and takes a shot at the empty net. When she retrieves it, she continues to skate around the rink, practicing her moves, skating over every circle, forward and back with a puck. She stops when she gets to the last one.

"Great practice," Ty says, skating toward her.

"Thanks," she says, surprised. She had to admit it was one of her toughest practices so far, not because of the comments made, but because the practice itself was a challenge.

"What are you doing after this?" Ty asks, standing tall, his blue practice jersey tucked into one side of his shorts.

She stops skating so she can see his upper lip curl when he asks her out. "When I leave here?"

He smirks before he answers. "Yes."

There is something about his curved smile that makes her smile back. Maybe it's the way he looks at her with those bright blue eyes, making her feel like no one else is in the room or rink. Or maybe it's the way he says her name in a flawless and endearing kind of way.

"I'm busy," she says.

"With what?" He twirls his hockey stick.

She arches an eyebrow. Did he forget she has other work to do?

"I was hoping we could grab a bite to eat."

"Hmm."

"We're supposed to be a couple, you know," he teases, nudging her with his shoulder. She finally looks over at him. When she doesn't respond again, he asks, "So?"

"So . . . what?"

"Pick another day then."

"I don't know." Eileen wrinkles her forehead in thought. How can she tell him they have to stop seeing each other?

"Why not?" he asks, shocked by her answer. "Wasn't it a good night?"

"I'm your skating coach, remember? I don't go out with guys I work with. Well, at least I try not to."

"You did the other night. Wasn't it worth it?" he asks playfully. "And why the sudden change of heart?"

She can feel her cheeks heat up. "Because I shouldn't have done what I did."

"I don't know why all of a sudden you're trying to pretend nothing happened," he says.

"I have to," she says. "Let's pretend nothing happened. I think it's best for both of us if we do."

"That's too bad. I haven't stopped thinking about it . . . or thinking about you," he corrects. "It doesn't mean we can't go out for dinner, right?"

"It can lead to other things," she reminds him.

"It did lead to something."

She puckers her lips in thought. This is what she was afraid of.

"What's gotten into you?" He tries to make eye contact. "I don't get it."

Eileen looks away not sure what to say. Does she remind him that there will never be another Saturday night like the one they shared?

Ty waits for an answer. He's patient and observant as though waiting for the opportunity to disagree. "We had a great time Saturday night. I didn't see a problem then, and I don't see one now."

Didn't he get what he wanted?

"What kind of guy do you think I am?"

"I don't have to explain," she begins. "I'm sure you've heard it before." She tries to shrug him off.

"I want to hear what you think of me," he states. "Because clearly you have a different opinion than you did on the weekend."

"No, you don't want to know," she argues, shaking her head.

"Yes, I do," he urges. "Come on, everyone has their own opinions, I know you have one. Let's hear it."

"As if," she mutters. "You're like the rest of them. All you guys want is attention from women and I'm not playing this game. I don't want to be like the others."

"Like the rest of them?" he asks, offended. "I think you're getting me mixed up with Visconti."

She looks at him with hurt-filled eyes as though he called her a bad name. The shame Mario put her through was upsetting enough, but he also broke her heart many times over and couldn't keep their relationship real. There was always someone else even when she felt like she was the only woman in the world. He was charming, like Ty, had incredible talent and looks that magazines flocked to, just like Ty. He paid attention to her and expected her to drop everything for him, just like Ty. But Mario wasn't persistent and encouraging like Ty. Nor did Mario give her the attention Ty does.

Why does this situation feel all too familiar? This time she will be proactive and not let Ty break her heart. She'll be one step ahead.

"You guys are all the same," she says. "But I'm to blame for the other night. I shouldn't have let it get as far as it had. Quite frankly, I'm mad at myself. Disappointed, really."

"I don't see it as a problem," he says, cradling his hockey stick.

"If this continues, it could be," she says. "I don't want to be a trophy you're trying to win. Trying to win another night with your skating coach."

He takes in a breath and pauses for a second before he responds. "By the sounds of it, you've had some bad luck with men."

He had no idea.

"Look, I just thought we could both use the company and have a drink, maybe even dinner, again . . . friends," he finally concludes.

"Friends?" she repeats, as though she doesn't believe him.

The look in his eyes tells her he's playing. He takes off his helmet with one easy sweep and brushes back his hair and wipes the sweat away from his eyes.

"Yeah, don't tell me you're Miss Popular and having another friend would be a burden on you. Come on," Ty encourages, getting her to smile.

They hold a gaze. "What do you really think of me?" he asks.

"Why does it matter what I think?"

"I'm curious."

"About my opinion?" she asks. The Zamboni driver opens the gate, and they watch from center ice as he starts up the ice cleaner. "You don't even know me." They skate together for the bench.

"Maybe not well, but I want to know you better," he replies confidently.

He never gives up.

"I don't think so," she says and skates slowly off the ice.

"I'm telling you that I do," he says, following her to the bench. "Why are you not letting me get close to you?"

Eileen sits on the bench and unlaces her skates. "I'm not. I'm giving you an honest answer." She grabs her duffel bag and puts on her shoes. "I've got to get back to work. I do have another job to get to," she reminds him.

"What time are you off?"

"I don't know." She sighs and zips up her bag. "Whatever time I get my work done will determine the time I'm home."

"Okay, let me pick you up. We'll grab a drink and dinner, and you can tell me all the reasons why we shouldn't see each other, okay? I think that's fair. I think I deserve to know your reasons."

"I can tell you right now," she says.

"I think you have more than one excuse."

"It's not a date," she reminds him.

Ty rolls his eyes, "Okay," he says with a sigh. "It's not a date."

"And how about we meet at a coffee shop for seven?"

Eileen swore that she didn't want to start a relationship with Ty and now it was happening, a relationship she wasn't expecting. A relationship she didn't want because it came with expectations. Didn't every professional sports player date a bombshell beauty, an ex-model or an actress? She was an athlete and not a woman who is comfortable with hanging off his arm like a charm bracelet.

The attraction for Ty Caldwell is real. She can admit she likes him, maybe a bit too much. If she keeps going with him, her fear is it could lead to further disappointment. Did Ty Caldwell make every other woman before her feel this special?

Eileen walks to her car feeling a bit light in her step, wondering if anything will become of them once this gig is over. When it comes time to settle into a relationship, she wants to be with someone who is willing to stand by her and be a friend as well as a lifelong companion. Was she wasting her time?

She takes out her keys from her purse and opens her car door. Her heart races as she zooms in on the note left on her window. She glances behind her to see if she sees the person who is responsible. She flicks the note off her window.

You have been warned. Only time will tell.

Only time will tell? Eileen asks herself as she drives away. Then what? Am I going to be physically hurt, again? Am I going to get fired? What does this all mean? Eileen needs to call her uncle Gary, a man who cares about her well-being, the only man she trusts, besides her overreacting brother, but that call will have to wait. She has to make a call to Constable Dundas.

Chapter 14

Eileen meets Kelly for a quick bite to eat. "Elle!" The warmth of a familiar voice shouts from the open restaurant door and the young woman in two-inch heels scurries to the booth.

"Hi," Elle says, relieved when her friend sits down.

"What's wrong? You're pale. Are you feeling all right?"

"I'm okay. Just got off the phone with the police. Those threats I was telling you about haven't stopped."

"Do you know who it is?"

"Not a clue."

Her friend sealed her lips in thought. "Can you trace the number?"

"I've tried. It's blocked."

"What did the police say?"

"Keep the notes, document the time and days I'm threatened. There's not much that can be done without knowing who it is. I just have to be careful. For now."

"Maybe Ty can be your bodyguard," Kelly says.

"Right." Eileen smirks. "You've probably heard the news, then?"

Kelly blinks, her eyes widening. "No, what news?"

Eileen sighs. "It's nothing then," she says, wishing she didn't open her mouth.

"What's the news?" Kelly presses.

"There was an article in the newspaper that said Ty and I are a couple."

"Are you?" Kelly asks with hesitation.

"No . . . no. I just thought since everyone else seems to be talking about it . . ."

"You can't be all that surprised, I mean, you are coaching the Warriors, it was only time before an article was written."

"I guess so," she says, opening her menu and skimming it.

"Have you talked to Ty about it?" Kelly glances up from the menu.

"Yes."

"And what does he say about all of it?"

"He doesn't seem to care," Eileen says sadly, folding her hands on the table.

"I'm sure you do though."

"Well, yeah," Eileen says. "How can I not?"

"So, what are you going to do?"

"I need to phone the reporter who wrote the article and ask him who the source was. I think it was made up. Who would tell him that we are going out? That's not much of a source."

"It must have been someone on the team. Maybe one of his teammates is jealous. You told me that there are always reporters there, trying to get a story, so maybe that's how it happened."

"I don't want a reputation. It's bad enough I went out for dinner with him."

"You need to get out more," her friend says, shaking her head. "You didn't do anything wrong."

"I have a job to do."

"The old Elle would have taken it as a compliment. Yes, you have a job to do, but you also have a life. You need to get out with the opposite sex and enjoy yourself."

Eileen lets out a breath and in a whisper, she asks bravely, "So what would you do?"

"I'd let it go and be flattered that I was picked as a candidate."

"Let it go, huh?"

"Yeah. That's what I would do."

The waitress comes by to take their order.

Eileen hands over her menu. "I can't pretend it didn't happen," she says, sipping her water. "I'm meeting him tonight for a coffee. He wants to talk. I can only imagine what that means."

"It's not like you slept with him, right?" Kelly asks.

"Uh," Eileen says, not sure how to answer her.

Kelly shrieks and immediately lowers her head. "You slept with him?"

Panic fills Eileen's face. She's not sure how to answer, since she doesn't want anyone else besides Brooke to know about her fling.

"You did, didn't you?" Kelly asks, her eyes large in disbelief.

Eileen can feel her face grow hot. How could she hide this?

"You can't tell anyone," Eileen blurts out. "Please," she begs, close to tears. "I don't want anyone to know. Please swear you won't tell anyone? It's horrible—I made a huge mistake!"

"Ohmigod, I don't believe it! I don't believe it!" Kelly squeals. "Wow! I didn't know you did that sort of thing."

"I know. I know. I can't believe it either," Eileen says regretfully, closing her eyes for a second and shaking her head. "What have I done? I can't undo this. Now he wants to see me again and I don't want a relationship with him."

"Why not? You're crazy! This isn't a bad thing. Stop beating yourself up."

"It won't last."

"That's up to you if you want it to last." Kelly's smile widens. "So, is he as good in bed as one might think?"

Eileen sucks in her lips, not wanting to brag about it, but it was good. Really good. "Yeah, he's pretty amazing."

Her friend bobs her head as though waiting for more information.

Eileen drinks more water. "Nobody knows about this except you."

"Who are you kidding?" Kelly asks. "If there was already a write-up on the two of you, there's bound to be more."

"I hope not."

"You can count on it," Kelly says. "I know you're second-guessing your feelings for Ty because of your failed relationship with Mario. But you can't compare the two. Mario was different. He was self-centered and didn't treat you like he should have. "I don't know how you stayed with him for a year."

"I loved him."

Kelly is right; the two are incomparable. But how can she not compare? They have similar personalities and professions.

"Look," Kelly says. "Mario is history. You have a new man now who is starving for your affection. Give him a chance. I know you want to; you're just scared of him being the perfect guy."

Eileen's face softens. "I didn't want to get involved with him."

"It's too late now."

"What do I do?"

"Look, you can pretend nothing happened, but what good would that do? You're better off enjoying this new relationship; it'll be good for you."

"We're not dating," Eileen says.

"Why not?"

"I don't mix business with pleasure."

"Please! You already have, so get over it! Now you have to figure out what you want out of the relationship. If you don't want anything to do with him, stop talking to him, or if you do—obviously you do—keep the relationship going."

"That's the thing—I really don't know if I should," she says, thinking about the threats.

"It's not hard, Elle. Do you like him or not?"

That question was embedded in her mind long after she left the restaurant and headed over to a coffee shop to meet Ty.

Eileen gets there early to finish up on some lesson plans before having a serious conversation with Ty about their relationship and where it is headed.

She's glad they're not meeting at a pub since that would require a few drinks and a few promises she wasn't sure she could keep. A clear mind is what she needs. What is she going to tell Ty? She is attracted to him, but doesn't want anything to do with him? It sounds crazier the more she thinks about him. It's hard to be involved romantically, while it poses a threat to her dream job.

"Is this seat taken?" a male voice asks and Eileen looks up from her day timer. Ty is standing in front of her casually with his charming smile.

"Now it is," she says, and he pulls the chair out from under the table.

"Coffee?" he asks, holding on to the back of the chair.

She lifts her cup toward him. "No, thanks. I still have some."

"I'll be right back." He leaves and comes back with a large coffee, two chocolate brownie desserts, and two forks dangling from his thumb. He sets down the coffee first and then the two plates. "Not much of a date if we buy our own coffees, is it? I had to buy dessert."

She clears off the table and places her work back in her bag on the floor beside her. "I had some things to finish up." She sits up and takes a drink of her warm coffee.

"Still working?" he asks lightly.

"I have three new classes starting this week and had some new ideas I could teach."

He slices off a bite of brownie and holds it up to his mouth. "You're a hard worker, Ms. Francis."

"I care about what I do."

He swallows the chocolaty dessert and says, "And it shows. Try your dessert. I can't eat two." He swallows a sip of coffee to wash it down.

She picks up her fork and takes a bite, enjoying the sweet and creamy taste of the icing. "That's how you succeed, right? Working hard pays off." She takes a drink.

"Yes, it does," he says, taking a sip. "Do you like what you do? Teaching kids?"

"Yeah, I do. I've always been able to coach."

"You keep pretty busy."

"By choice." She takes another bite of her brownie, enjoying the satisfaction of sweetness. "It's supposed to keep me out of trouble."

"No wonder you don't want a relationship."

Her head shoots up from the plate. "I never said that I don't."

"Yes, you did."

"No, I didn't. I said I don't want to mix business with pleasure."

"Nobody cares if we date or not." He puts down his fork with one bite to go.

"I care. Ted cares. He'll fire me if he knows about us. Besides, this isn't a permanent job," she reminds him. "I'll be around for three months, tops. We're already into the second month."

"So, where does this lead us? We can be more secretive if that's what you want. I'm fine with that. It could be interesting, listening to people talk and us denying it. . . ."

"We tried that and you couldn't keep it a secret." Why did this have to be so hard? Why couldn't he understand that if they just waited a few months everything would be fine?

"If that's what you want, to keep it a secret, I'm in." Ty sounds so sure of himself.

"Can we take a break?" she finds herself saying and then suddenly bites her lip.

Ty laughs. "We just started something and you need a break?" There's an intensity in his voice, and she knows she caught a nerve. She can see it in his eyes. He's not happy.

"Just until I'm finished with my job and then we will."

"What you're saying is you want to be single until your job is over."

Eileen's face drops. Maybe she was single for a bit too long and she is now set in her ways, doing what she wants to do and being who she wants to be. Then Ty comes along and makes her feel attractive and wanted, a person she never thought she was capable of being, and he's calling her out, telling her it's his way or nothing.

"What am I to you?" There is a hint of sadness in his voice. "A toy you play with and then put away until it's convenient for you?"

She gasps and glances around her to see who is listening. That's all she needs, someone reporting to the media that Eileen and Ty are having a falling out. "No, that's not true at all!" she interjects.

Ty takes his coffee in hand, swallows a gulp, and stands up. "Elle, I really like you, but I can't be on a string. That's not me. I guess we're on a break until your contract is over," he says, firmly.

"I don't have a contract," she whispers. She wishes she could stop him, but she can't because this is all her fault. She didn't want a relationship in the first place, and now that Ty was breaking it off she wasn't ready to accept it.

"Then whenever is convenient for you." He walks out of the coffee shop casually as though nothing is wrong. She waits for Ty to come back and tell her that after the job is finished she will have his heart, but for now she wonders if she will ever get the chance to mend a relationship with him. She closes her eyes for a second, takes a deep breath, and packs up her things.

Chapter 15

The Oasis Pub is crowded on Friday night. The music is loud and most of the women are all dressed to please a man's eye: short skirts, high heels, and tight tops. If Eileen didn't know better, she would have thought she was at the Midnight Oil, a strip club downtown. Not that she had ever been to such a place, but she is feeling rather sophisticated wearing her straight-leg, dark denim jeans and loose cotton-blend top.

The waitress comes by to take another drink order, and Eileen then turns her attention over to Brooke, who is sucking on a straw, trying to get the last drop from the bottom of her glass.

"I'll get another one, please," Brooke says and then moves the glass over for the waitress to take with her.

Eileen hears her cell phone vibrating so she reaches for her purse that's hung on her chair and takes out her phone.

Elle, it's Mario, I've been thinking of you. Call me . . .

"What's wrong?" Brooke asks as she studies her friend's face.

"That's weird," Eileen says, staring at her phone. "I just got a text from Mario. Strange. Haven't heard from him in what, two years?"

"Maybe he's heard about you and Ty and now he's jealous," her friend says mischievously. "I've heard that some guys want a woman back when they see their ex with somebody else. What are you going to do about Ty?" Brooke asks, taking a sip from her straw.

"I don't know," Eileen muses. "Ty seems really persistent in wanting a relationship with me. Although I told him we can't see each other anymore."

"You've been seeing him for weeks and now you want to call it quits? Guys don't get that. He likes you! He's probably scared to lose you if you both cool it off."

"You think so?"

"If you really care about him . . ." Brooke looks at her friend. "You do, don't you?"

Eileen smiles instead of answering.

"Okay then, you have strong feelings for Ty. There is nothing wrong with having a relationship with someone you care about, even if you did meet him at work. It's not a big deal where you meet the love of your life," she says. "Call it fate. If it's meant to be, then it will work itself out."

Eileen's phone buzzes and she jumps to answer it.

"It's Mario again: 'Do I have the right number?' How do I respond? He's obviously waiting to hear back from me."

"Find out what he wants."

"I'm not sure it's such a good idea." Eileen puts down her phone and takes a drink from her straw.

"Why not? I'm curious what he wants."

"I know you are, but I have to figure out what's going on between Ty and me first. If Ty finds out I was in touch with my ex-boyfriend, that doesn't look good either, especially since it's Mario. Every time Ty says his name it's like he's annoyed by him or something."

"No, but this is harmless. You're not jumping into bed with Mario. There's no reason why Ty needs to know anyway."

"True." Eileen sucks in a breath as though she is making a big decision and then picks up her phone and texts Mario back.

You've got the right number. I did miss you, she texts, **but it's been two years! What's up???**

She hits send. Does he want her back? She puts her phone down on the table. "I don't get it. Suddenly he's texting me? It's been a long time and suddenly he misses me? It seems kind of strange."

"Maybe he's lonely and you came into his thoughts," Brooke says, trying not to laugh.

"Jeez, thanks. That makes me feel better." Her eyes drop to the table, where her phone is buzzing. She picks it up and reads it aloud:

I've always missed you. I'm just sorry how we ended things. Call me, I want to hear from you.

"Well, are you going to call him?" Brooke asks with eagerness.

"I don't know . . ." Eileen says, puckering her lips. "Should I? He's probably bored and looking for attention." She grips her phone, trying to decide whether to call Mario or just forget about him.

"Speaking of attention," Brooke says and sits up straighter, pulling her long blonde hair in front of her. She plucks through the strands looking for split ends. "I need your opinion," she says and then combs her fingers through her mane and tosses it behind her. Brooke folds her hands on the table so that she looks prim and proper, like a young girl who's gone to boarding school. "I was thinking of getting Botox on my lips to make them fuller," she says, puckering up. "And getting liposuction on my thighs."

Eileen squints her eyes as though missing something in the conversation. "What for? You're selling purses, not your body. What makes you think that having bigger lips and thinner thighs will help you sell your product?"

"I want to feel refreshed and new," Brooke says, lifting up her shoulders and tilting her head to the side. "I need to feel like I'm one of those Mary Kay ladies, you know? Walking around like I just won the lottery, feeling glamorous and princess-like. Besides, I need a change."

Eileen slouches, resting her elbows on the table, cuddling her drink. "Why not go to the spa for a facial and pedicure if you want to feel refreshed? Or go to the gym if you want a change?" Eileen asks. "That's what normal people do. And it would be cheaper, plus the results are guaranteed."

"The gym takes work," Brooke whines and pouts her lips. "So, you don't think it's a good idea? What about getting just my lips done? Men love full lips."

Eileen makes a face and says, "I'm sure you can buy a lipstick that does the same thing, can't you? And it won't cost you a month's wage."

"I don't have time to go to the gym right now, and if I get Botox on my lips and cellulite treatment on my thighs, it would feel natural after a while, wouldn't it? Waking up to thinner thighs and bigger lips? Besides, what woman doesn't want that?"

Eileen looks at her friend with wide eyes.

"Okay, besides you," Brooke says. "You're not exactly the average woman."

"What's that supposed to mean?"

"I'm not telling you something you don't already know," Brooke says. "Come on, you're not the type of woman who cares about feminine things."

"Yes, I do!"

"Elle, you don't care about shopping or owning a Louis Vuitton handbag."

"That has nothing to do with being feminine. It has a lot to do with priorities," Eileen says and takes a sip of her drink. "So, I'd rather not worry about makeup. If you want my advice about artificial beauty, you don't need it. Think about it. Whatever happened to natural beauty anyway? Women have forgotten about trying to look good by working out—instead, they get a quick fix at some clinic. Look around us. This pub is filled with women trying to look the same." She glances at the full tables. "They're all wearing low-cut shirts to show off their cleavage and a ton of makeup. My advice to you is if you want a change, make time to go to the gym, get a personal trainer."

"That's the thing with working all day, coming home, and designing and making purses. I don't exactly have a lot of time or a lot of energy."

"Of course not," Eileen says.

"Really, by the time I get home it's five-thirty. I eat dinner and sew, and it's time for bed. If I get a little treatment, it would help me look and feel beautiful so when I am selling my original designed purses. I'd look the part, you know?"

"And what's the part?" Eileen chuckles.

"Perky lips, thin legs, and good height—of course that would be thanks to my Christian Louboutin heels and a black fitted dress that I will one day purchase when I sell my collection to the highest bidder." She laughs.

Eileen arches an eyebrow and takes a sip of her drink. "Kinda like a game show hostess," she says. "Those heels are probably a paycheck, too."

"Some things in life are worth the money."

Eileen smiles. "Like a designer Brooke purse."

"Exactly!" Brooke says with joy. "One day, I hope."

"Well, I have to hand it to you—I think it's just a matter of time before your purses are in demand."

"You think so?"

"Sure! You're talented and unique—just what the fashion world needs."

"Thanks, Elle. Have you been reading *In Style* or *Vogue*, or something?"

"No, but your designs are one of a kind. I've never seen anything like them," Eileen says and then cradles her glass with her hands. "One of these days, you'll have your own store and you'll be shipping your purses all over the world."

"That would be nice," Brooke says with a full smile. "I'd love that. Maybe even go to L.A. or New York to showcase my work. Wouldn't that be fun?"

"You could be going to those fashion conferences and hooking up with some big company that'd be willing to distribute your purses."

"Ohhhh, wouldn't that be cool? Say, what happened to the purse I made you for your birthday?"

"I use it, but occasionally I like to use this one," Eileen tells her and glances at her faded black purse.

"That one is so old," Brooke says with disgust. "Didn't you buy it like five years ago on a clearance rack?"

"I don't remember exactly, but I don't care. It's leather and it will last forever."

"So will my purses," Brooke says with a tap of her hand to her chest. "As long as you take care of it."

Eileen looks down at her purse hanging off the chair. "I think it's fine. It does its job and besides, the purse you made me is really fancy. I use it for work or for dinner dates."

"That means you don't use it," Brooke says with a pout.

"I do, too."

"When?"

"When I had my interview with the Warriors."

Eileen reaches for her phone, which is vibrating again, and reads the message:

I'm coming to Vancouver. Can we meet?

"What? When?" Eileen shrieks. "Mario's coming here and wants to see me!"

"What are you going to do?"

"I don't know."

"Do you want to see him?" Brooke asks.

"Not really."

"Then tell him you don't want to see him."

"I don't think I can."

"Of course you can. It's never stopped you before."

"I loved him, Brooke. It took a year to move on."

"Elle? You'll always love him," her friend tells her before taking a sip. "It will just be a different love now because you'll never be able to trust him again."

"I wonder what he wants." She picks up her phone. "Maybe I've got it all wrong. What happens if this is fate?"

"It's not! After two years?"

"I don't know. It would be great seeing him again." She picks up her phone and texts him back: **We can meet. Where and when?**

"There," Eileen says, putting down her phone. Her hands tap the table. "He's probably trying to see if I would see him again. Why would he be coming here? Unless the Warriors signed him."

"Wouldn't that be crazy?" her friend asks.

Her phone vibrates again.

I'll let you know when I book my flight.

"I'm curious. What does he want to see me about?"

"What are you going to tell Ty?" Brooke asks.

Eileen's eyes widen. "I can't tell him about Mario. I don't want him to get the wrong idea."

"He's going to get the wrong idea if you don't tell him."

"We'll see," Eileen says.

Brooke makes a face.

"What?" Eileen asks. "It's not like I'm cheating on him. We're not even together."

"Yeah, right." Brooke smirks. "You're so in denial."

"No, really. Ty doesn't want to see me right now, anyway, so seeing Mario isn't cheating," Eileen decides. "Mario and I had something, and I can't figure out why Ty doesn't understand how the job with the Warriors is so important to me. I don't want to lose it. I was already warned by the owner to put a stop to it, but Ty doesn't get it. He thinks it's nobody's business if we're seeing each other."

"He has feelings for you, obviously," Brooke says. "If he didn't care, you wouldn't hear from him again."

"Yeah, I guess. It's just that he can't tell me who I can see; I'm not stopping him from seeing anyone." With that, she downs her drink and asks for another. How did her love life get complicated when she wasn't asking for it in the first place?

Chapter 16

After practice, the team disperses, but Ty hangs around, cradling the puck with his hockey stick. He skates toward Eileen with a crooked smile. "Do you wanna play one-on-one?"

Hesitant, she slows down and looks up at him; his helmet strap is hanging past his stubble-covered chin. How could she resist? "Sure."

"Good, I'm going to kick your butt!" Ty says and takes a slap shot, aiming for the net and getting in. He then skates to the boards, where there is a pile of pucks, and clears them with a sweep of his stick, getting them to center ice. She follows.

"Here's how it works," he says. "You have to skate around a face-off circle." Ty points to the far end of the ice with the end of his hockey stick. "Then you take a shot at the far-end net. Second time around, you skate around the next circle. The third time, it's center ice. We skate all face-off circles. Best score wins. Got it?"

"Yeah," she says. "I got it."

"Okay then. Whoever gets the most in wins," he tells her, cradling the puck with the blade of his stick, rocking it back and forth.

"What does the winner get?" she asks, trying to sound interested by managing a straight face.

With a half-smile, he replies, "Don't worry about that. I'll win." His smile widens and Eileen wonders if he's teasing.

"What makes you so sure?" she asks.

"I always win," he says and shoots the puck at the net. "Look at that, one point for me."

"That was easy. Even my six-year-olds can do that," she taunts him.

Ty glances at her, revealing his Caribbean-water-colored eyes and rosy lips that are perfectly formed, remembering how they felt against her bare skin.

He leans on his stick and says, "You think so?"

"Absolutely!"

"It gets harder," he warns. "The winner gets a date with me tonight for dinner."

"Hmm . . . and if I win?" she asks.

"If you win, dinner with me. It's a win-win situation."

"What happens if I don't want to have dinner with you?"

"Why wouldn't you? It's not like you're seeing anyone right now."

"There's a reason for that. People care too much that I'm here, and I want to finish my job with the team."

Didn't he get what he wanted from her? Can't he just forget about her until Ritchie comes back to work?

"Didn't we talk about this? I thought I made it clear," she says.

"I don't remember having that conversation."

"Of course you do!" She can feel her frustration grow. "At the coffee shop? You left because you didn't get your way."

"No, I left because I didn't agree with your answer and I'm tired of hearing what you want. How about what I want?"

She puffs out a breath. "You don't make it easy for me," she says, skating around the blue face-off circle. She shoots and misses. "Damn!"

"I get you don't want a relationship. I'm just asking for a dinner date." He skates off, takes a shot, and scores. They meet back at center ice.

"If I win this game, you have to make an appearance at one of my skating classes."

"That depends, kids or adults?" he asks.

"You can make a bet, but you can't play fair?" Then she says, "Kids," before skating for a circle. She shoots and scores.

"It's a deal," he says and skates off.

"I can't believe Ty Caldwell is willing to make a deal," she banters.

"I'll still win," he boasts and skates around center ice. Eileen stands at the face-off circle, watching his long, quick glide before stopping to shoot.

Eileen picks up a puck and skates around the circle. She winds up and, with all her might, takes a slap shot, firing the puck into the net. Trying hard not to smile, feeling like she's won the game, she tightens her lips, scoops up the puck, and gives a hard pass to Ty.

"I bet you didn't think you would be challenged, did you?" she asks, skating past him. Eileen doesn't want to admit it, but she is enjoying putting him in his place. She grimaces at the fact that she is able to make a professional hockey player work hard for bragging rights even though he's winning by one point. They finish off the next circle.

"Oh, Francis, I think you'll be going on another date with me," he says and then takes a shot. "Yup, that oughta do it."

"Not so fast, Slick. We have one more circle," she says, gripping her stick and eyeing the net. She winds up for the shot and with all her strength she shoots, but just as she slaps her stick down, she loses her balance and fans on the puck, hitting the crossbar.

Without a word, she skates to the red line and waits for Ty's smart-ass comment.

"Nice try," he says. "You're good competition."

That's it? Wasn't he supposed to say something like, "That shot cost you a night out with me," or "Had you kept your eyes focused on the net, it would have gone in."

Ty shoots the puck and gets it in the net as planned. He then skates after it to call it a game.

"I guess I win," he yells as he skates toward her.

"I guess so," she says, hanging her head.

"I know, it's tough when you lose, eh?" he jokes. "So where is it going to be? You pick the place, but a pub would be a good choice."

"You'll have to take a rain check."

"That's not the deal."

"Yeah, well, Ted warned me that if I saw you I'd lose my job here."

"He doesn't have the right."

"I know, but he will do what he can," she says.

"Eileen!" a voice shouts and she looks over at Steve, still in his tracksuit and wearing a straight face, standing at the bench and waving her over.

"Can I see you for a minute?" he calls out.

She skates to the bench. "Yes?" She hopes there's news he has a contract for her.

"Rick and Ted want to see you upstairs."

"Now?" Eileen asks.

"Please."

"Is everything okay?" she asks, trying not to sound concerned. She steps off the ice to unlace her skates.

"Just a quick meeting, that's all."

"Okay."

Ty skates over to the bench, leaning one elbow on the boards. "So, what do you say?" he asks, ignoring his coach's presence.

She glances up at Ty, holding a steady gaze, and she says firmly, "Not now. I'll talk to you later." She slips on her running shoes.

"Yeah, we need to keep our bet," Ty says. "Don't forget."

"Bet?" Steve says. "You two have a bet going on?" His face is childlike, as though he's missing out on something.

Eileen gives Ty a sharp eye. *Don't blow it.*

"Just a little wager," Ty says. "No big deal . . ."

Eileen puts her skates into her gym bag. "All set," she mutters as she stands and then walks away with Steve.

When they enter the boardroom, Steve tells her to have a seat and waves his hand toward the chair she sat in when she got hired. Is this going to be her chair from now on, like at the dinner table where everyone has assigned seating? Perhaps this is the start of her involvement off the ice.

She sits down. "What's going on?" she asks, looking at the emotionless faces.

Her heart races and her mind is scrambling to think of what this urgency could be about. It feels serious; the room is tense with stiff faces. Suddenly her stomach is feeling uneasy.

"Thanks for making it," Rick says. "I know you need to get to your other job, so we won't take up too much of your time." He's speaking calmly, as though he's performed this speech many times before. "Having you here has been great and we appreciate your skills and your superior hockey attitude, but most importantly your commitment. That in itself has made you a prime candidate for this job." He folds his hands on the table, where there are stapled papers and a notepad. He looks down as though gathering his words and then looks up to express his gratitude. "We have been pleased with your skills and ability to work with the team—"

Just get on with it! Will you? Just give me the contract and I'll sign!

"Unfortunately, as much as we appreciate your talent, we are under obligation and cannot keep you on board for the pre-game season."

"What?" She tilts her head, not sure if she is hearing what she thinks they are telling her.

"I'm sorry, Eileen. It's been a pleasure getting to know you, and I wish you much success in your future. I know you'll do well in your career wherever it will lead you."

She tries to comprehend what he's telling her. What did she do to deserve this? If only she pressured them into signing a contract when they first hired her. What are their grounds for getting rid of her? She missed that part.

"So, please explain to me," she says as she clears her throat. "You're telling me that my job here is finished?" She tries to keep her voice at an even tone so that her frustration and anger won't seep through.

The men's faces are like statues; they freeze, not uttering a word.

"And all along I thought I was doing you a favor," she concludes.

"We'll compensate you for the early termination," Rick says.

"That's supposed to make me feel better?" she says. "It's not about the money."

"We're sorry," Rick says.

"Me too! I've been here two months."

"I'm really sorry to have to do this," Rick continues. "But—"

"But unfortunately it didn't work out the way we had planned." Ted raises his voice, finishing off Rick's sentence.

"What didn't work out? I'm missing something here. You still didn't give me reasons for letting me go," Eileen pushes. "I think I deserve an explanation."

"Technically, we don't have to give you one," Ted says.

"That's not fair, is it?" Eileen retorts. "If I did something to influence your decision, although I don't know what that possibly could be, I have the right to know, don't I? I've been pretty honest with you and instructed the team the best way I know how, and without warning you tell me I'm done?"

Ted presses his lips together. All Eileen can see are his bushy eyebrows that sprout in all directions.

"Did I not do a good enough job?"

"No, that's not it. I wish I could tell you different," Ted says. "You know how this business is. It's not about feelings, and it's about sacrifice. We need to do what's best for the team—that's the sacrifice. If we worried about personal feelings, we would have a lousy hockey club, now wouldn't we?"

Eileen chooses her words carefully, not wanting them to come back to haunt her later in life when she has other hockey opportunities, if that is at all possible.

"So, let me get this straight," she says, controlling each breath. "Just so I understand where you are coming from. You're telling me I didn't do a good enough job? Is that it?" she asks, looking at their numb faces. "If I didn't do a great job, tell me. Don't you think I should know? I think I deserve to know. You can't get rid of someone and expect not to give them a reason."

"Eileen?" Rick speaks up. "You did a good job. You are doing a good job—"

"Now you've just confused me. I'm doing a good job, yet you need to get rid of me? I don't think my skills have anything to do with my termination."

"You're right," Rick agrees.

"I think I'm damn good at what I do. I instruct skills that are worthy in a game situation. I work one-on-one with players, giving them tips and suggestions. I encourage and expect only the best from each of them, I—"

"Eileen?" Rick says.

"I study the game and work with other coaches to master a particular skill—"

"Eileen?"

"I'm always looking for more interesting ways to teach and I love to share the skills I have with others."

"Eileen," Rick says again, but this time in a more assertive and direct tone that grabs her attention.

She looks at him, closing her mouth and fluttering her eyes, waiting for him to tell her if she doesn't leave now, security will be here shortly to haul her out of the building. *Oh, no, this is it. This is when he's going to tell me it's unprofessional to have a relationship with a coworker.*

"Ritchie's coming back to work," he tells her.

Her stomach flips with anticipation at the realization she is no longer a part of the team. "I thought he was taking at least eight weeks off," she reminds them.

"Yes, but it's his decision," Ted chimes in.

"I didn't know," she says softly. "Why didn't you tell me that in the first place? That is good news. I'm glad he's doing better with whatever family issues he had to deal with," she says and then releases a smile with relief. "Please wish him all the best for me."

Rick grins, his chubby cheeks dimpling and the creases under his eyes turn into craters.

"I'd like to call Ritchie and wish him well." Eileen stands up, and the men all stand to signify that the meeting is over.

"I don't know," Rick says. "He might need some time to adjust."

"Okay then, will do," she says. "Thank you for the opportunity. I enjoyed working here." She extends her hand to Rick, Steve, and then finally Ted. "Good luck in pre-season."

She can't get out of the building fast enough. Eileen heads downstairs, back to the rink to her parked car.

"Hey! Elle! Wait for me!" Ty yells as he spots her walking toward the exit.

Eileen stops and turns around. "Hey."

"What was that all about?"

"What?" she asks.

"Upstairs," he says, pointing up. "Is everything okay?"

"No, not really," she admits, wondering if the situation changed because of the way Ty feels about her. "I was let go."

"No way! Why? What did they say?"

"I guess Ritchie is coming back so I won't be needed, which is strange because I was told he would be out for eight to twelve weeks."

"Well, that's good that he's recovered so quickly."

"Yeah," Eileen says, nodding.

"Are you still up for a dinner tonight?" Ty asks.

"I don't think I'm up for much—"

"That's too bad. I was hoping you would join me for a drink and a decent Italian meal."

"That sounds more like a date."

His lips break into a smile. "I guess it can be. . . . It doesn't have to be a secret anymore."

"Not that it ever was," she reminds him.

"What time can I pick you up?"

She thinks about it before answering and takes a breath. "Six o'clock will be fine." She could use the night out.

"Okay, it's a date," he says, smiling from ear to ear.

"Yes, it's a date," she agrees, smiling back.

They sit across from each other at an Italian restaurant, which smells of fresh herbs, red wine, and old cheese. They order pasta dishes that are the size of footballs and a jug of sangria.

"What are you going to do now?" Ty asks as he forks a bite of spaghetti, wrapping it around to make a ball before popping it into his mouth.

"I don't know—continue teaching, focus on my hockey school," she says with relaxed shoulders, taking her glass in her hand. "I would like to play on a team again, too. I miss that."

He watches her trying to sip her drink, the piece of apple in her glass bobbing toward her mouth.

"I would like to refocus and take some time for myself. I haven't done that yet since my parents passed away."

"Maybe that would be good for you."

"I think so," she says, placing her empty glass down on the table.

Automatically, Ty reaches for the jug and fills up her glass. "For me, I either have a lot of people around me or nobody. It's strange. Sometimes, when I am on the road, I look forward to an early night just so that I can have time for myself."

"We all need it, time for ourselves. That's how we keep our sanity. That's when you discover things you love and want to pursue," she says.

"And what have you discovered?"

She tilts her head to the side, thinking of what it is that keeps her going.

"I don't need much to make me happy," she says and takes a sip of her wine.

Ty's eyes widen. "Oh, yeah? So, what makes you happy?"

"Walking dogs at the shelter, although I haven't done that in weeks. I've had no time. But I love skating, teaching kids. Of course it's a lot of fun. It's rewarding. I also like to stay home and put my feet up, watch movies and order take-out."

"Yeah, I like to stay home too, sometimes. Although I do like to cook on occasion."

Eileen smiles.

"Will you miss working for the team?" he asks, forking a meatball.

"Of course! It was my dream job. And I do mean dream, since women don't usually get these jobs."

"No, they don't," he says. "How do you think our team looks for the new season?"

"You're asking me?" she asks with a laugh.

"Yeah, your professional advice."

"Well, I think your team has a lot of strengths. You all seem to work well together, especially on defense. I think that's the team's strength, which will really help since last season your poor goalies struggled, not because they're not excellent goaltenders, but because it wasn't much of a team effort."

"This year feels pretty good. You know your uncle is a good guy. He's really encouraged me. He's a smart man. I guess that's why he's the senior adviser to Ted."

"I've looked up to him since I was a kid. You can always count on him. He's very dependable and will always give you an honest answer. I guess that's where I get my say-it-how-it-is attitude."

"You can tell you're related."

"You think we look alike?"

"No, not at all. But you both have strong personalities, and a soft heart."

"You've only seen one side of me." Eileen laughs, taking a bite of her saucy bow-tie pasta.

"No, I believe I've seen both sides now, and it makes me want to keep on your good side."

She swallows her bite. "Come on, I'm not a bad person."

"I never said you were. You're just strong minded and you know what you want."

For a moment, Eileen looks at Ty, his eyes glistening even through the dim light.

He reaches for her hand and gently holds her fingers in the palm of his hand. For the first time in a long time, she's really relaxed with him. She no longer has to hide her feelings for Ty.

They stare into each other's eyes for a moment in silence, and then Ty whispers, "We don't have to keep quiet anymore."

She laughs. "I was just thinking that."

"Really?" He smiles, showing off his dimple.

"I guess I'm over the fact that I am no longer a Warriors employee. No free hockey tickets this season," she jokes.

"I'm sure between your uncle and myself, we can manage to get you into all the home games."

She smiles. "It's not the same. It would have been nice to earn my own," she says, reaching for her glass with her other hand. "It's not like I have a lot of spare time anyway. I don't know how I managed without working for the team."

"I don't know either," he agrees. "But you'll manage."

She swirls her glass around, watching the orange slice hardly move.

"You must like kids if you teach them."

She grins, putting her glass down and thinking how happy her parents would have been if they could have one day seen her as a mother. "I do."

"Do you want kids one day?" He takes the last sip of sangria and puts his empty glass down on the table.

"Yeah," she says, meeting him eye to eye.

Ty grins. "How many?"

"Three or four."

"Really?" he asks. His lips curl up as though he's trying not to smile.

"At least three. I look forward to a family life," she says. "Hopefully one day I can experience what my mom experienced with my brother and me. One day. I'm still living the city life though."

"You and me both."

After dinner, Ty drives Eileen home. She undoes her seat belt. "Thanks for the date. I really enjoyed it."

"See? I'm not bad company," he says with a warm smile.

He thumps his hands on the steering wheel. "So what does it mean for us?" he asks, looking over at her.

She pauses, glancing out of her side window. "I don't know. I didn't think we would see each other as often as we have."

"You didn't believe we could date, is that it?"

"To be honest, I didn't think we would last this long."

He undoes his seat belt and turns in her direction. "I like where this is going, don't you?"

She studies his blond curl over one ear and his face, which is freshly shaven, revealing his rounded chin and a small scar on his cheekbone. *Hockey is a rough sport*, she thinks, but admires his competitive nature.

"So far—" But before she can say "so good," Ty leans over. One of his hands brushes the side of her face, bringing her closer to his body. Eileen closes her eyes, feeling his soft, gentle lips on hers. He breaks away and she opens her eyes as their lips part.

"I noticed you didn't hold back," he says. "You just can't admit that you like me, can you?"

"Very funny," she says, enjoying his touch and wanting him to kiss her again. She's been waiting for that kiss all night.

"Elle," he says softly. "I really like you. Just give me a chance . . . give us a chance."

She looks at him, not wanting to lose Ty or what they share, but she also knows the consequences of dating a man who spends half his time on the road. "I don't want to waste your time or mine. . . . That's all. We both have commitments, or I did have a commitment to the team, and that is the number-one priority, right?"

"That's what I like about you, Elle. You understand my job, and you're fun to be around. I don't know why we have to fight what we both feel," he says. "I can be myself around you."

She looks at him and observes the inside of his clean truck and his beautiful eyes, his sweet scent. . . . How can she not find him irresistible? She is falling in love with him, and as much as she is trying to resist him, she gravitates more toward him and doesn't know why.

"Let me walk you to your door," he says, getting out of his truck. "I want to make sure you get in safe."

"Are you sure that's all you want?" She jumps out of his truck and shuts the door behind her. "I'm quite aware of my surroundings tonight," she says, trying to make light of it.

"Just say the word and I'm yours," Ty says, grabbing her hand as they walk to the entrance. Ty follows her into the building and up to her suite.

"What makes a guy like Ty Caldwell want to commit to a relationship? Doesn't he have a list of women he plans to get with?"

Ty smiles as they wait for the elevator. "You're the only one on my list."

Eileen smirks as they walk into the elevator and presses the button. "Is that how you get women into bed with you? Tell them what they want to hear?"

"No," he says sharply. "I'm not like that."

"You're not?"

"No, I have more class than that."

They walk out of the elevator and down the hallway. "Really? Or is it a lack of women in your little black book?" she teases, getting her keys out of her purse.

"No, really," he says, trying to sound convincing. "Since you've been playing hard-to-get."

She turns her key in the lock of her front door. "Now that you have what you want, how does that change things?"

"You're admitting that we're dating now? That's good news and I'm sure the newspapers will love to hear about it." He steps inside.

"Can we keep it under wraps for a while? I'd like to go to work in peace."

"I think I can manage it," he says.

Eileen walks into her kitchen and stands on her tippy toes to reach for the top cupboard. She doesn't see what she's looking for, so she pushes herself up onto the counter. Ty watches her from the corner, staring at her with arms crossed like he's admiring what he's seeing. "What are you doing?" he asks.

"I'm looking for a bottle of wine. I'm sure it's up here somewhere."

"Here, let me help you," he says as he reaches a hand in the cupboard by her head. "Is this it?" He pulls out a bottle of merlot without any effort.

"That's it. I don't know how good it is—it's been up there for a while."

"I couldn't tell." He blows dust off the bottle and puts it down to grab hold of her small waist, taking her into his arms. She puts her hands on his broad shoulders until she has two feet firmly on the ground. "Where are your glasses?"

She pulls out two wineglasses. "They're a little dusty too. I'll give them a rinse," she says and places them under the tap to clean them off.

"You don't drink at home?" he asks, opening drawers, looking for a wine bottle opener.

"Not very often," she admits, drying off the glasses with a tea towel. Eileen knows what he's looking for, so with a glass in hand, she points and says, "The wine opener is in that drawer."

With little effort, he opens the wine and pours two generous glasses, handing one to her.

They settle in the living room. Eileen lies against Ty as though he's a recliner chair, holding her glass of wine up to her mouth. It's a blissful moment, and even though she lost her dream job, she has a dream guy. What more does she want? She still has her skating classes and potentially a franchise. What else does she need?

Ty brings his lips to her neck, kissing her in a delicate motion. A ray of goose bumps covers her arms and she squirms with enjoyment, trying not to laugh too hard.

"Looks like I found a ticklish spot," he says and kisses her again.

"I'm going to have to put my glass down if you keep doing what you're doing."

He takes the glass from her hand and sets it down on the coffee table. Ty then leans in to her and kisses her mouth.

She closes her eyes, rolling her head to one side, letting him kiss her more and explore her neck, feeling the rush of satisfaction come over her. Slowly he pulls off her shirt and kisses her shoulders, then her neck and the tops of her breasts. She can't stop him. Even if she tries, she loves the way he loves her—it feels right.

Ty lies down on the couch, pulling her on top of him, running his hand through her hair and kissing her deeply on the mouth. His hands run along the sides of her body and land on her back, securing her delicately against his hard chest. Their noses are barely touching when Ty whispers warmly, "I'm falling in love with you."

She bites her bottom lip. How does she agree when she's so scared of losing him?

He sweeps his fingers along the full length of her arm. Nervous maybe? Certainly he's said these words before.

He swallows hard and she watches his Adam's apple move up and down. "I think we have something special," he whispers. "Don't you?" He leans into her and begins kissing her earlobes and trailing his lips down her neck. Eileen grabs for his shirt and lifts it up, dying to feel the ripples of his well-worked muscles. He helps her accomplish her goal by reaching his hands across him and pulling off his shirt without doing a full sit-up.

She presses against him so she can be held and he kisses her passionately on the mouth, giving into her puckered lips and active hands that can't seem to hold still. She wants to feel all of him again, so she takes charge and opens his button, running her finger along his boxers. He continues to kiss her, caressing her body and running his fingers through her long, brunette hair. With one hand, he unclasps her bra and throws it to the floor. Her body tingles as he runs his smooth hand over her breasts before kissing each one. He slides off her jeans, getting to the moment neither one of them can resist. And as their kisses become more heated, their bodies connect in a way that is desperate and beautiful.

Yes, Eileen thinks. *I'm so in love.*

Chapter 17

A guilty pleasure. That's what Ty is, Eileen tells herself over and over again. In the heat of the moment she admitted she was falling in love with him, not because it was automatic, like saying, "I'm fine" when someone asks how you are. It came naturally. Eileen rubs her forehead in frustration. Feeling tired and bogged down at work, she tries to think straight. Her job depends on a clear mind, and yet Ty has consumed her once again.

She sits at her kitchen table, on the phone. "Uncle Gary, are you sure that Ritchie is not back at work?" she asks hopefully.

"I'm positive, Elle. I haven't seen him. I haven't been kept in the loop the past week. I asked Steve and he says Ritchie is not back at work."

"That's funny. Do you think there's more to the story than what they're telling me?"

"Could be, but I don't know for sure. Give it a few days and see. I'm sure Ritchie is just easing himself into things."

"Yeah, I guess. Thanks. I'll talk to you soon," Eileen says and hangs up the phone.

"I don't believe it," she whispers to herself as she searches the Internet for the *Vancouver Daily* newspaper's phone number. There has to be more to the story. She deserves to know the truth.

Eileen opens up a notebook and taps the pen on her paper, anxiously wanting to know what is going on with Ritchie Forbes. "Bill Braxton, please," Eileen asks when she gets the receptionist.

"One moment," the female voice says and transfers her call. After two rings, a man picks up.

"Bill Braxton here."

"Hi, Bill. It's Eileen Francis calling, the Warriors skating coach?" she says and then corrects herself, "or I mean ex-skating coach."

"Yes, hi, Eileen," Bill says. "What can I do for you?"

"I've got a problem and I'm hoping you may have an answer for me," she says, doodling on the page in front of her, suddenly nervous. "As you probably already know, I'm no longer the skating coach and the reason I was let go was that Ritchie has come back to work. However, I have tried to get in touch with Ritchie, but I am put directly to his voice mail and he doesn't return my calls. So I asked a dependable source and he says he was told that Ritchie is still not back from his leave. I want to find out the real reason they let me go, but I haven't had any luck with finding out an answer and I suspect there is more to the story."

"Huh, well, neither Steve nor Rick ever mentioned it to me when we were talking yesterday."

"It's like they're covering something up. I don't know what, but I would love to find out."

"It does sound a little sketchy. When did this happen?"

"After practice Wednesday."

"You instructed a practice and then they let you go?"

"Yes."

"What was the reason?"

"Ted told me he didn't have to give me one, and Rick said it's because Ritchie is coming back to work."

"I see," Bill says.

"And Ted said that in this business it has nothing to do with feelings and is all about sacrifice."

"Is that so?"

"Uh-huh."

"What does your contract say?"

Eileen lets out a heavy breath, disappointed in herself for not signing one. Nick was right, she should have. "I didn't sign one," she says with irritation.

"They usually work from contracts," Bill says. "I can definitely look into this. And there was no indication from the beginning that this position was for a short period of time?"

"No, I mean I knew I was covering Ritchie's position for at least eight weeks, but not less than that."

"Right. Well, I've never seen them do this before. Why do you suppose they've let you go? Do you have any idea?"

"I don't know. I've been trying to figure it out. I did a good job. I was loyal. My only guess is that it's because I'm female," she says. "I just don't understand."

"They knew your gender when they hired you. That can't be the reason," he says confidently. "And you're sure Ritchie isn't back?"

"Yes. Like I said, I spoke to someone—"

"Your uncle?"

She doesn't want to admit she heard the news from her uncle—she swore that she wouldn't tell anyone where she heard it.

"No," she lies. "But it was someone who is trustworthy."

"I see. It would be surprising if Ritchie did come back this soon," Bill admits. "I can look into this and let you know."

"That would be great, thanks," Eileen says. "I appreciate it."

After work, she changes into shorts and a T-shirt and drives over to the animal shelter, looking forward to her hour of volunteering since it doesn't require email or a telephone. All she needs to do is show up, take two or three dogs from their pen, and comb the streets of Vancouver. Easy. And she feels good about it every time.

Her cell phone rings and she blindly clicks on her Bluetooth with one hand on the wheel.

"Hello?" she answers.

"Hey!" Ty says. "How are you?"

"Fine," she says, staring at the car in front of her. "How 'bout you?"

"Great! Where are you?"

"I'm driving, just about at the animal shelter."

"I want to see you."

"You do?"

"Why do you sound so surprised?"

"I don't know . . ." she says, but the truth is they just saw each other last night and she didn't expect to hear from him so soon.

"I miss you."

"Really? You do?" she gushes.

"I do."

She can feel his smile through the phone, his upper lip curving in an Elvis grin. Did she miss him too? But before she can decide whether or not she should say it back to him, he gently says, "Would you mind if I came with you?"

"To the shelter?"

"I'd like to see what's involved."

"Why? Are you planning on volunteering, too?" she asks, ending with a laugh.

"Maybe."

"They're going to love this," she says, still laughing. "I show up with a superstar and they'll be all over you wanting your support and making it public. Next they'll be asking if you can donate to the cause."

"I can handle it," he assures her.

"All right then, I'll see you in a few." She hangs up the phone. What has gotten into him? Eileen doesn't mind though; she feels the same way. The thought of being in love scares her, but she can't help the feeling that is building inside her every time she sees him.

Ty shows up at the shelter and Eileen is relieved that the supervisor, who resembles a Havanese dog—long gray hair and tiny face—doesn't even recognize him. The lady hands over a bunch of leashes. "Eileen?" she asks in a squeaky voice. "Can you and your friend take four dogs, two each?"

Eileen takes the leashes from her hands. "Sure, we can!" She bends down to pet each one, scuffing their necks.

They set out for a brisk walk, each handling their own medium-size dogs.

"So this is what you do in your spare time," Ty says as they stroll the streets. "Why do you do this?"

"Who else will? I do what I can for these poor animals," she says, eyeing the mixed breeds walking side by side. "Look at them—they're so happy right now. Tongues hanging out." She laughs.

"They look thirsty."

"They're smiling!"

"You really do enjoy this, don't you?" he asks, making eye contact.

"I do. If I could take them all home I would."

"I'd love to have one too, but it wouldn't be fair since I spend a lot of time on the road. Maybe one of these days when I settle down."

Eileen looks at Ty. "When someone else's home," she says, thinking that it would be nice to come home to someone or something, even if it were just a mutt from the pound.

Her cell phone vibrates and she reaches for her pocket to look at her message.

I've booked my flight! Can't wait to see you!

She quickly snaps her phone shut and puts it back in her pocket. What would Ty say if he knew she was communicating with her ex?

Ty invites Eileen back to his place for dinner. She drives home so she can change into a pair of jeans and a colorful silk blouse, a little dressy, a little casual, and perfect for another date.

She reaches his apartment, parks in visitor's parking and walks to the front door.

The concierge nods his head. "Good evening, miss," he says and holds the door for her. "Which floor?"

"Twenty-eight."

"Whom are you visiting?"

"Caldwell," she says confidently. "Ty Caldwell."

"Very good," the man comments and leads her into the new building, which has a modern design: tall glass windows and a spacious entrance with a large seating area in the lobby.

"Thank you," she says, feeling the need to thank him just because he is standing there making conversation with her. She enters the elevator and presses the twenty-eighth floor, and within a minute, she is stepping out, remembering what door to go to.

Eileen knocks on Ty's front door. He answers, wearing a pair of faded jeans and a golf shirt. His hair looks messy, as always—his signature look.

"Hi! Come in!" he says, holding the door open and greeting her with a warm smile and a peck on the lips.

The smell of something fabulous cooking makes Eileen's stomach growl.

Eileen smiles at him and he bends over to kiss her on the mouth.

She lets him. After all, they are dating and he is now officially her boyfriend. Isn't he? Her body tingles from his touch; even when he lets go of her arm, she feels blissful and charmed by him.

"You look great," he tells her.

She wants to tell him he looks great, too, but that would sound unnatural and not as sincere, so she says, "Thank you."

Eileen takes off her yellow cloth espadrilles and says, "Something smells good."

Ty shuts the door behind her. "Thanks! Welcome to the Ty Caldwell kitchen," he says, imitating a dining room server. "We will be dining in candlelight this evening, miss. Dinner tonight features the slow-roasted cashew chicken over jasmine rice and asparagus, paired with a pinot gris."

She follows Ty into the wide-open space, where they stop in the kitchen. "Sounds delicious," she says, giving him an eye. "Did you cook it?"

He nods. "Can't tell you how good it tastes."

"I'm sure it does."

"And for dessert, chocolate mousse," he says, reaching for two wineglasses in the cupboard. "With fresh strawberries."

"Wow! Caldwell, I'm impressed," she says, leaning on the granite-tiled island as she watches Ty take the wine from the fridge, open the bottle, and pour two glasses.

He hands her a glass. "Here you go," he says and lifts his glass in the air. "Cheers! To a lasting relationship."

"To us!" she says, surprised how easily the words flow out of her mouth.

They clink their glasses together and take a sip, both letting out a satisfied sound, pleased by the brilliant taste that coats their mouths.

"Very good," she says.

"Not bad," he says, putting his glass down on the island and taking her into his arms. She holds his gaze steadily as though a powerful force were pulling their lips together. Ty runs his fingertips down one side of her arm. She feels his breath on her lips and is carried away by the firmness of his embrace. There is tenderness in every move. She follows him into the bedroom and lets him pull her down on his bed. His eyes drop from her eyes to her breasts. He slips the flowy blouse over her head and kisses her flesh along the silk trim of her bra. He murmurs the words, "beautiful" and "turn-on," not sure what he's saying. His head is at her tummy, exploring her crevassed abs. She doesn't react to his neediness, but settles back into his comforter, enjoying the touch of his lips against her skin. Why did she believe dating Ty was against her rules?

He presses his body into hers, completing their desire to feel loved, wanted, needed. . . .

As they lay in each other's arms, catching their breaths, she realizes this is more of a committed relationship than she planned and it feels great to be loved, yet she can't bring herself to say the words, afraid to have her heart broken.

Ty jumps up and says, "I have to check on dinner!" He gets out of bed and dresses as he races into the kitchen.

Eileen lies in his bed for a moment, dreaming what it would be like to live with Ty and share a bed permanently. The funny thing is, it doesn't seem like a crazy idea. She reaches for her bra and panties and, once she is clothed, wanders into the kitchen, where an aroma fills the air.

"It's been a long time since someone has cooked me dinner." It's been a long time since she's felt excited about a home-cooked meal.

"It won't be the last," he tells her, dishing out the rice and putting it into a serving bowl. "Dinner is ready!" Ty announces, happily taking the dishes to the table set for two. "Have a seat," he says, pulling out a chair for her and then returning to the kitchen to grab the chicken and his glass of wine.

Eileen can't help but smile. "Looks great!"

"Dig in!" he says, waiting for her to start scooping out the rice before he helps himself.

She dishes out a piece of chicken from the platter. "I'll have to cook for you next time, but there's no guarantee that my supper will turn out this delicious."

He tops up their wineglasses. "Timing is everything and dinner is always good when you have a glass of wine with it."

She cuts up her asparagus and before taking a bite, she says, "I think it goes with everything."

"I think so too."

"So have you seen Ritchie at work yet?" Eileen asks.

Ty swallows and brings his fist to his mouth, clearing his throat before answering. "No, I haven't. I heard soon, though."

"Yeah, I wonder what soon means. It could mean the end of the week or next month."

"Don't let it bother you tonight. Just sit back and forget about work. Drink your wine and taste Tyler Caldwell's cuisine."

Eileen grins. "I don't think I have ever heard you or anyone else refer to you as Tyler."

"Just my mom," he admits.

"And Slick? How long have you had that nickname for?"

He lowers his fork to the table and clenches his jaw as if not wanting to admit it. "I think it started when I played junior."

Eileen nods. "I don't think I want to know why you got that name."

"No, I don't think you'd want to know."

"Of course you've piqued my interest," she says playfully and then takes a bite of her chicken. She swallows her food. "I can only guess why you have a nickname like that."

"You know what guys are like when they get together."

"Yes, I do. Too well, I think," she says. "Where did you learn to cook like this? I had no idea you had a hidden talent besides hockey."

"That's right; you thought you were getting just a jock."

"I had no idea!" She giggles.

"My mom's a great cook. I have to admit when I'm stuck on a recipe, I give Mom a call."

"Yes, moms are wonderful," she says. "What's your favorite meal she cooks you?"

"That would have to be her cabbage rolls. They're to die for," he says, placing a hand to his stomach. "I'd love for you to meet my parents one of these days. My mom would love you."

"Thank you. That would be really nice," she says. "I am curious what they're like."

"My mom's easy to get along with."

"I'm sure she is."

Eileen's cell phone rings.

Ty stops chewing. "Is that your phone I hear?"

"It is," Eileen says, ignoring the ring.

"Are you still getting threats?"

"No, not since I was let go. Obviously it was someone tied to the organization. How else would someone know where to find me?"

Ty shrugs. "Coincidence?"

"Whoever it was, I'm glad it's over."

"Go ahead and answer it if you want, I don't mind."

"No, that's okay. We're eating," she says, taking another bite, fearing that Mario is trying to get in touch with her. When she swallows her food, she says, "Whoever it is, I can call them back. Look at that—it stopped ringing."

A moment later, Ty says, "I think I hear it ringing again."

Eileen stands up from the table to retrieve her purse. "Sorry, it's probably my friend Brooke phoning to tell me that she's sold another purse," she says with a nervous laugh. "Her business is picking up." Eileen opens her purse up and pulls out her cell phone, which is still ringing. "Hello?" she answers, a little irritated that it's cutting into her romantic dinner date. She knows the number and it better be important.

"Elle!"

"Nick?"

"Uncle Gary's been in a car accident. I'm at Vancouver General." The color in Eileen's face drains. Her stomach feels tight, her heart beats faster, and she brings her hand to her forehead. Suddenly the memories of her parents come to mind, her brother calling her to tell her the bad news. It was five years ago, yet some days it feels recent. Eileen remembers that cold November day. She came home late from the veterinarian clinic where she worked as an assistant when Nick called to say there had been an accident. At first, she thought her mom had a broken arm or her dad had some cuts and scratches. Nick was calm on the phone. He didn't alarm her or suggest that she should expect anything serious. She didn't even change her clothes. It was only nine-thirty; she could shower when she came home.

Eileen remembers parking her car in the first stall she saw and rushing into the emergency room, where a nurse met her to take her to Nick. It was like a whirlwind. One minute, she was walking down the hallway of the hospital; the next, she met Nick and Cathy, who were crying, at a waiting area. She knew something bad had happened. Even though her heart was telling her what she didn't want to know, the fear overcame her when Nick opened his mouth. It was a blur, all those emotions. The devastation and reality of her parents' death was nothing she ever expected. What hurt the most was that her parents were good people and were deeply loved. She was close to both of them. The car accident didn't have to happen. It was timing.

If only they left earlier or didn't go to the party at all, her parents would be alive. She'll never get over her loss.

She squeezes her eyes shut.

Oh, please let Uncle Gary be okay.

Eileen glances over at Ty, who is sitting at the table, not eating, but listening closely to her conversation. "I'm on my way," she says frantically and throws her phone into her purse.

Ty's eyes lift in curiosity. He sits back in his chair as though bracing himself for the news. "What is it?"

"Uncle Gary, he's been in a car accident. That was my brother calling me to let me know," she says, looking at him. "I'm really sorry, Ty, but I have to go."

"Don't be sorry," Ty says, jumping up from the table. "Let's go!"

They arrive at the emergency ward of Vancouver General Hospital. The room is packed to bursting, so they opt to stand outside for some fresh air as they wait for the prognosis.

Nick walks out of the ER doors to where Eileen and Ty are standing, embracing each other. Nick looks at Ty and then makes eye contact with his sister and says, "I thought I told you to be careful, Elle." His tone is bitter. There is no doubt he is disappointed that she's not alone and she's with a hockey player, of all people.

She breaks away from Ty and shoots Nick a puzzled look. "I am careful," she says.

"No, I don't think you understand."

"I do understand," she snaps, knowing exactly what he's referring to. "You don't have the right to tell me who I can be with."

"No, but someone needs to look out for you," he counters.

Ty cuts in, "Look, we're not here to fight—"

"Stay out of this!"

"I love your sister. I'd never want to hurt her, and I won't." Ty glances at Eileen, and it's a pivotal moment when she knows he feels the same about her.

"I respect that you are looking out for her, and as her brother, you should. Now, if we can all get along . . . right now, there's a man lying in a hospital bed, hurt and waiting for a prognosis, while we're out here arguing about who your sister can have a relationship with."

Eileen is distracted by her aunt walking out of the sliding doors of the hospital, looking distraught, no makeup on and wearing a long skirt and dress top.

"They say he's going to be fine," Auntie Lin says, exhaling a breath. Her eyes are teary. "He really had me worried."

"How is he feeling?" Nick asks.

"Okay," she answers, wiping an eye with a finger. "He has a gash on the side of his head, some bruising. . . . He looks rough, but he'll be okay."

Eileen relaxes her shoulders. "That's a relief."

"He really had me worried," Auntie Lin says again weakly, bringing her hand to her heart. "I can't live without that man. He's my life, my best friend. . . ."

Ty reaches for Eileen's shoulders and pulls her into his chest.

Suddenly Eileen has a better understanding of what it feels like to be loved by a man. She needs to find the time to tell him, tell him she was wrong for doubting him and to promise to never doubt him again. After she meets with Mario tomorrow.

Chapter 18

Eileen walks the pier at Granville Island, watching people peel off crust from their sandwiches and throw it to the pigeons. Summer is almost over, but one would never know from the public enjoying the sunshine. A busker plays the accordion and a clown entertains the crowd. She walks back in the direction she started from. Her hands are clammy, and her toes are moist in her sandals. She feels her cheeks warm with worry, as she looks around and wonders if Mario is a no-show.

She looks at her watch: quarter after two. He's not going to show. Did she really expect Mario to show up pleading for her to come back to him? He's probably done some thinking and is tired of sleeping with the same women over and over again so he's coming back to her to try and reconcile the relationship. Is it possible after all this time? What about Ty? She's in love with him and can't imagine life without him. Why didn't Mario contact her two years ago to say how he feels?

"There you are!" a voice yells out. Mario is walking toward her wearing dark sunglasses and a tight T-shirt showing off his athletic build. A thick gold band with diamonds is on his right index finger, his souvenir for winning the Stanley Cup last year.

Eileen turns to him and smiles with uncertainty. She lifts her sunglasses off her face to reveal herself and takes a good look at her ex-boyfriend. She is stunned by his saunter and easygoing smile. The

Mario she remembers is a tough-guy, hard around the edges, with lots of attitude and a healthy dose of self-assurance. He would raise his chin every time he made a statement and hold out his chest as though proud of his attitude.

"Hi," she says, smiling, staring at his well-formed physique and noticing his tanned skin.

If he thinks I'm going to take him back, I'm not. I'm not going to be his second best. I need to show him that I don't miss him and I'm much better off without him. Kill him with happiness, that's what I have to do, and don't forget to smile, lots.

"Sorry, I'm late. I'm so glad you're still here," Mario says. "I couldn't find parking."

"I was just about to leave," she lies, still studying him, his dark mop of hair, his thick eyebrows, and his white teeth, none of which are real—he's been wearing dentures since he was twenty-five after he got punched in the mouth in a game.

"I'm glad you didn't," he says, looking content and peaceful, not so uptight like she remembers.

Eileen smiles.

"You look great, Elle. Really good," he says, eyeing her up and down and then pulling her in for a hug and a quick release.

"Thank you. You look good yourself," she says, grinning.

"Lost ten pounds," he says, patting his stomach. "Changed my diet and my workout."

"Good for you! Congratulations on winning the cup."

"Thanks! A lot has changed. Actually, I've gone through a lot of changes since . . . since you and I . . ." he says, his voice trailing off.

"You and me both," she says quickly, saving him the explanation.

They walk together to find a place to sit.

"Would you like something cold to drink?" he asks. "I could use a lemonade."

"Make that two," she says, making their way to the walk-up counter.

"What have you been up to?" he asks, paying for their drinks.

"A lot." She's unsure of where to start.

"All good, I hope." He hands her a tall plastic cup half filled with ice, and they wander over to find a bench facing the water.

"Yeah. But I want to hear about you," she says, taking a sip from her straw. "What makes you travel across country to see me?"

If he tells me he's coming back for me, I'm not falling for him, no way. I don't care how charming he is. I'm with Ty now.

"I had some unfinished business to take care of."

"Really?" she asks, not believing a word he's saying. He never played for the Warriors so the only unfinished business here is to see her. "In Vancouver?"

"First of all, I really wanted to see you to tell you that I've missed you, Eileen."

He really does want me back!

"And I want to tell you that I'm sorry how things ended between us. I wasn't fair to you." He looks out onto the water filled with sail-boats and water taxis.

"It took you two years to realize that?"

"I know it seems unreasonable to come back here and beg for for-giveness."

"Are you begging?" she asks sarcastically and then laughs.

He shakes his head, grinning slightly. "Do you forgive me?"

Did she? For a year, Eileen has held a grudge against Mario and never thought she would see him again. Now he's sitting beside her drinking lemonade and she's stuck for words. If Nick were here, he'd want to knock him out.

"Mario." She clears her throat. "You hurt me," she admits. "I was caught up in Mario Visconti the romantic, charming boyfriend, not the tough-guy hockey player you're famous as. What you did to me wasn't fair—you really hurt me." Her voice softens. "I tried to forget, but I trusted you—"

Mario turns his body to face her, lowers his drink to his lap, and says, "I do feel bad. At the time I wasn't thinking of us. Unfortu-nately, I was thinking of myself. I guess the saying 'you hurt the ones you love' is true."

Her heart races and a pang of guilt hits her. She thinks of Ty. Love is such a strong word.

Eileen tilts her head toward him. She has to be bold now and ask him the question she has been pondering since she broke up with him. "Are you saying you love me?" she asks, finding her strong voice because she knows he didn't love her the way she loved him.

It takes a moment for him to answer. "Well, yeah, Eileen, I still do. Just because two people aren't together doesn't mean you don't have feelings still, right?"

"I guess so."

But he isn't acting like the Mario she was once in love with. He's acting distant as though he's a stranger to her now. Did he forget how close they once were?

"Mario, you don't have to say it because you think it's the right thing to say."

"I'm not." His coffee-colored eyes find hers.

She swallows hard, caught in a cloud of emotions. "Why are you telling me this now?"

"I've been in therapy," he admits. His head bounces slightly as though ashamed. "The doctor told me that one of the things I need to do is ask for forgiveness from the people I love."

"Oh," she says, trying to understand. "Really? Therapy? Why?"

"You know . . . I've had some personal issues over the years, trying to accept myself . . . been in conflict with a lot of people all the time. It's not healthy," he says, staring out at the water, unable to look at her now. "I've come to the realization that my life won't change itself. It will take work to fix it."

"What made you decide to deal with the issues?" she asks again, still trying to understand his point of why he needed to fly from Pittsburgh to Vancouver to ask her for forgiveness. "You flew out this way to see me?"

"Yes." He finishes the last of his drink, gives his cup a shake, and then tries sipping for another drop. "My girlfriend, Brandy. She's the reason for my therapy."

Eileen nods her head. "You're still with her?"

"Yes, we're engaged."

Eileen's eyes widen.

"Surprised?"

"Yes."

He laughs as he leans back on the bench. "Aren't I the marrying type?"

Eileen thought he was and would have considered him too if she didn't catch him cheating on her.

"I guess," she says doubtfully, clasping her hands together, although she feels relieved because she has Ty. She didn't want it to get complicated, but at the same time she feels a pang of loss. "That's fantastic. I'm happy for you. Congratulations!" She gives him a smile.

"How long have you known . . ." Eileen stalls, trying to remember her name.

"Brandy?"

"Six months."

"You knew that soon?"

"I did." He squeezes his lips together as though refraining from his feelings, and then he says, "When the right person comes along, you can't let them go."

"Huh," she says. She and Mario were together for a year and he never proposed.

"How are things going for you and Ty? You don't have to tell me, but since I'm here with you—"

Eileen shoots him a surprised look. "How do you know?"

"Word travels."

"No, really, how did you know that?"

"It's not a secret." He shakes his head. "I still talk to Mark Buckley. We met in Pittsburgh. What's the big deal?"

"I don't want people getting the wrong impression of me. I dated you and now Ty. I didn't expect for it to happen. I took the job with the Warriors because of the job, not because I needed a date."

"People who know you know the truth. I wouldn't worry about what other people think. How is it going?"

She knows he's referring to her relationship with Ty. She smiles. "It's going well. We really have something, you know?"

"I'm happy for you, Elle."

"Thanks."

"You forgive me?" he asks.

"Sure—I mean, yes, I do," she says, realizing now that Mario Visconti is the last guy she would dream of being with. As she looks into his eyes, she doesn't feel the tug at her heart that Ty makes her feel. She looks at her watch and suddenly feels a rush to leave. With a friendly hug, she says good-bye to Mario and wishes him all the best. What surprises her most is how easily she says it and how happy she is for him. If she stayed with him, he may never have become the new person he's striving to be and that in itself makes Eileen content and at peace with what is now their happy ending.

Chapter 19

"Good goal, Slick!" a voice praises as the team enters the change room after a four-two win.

"Thanks, man." Ty automatically tears off his jersey, feeling great after playing hockey with his new graphite stick and looking forward to using it in a real game. He didn't get too excited playing in the pre-season; they were like practice games.

"Did you know you were putting it top shelf?"

"Na," Ty says with a gentle grin. The locker room gets louder with excitement. "I was going for the five-hole, but changed my mind last second when the goalie closed in. Thought I'd surprise him."

The player laughs. "Nothing like faking out the goalie, eh?"

The head coach steps into the middle of the room, one hand in the pocket of his dress pants. "We're off to a good start, boys," Steve says in a big voice. The players pay attention as they change out of their gear. "We have a practice at home, a day off, and then a game against the Oilers. Let's keep this going. We came out strong," Steve says with an air punch. "We are strong and we'll prove we're strong. Thanks to Eileen—she's put us in good shape."

Bret snickers as he dries off his skates with a towel. "You have a good team, Coach. Don't think Eileen's the reason," he says, concentrating on getting the water off the blade.

"It's hard to admit," Steve says. "But the only way to win games is practice."

"How 'bout that, Slick?" a player shouts. "Your lady friend gets the credit!"

Ty rips the Velcro from his shoulder pads. "She knows her stuff—what can I say?"

"And you were against having her work for the team."

"Most of us were. . . . She proved me wrong," Ty says with a shrug as he takes off his elbow pads.

"I want to see the same hunger and confidence for our next game . . ." Steve says, heading for the door.

"It's too bad she got fired—"

"She didn't get fired," Ty says, peeling off his sock tape from his pads. "Ritchie came back, right?"

The player chuckles. "So they say."

Ty rolls the tape in the palm of his hands forming a ball. "He should be back. It's expected. Otherwise, Elle—" Ty clears his throat. "Eileen should still have a job." He throws the plastic ball in the garbage can, getting it in.

"One would think," the player beside Ty says as he unlaces his skates. "I haven't seen him. But then it wouldn't be the only lie I've heard."

Ty cocks his head, staring at the young defenseman.

"I heard Eileen got hired because Ted wanted to please Gary and it was an easy solution. The truth is, Joe wanted the skating coach position."

Ty's eyebrows come together. "What are you talking about? Wouldn't Joe want to be head coach?"

Thankfully the room was loud and distracting. The less he talked about Eileen, the better. He didn't want the criticism and banter that would go along with it.

"He used to be the skating coach for the Islanders. Didn't you know?"

Ty clenches his jaw. He thinks for a moment. Could Joe have had something to do with the threats?

"Maybe Joe wants the credit for our wins. He's getting overshadowed by Steve." The player chuckles to himself and takes off his chin guard, leaving it on the ground. "This team is full of surprises, isn't it? Next we'll be assigned a gym instructor."

"As long as I can improve my game," Ty says, grabbing for a towel and wrapping it around his waist as he heads for the shower.

* * *

Eileen drives home from meeting Mario when her cell phone rings.

"Hi, Eileen. It's Bill Braxton. I wanted to give you a call to let you know what information I've found out. You're right. Ritchie is not back to work yet—"

"I knew it!" she screeches, stopping at a red light. "What did they say? What were their reasons?" She leans forward to break away from the seat; she is hot from being outside and sitting by the water. "Did they admit it?"

Bill takes a breath before answering. "I was told that there were a couple of players who complained."

"Complained? Really? About what?"

"Apparently they didn't like the idea of a woman teaching them, but that's no surprise to you, is it?"

"Well, besides the whole 'female working in a men's profession' thing, I did a great job."

"I'm sure you did."

"I was only incorporating their talent into practice. I was encouraging them and helping them. Sure, I was tough on them, but that's the job. I needed to prove myself—you know, being a woman."

"I know, I know. It can be hurtful," Bill sympathizes. "It's a tough business and if they change their mind on who they want running the show, then they do it, no questions asked."

"You would think in this day and age that it wouldn't be a big deal." She steps on the gas and drives through the intersection.

"You have to remember that if there are players making a stink about who's coaching them, higher management will talk about it, especially if they're respected players. They'll do something about it."

Like making threats.

"They don't want it to affect their game, especially going into a new season. They want the team to be as seamless as possible."

"Whose decision was it to fire me?"

"I don't know."

"Ted wanted to get rid of me, I'm sure."

"I don't think so. He only spoke highly of you."

"Steve was on my side," Eileen says, her heart pounding. "I don't know about Joe. Did you speak to him?"

"I did."

"And?"

"He didn't say much. Clammed up when I asked him questions about you."

"What did you ask him?" Eileen needs to know. Did Joe have something to do with the notes, the threatening phone calls and vandalism to her car?

"If your coaching style influenced the team."

"What did he say?"

"He said no."

"Go on," Eileen says, sensing this could be the reason why she was let go.

"He didn't like you coaching. In fact, he said he didn't want you on the team."

She gasps. "I knew it!" Did Joe leave the notes? *Think again about your career. You'll regret it later.* By not quitting the Warriors, she got fired instead.

"Was there anyone else?"

"Uh . . . hmm . . ."

"Please tell me. I need to know!" Eileen says. It's not going to make a difference, but it would settle her mind to know that it really wasn't about her ability to do the job.

"Okay, I will tell you, but you didn't hear it from me, got it?"

Eileen grips the steering wheel so tightly her palms are sweating as she turns onto a street.

"First of all," Bill says. "I did hear from players that they didn't like the idea of you and Ty together. They said it was unprofessional."

She thinks of Ty and misses him while he's away playing a pre-season game in Anaheim. "We weren't together when I was employed!"

"You know the truth," Bill says. "I spoke to Joe and he backed the players up. He believes if you're coaching, what's next? Are women going to play in the NHL? Quote, unquote."

"That's crazy talk."

"I know, but that's what he said."

"Who were the players that complained?" Eileen asks. Whoever the players were, she would somehow confront them without getting Bill in trouble. She had to. What man would be so insecure about having a woman teach him that he would complain to have her terminated? They all know it was for a short time.

"It was Bret Thompson—"

"Okay, no surprise there, he tried crippling me on the ice. That guy has a lot of anger. Who else?"

Eileen's throat is dry.

"Fitz and Price."

"Okay." Eileen accepts she can't be liked by all.

"And I was told Ty had something to do with it, too."

Did she hear him right? "Can you say that again?"

"Ty Caldwell."

She smacks her lips together and rubs her eyebrow trying to absorb the hard news.

Why would he do this to me?

A stream of coolness comes over her and she is lost for words. Of all the guys, why Ty? Why? Why did he not want her there? She didn't understand. He knows how much the coaching job means to her. Why did he want to hurt her this way?

I thought he said he was in love with me?

Why would he do this? She has a lot to talk to him about when he gets home. She's just unsure how to tell the guy she loves she doesn't want to see him again.

Chapter 20

She's preparing for her usual Saturday routine of teaching at her local ice arena for her mid-morning classes with six- and seven-year-olds. It was a good way to clear her mind from her personal life and concentrate on the children who were there to practice their skating.

Eileen grabs her phone when it rings in hope that it's Ty. She hasn't spoken to him since his road trip. She looks at the call display and decides to not answer it even though she's missed him terribly the past two days. She needs to focus on work and get back into a regular schedule. She drives to the rink, listening to her voice message.

"Hi, Elle. It's Ty. . . . Can you call me? I'm at home for a bit. If I don't hear from you, I'll try calling later."

Didn't he get what he wanted from her?

She has been thinking about how to confront Ty and ask him if it was true, that he helped get her fired.

People don't hurt the ones they love.

Eileen skates around the rink with the puck a couple of times and then proceeds to skate all five face-off circles, forward skating and then backward skating, a drill she was taught to practice when she played in her younger years and she continues to practice. She does this continuously until her students start to make it onto the ice. Once her class is all accounted for, she instructs the students to skate laps to warm up. Eileen stands at center ice watching each student make the effort to keep up with the group.

"Can I have everyone along the goal line, please?" she yells and watches everyone skate in and stand on the red line facing her.

"Hi, class," she says, trying to sound cheery. As she looks at the smiling faces staring back at her, she finds joy in their inquisitiveness.

"Hi, Miss Eileen," the children say in unison.

She smiles at their effort, reminding herself that the kids are all there to learn and want to hear what she's saying. She can see their alert faces, taking in everything she is telling them.

"Today we are going to work on skating," she says, making her voice loud and clear. "First things first, you're going to skate with long strides to the other end and back." She emphasizes the word *long*. "Think about extending your legs with every stride." She demonstrates a lunge position. "This is not a race, so don't worry if other players pass you. Concentrate on what you are doing. Does everyone understand? Ready?" she asks, hearing the bench door open up behind her and then slam shut. "Go!" she shouts and blows her whistle as she looks at her surprise visitor skating toward her.

At first, she doesn't say anything; she just stares at him, thinking about what he did to her and how much it hurts, yet she can't seem to get past his blue eyes and dimple. Ty skates closer to her slowly, as though anticipating the moment. He is wearing black pants similar to hers, his hat is on backwards, and his blond curls are sprouting from the sides.

"What are you doing here?" she asks, keeping one eye on her class, trying to keep mellow.

"Hello to you, too. I thought I could teach the kids a few things," he answers. "Now that we're a couple, it doesn't matter if I show up to one of your classes."

Eileen keeps her eyes on the kids.

"Hope you don't mind," he says. "I tried calling you, but you didn't answer your phone."

She glances at him.

"What's wrong?" he asks. "You look upset."

"I am," Eileen says and then turns her attention to her class, who are all skating back to the starting line.

"Very good," she tells her students, who are all eyes on Ty. "Now this time, I want you to skate, making a sharp C-cut with your skate, like this," she says, demonstrating by digging her skate into the ice, making the sharp curve with clean indents. Her students are staring at Ty. "Okay! Stand on the line and let's see you try it with your right leg. C-cut," she says, getting their attention as she digs her skate into the ice again so they get the right idea. "Very good, now try it with your left leg. You're going to find that one leg might be stronger than the other. . . . Very good," she says again, watching the smiles on the kids' faces as they try to find their balance. "All right, that looks good. I want you to skate to the other end and back concentrating on the C-cut using only your right leg.

"You'll feel awkward at first until you get the technique in place. This isn't a competition to see who can skate the fastest; it's all about making a sharp C, okay? So, think about it when you're skating. . . . Go!" She blows the whistle.

"I like when you talk all superior. It's kind of a turn-on," Ty teases.

"Shhh." Eileen shakes her head. "Please, not here."

Ty laughs at her seriousness.

Eileen watches her class, ignoring Ty. She skates a couple of feet, paying attention to the kids trying their hardest to make it to the other end. "Good job, Tommy! That's it! You're doing great. Good job, Michael! You got it! Keep going."

"You're not yourself. What's wrong?"

How can Ty think she is not bothered that he got her fired from a job she only dreamed of? "I found out something and I just hope it's not true."

"What is it?"

Her class skates toward her, and she ignores Ty and turns her attention to her class. "How did that feel?" she asks the group of kids with a forced smile. "I noticed some of you were not extending your leg far enough. When you are skating, you want a long stride; this will give you momentum to skate using your legs as your power-house. Okay, now I want you to try it again, only you will be using your left leg. Okay? Let's go!" She blows the whistle.

"You didn't answer me," he pushes. "I know something is bothering you and I wish you would tell me." They both look at each other at the same time. He is leaning on his hockey stick, the blade between his skates. He hesitates before asking, "Are you pregnant?" His eyes grow wide, anticipating the answer.

"No!" Her lips curve into a smile.

"You're not? Whew! That's a relief, not that I wouldn't support you if you were. I just mean that I'd rather be married before having kids."

She nods her head. "I made a mistake," she whispers, watching her kids skate.

"If you're worried about us sleeping together, we're not seventeen and it wasn't a terrible mistake," he informs her, lowering his hockey stick to his side. "I don't know why you would think it was a mistake, but we're adults and we made a conscious decision. You wanted it, I wanted it, and there is no mistake."

Her face deepens with color. "You don't get it, do you?" she asks, unable to look him in the eye. Her stomach tightens, still in disbelief.

"Elle, you can't be embarrassed about it."

"It shouldn't have happened," she whispers, looking at the kids rather than at him.

"What's wrong? I know you don't sleep around with just any guy. I get that, and to be honest, I like that about you."

"That's what makes it so ridiculous. I had no intention of ever sleeping with you," she retorts in a low voice so that her class can't hear what she is talking about. The nerve he has to come here and discuss their problems in public. "Anyway, that's not what I'm mad about."

He furrows his eyebrows. "It's not?"

Her students skate back to the red line.

"Grab some water," she tells them and watches her students skate for the bench as she thinks about Ty, standing beside her looking confused.

"What's done is done," she says with determination.

"What is it, then?" he asks.

"I can't talk about it here." Her eyes soften and she feels weak thinking about his betrayal of trust.

Her class skates back to the goal line for their next instruction.

"Okay, we can talk after class," he says.

"While you're here, you might as well make yourself useful and show this class a few things," she tells him, trying to contain her emotions and focus on anything but Ty.

"I could do that," he says. "What are you working on after skating? Passing?"

"No, that's next week."

"Hmm . . ." He hums, thinking about what to teach them. "Well, you can have them skate circles like you were doing earlier."

"You were watching me?"

"For a few minutes," he says as he leans on his stick with two hands looking at the kids.

"How about a relay? Two teams?" he suggests.

"No, that doesn't really teach them a skill."

"I guess not, huh?" he says. "How about skating lines? That's always a good one to learn."

"Would you like to show them how it's done?"

"Sure," he agrees, watching the last of the students return to the starting line.

"You did a good job on the C-cuts," she tells her class. "Just remember to extend your leg. We'll come back to practicing the C-cut another time, but for now, we are going to practice stopping skills. This exercise is called lines. My friend Ty, here, will show you how it's done," she says, extending one hand as if to say, *Now over to you.*

One kid looks up at Ty with amazement, as though he's a giant. "Do you play for the Warriors?"

Ty smiles. "Yes I do," he says, proudly.

"Cool!" the boy screeches. "Are you going to be our teacher every week?"

"No, that's Eileen's job. I have games to play," he reminds them.

"Oh, yeah," the boy says with disappointment.

"Are you Ty Caldwell?" another boy asks.

"Yes, I am," he says proudly, leaning on his stick.

"Well, Ty's here today, so let's work as hard as we can," Eileen encourages, trying to turn their attention away from Ty and back on what they were here to learn. "Okay? Let's show Mr. Caldwell what you can do."

"Are you able to sign my jersey after class?" one boy asks, pulling at his jersey to indicate where he wants his signature.

"Sure," Ty says.

"Cool!"

"Let's talk to Ty after practice," Eileen tells them.

"I just got a Warriors jersey for my birthday," another boy tells Ty, his eyes wide with admiration.

"Great," he says. "What number did you get on it?"

"Thirteen."

"So you're a Keller fan."

"He's really good."

Ty laughs, enjoying the conversation.

"You know, you could give your jersey to Eileen. She's a real close friend of mine and she could give it to me to sign for you if you would like."

The child's face lights up. "That would be awesome!" he shouts.

"Okay, class, we can talk to Ty after our practice?" she asks with frustration.

"Let's practice lines," Ty says simply. "This is a drill I still practice. When you're skating, you are building up speed and when you need to stop, you'll carry a lot of force with you, so when you stop, you're putting your body weight into it," Ty says, showing them how it's done. "For this drill, skate to each line and stop on your left leg, so you'll be facing the boards," he says, pointing his stick. "Make sure you bend your legs and dig your blade into the ice. When you get to the end, you'll come back, stopping, facing the opposite direction. You got it?"

The kids nod their heads, starstruck by Ty's presence.

"Now give it a try," Ty says loudly and then looks at Eileen.

The children skate off. Some are more cautious than others, looking up to see if the hockey player is watching them.

"You're good with kids," Ty says, eyeing her. "I took notes."

"This is just a test," she says.

"Test?" he asks with concern.

"Working with kids tests your patience."

"Are you testing me?" he asks. "Seeing if I will be good with kids?"

"Not at all," she says.

"That's not what it sounds like."

His eyes study her for a moment. "So . . . what do you say we grab a bite to eat after this?" he asks and then lowers his composite hockey stick, letting it fall to his side.

"No, I don't think so," she says. "Sorry."

"I don't get you," he says, giving his head a shake. "I've never met a woman so, so . . ."

"Independent?"

"No."

"Compassionate?"

"That's not what I was looking for," he says. "More like the most difficult woman I have ever been with."

"Shhhh," she says.

"What?"

"I don't want the kids to know." Yesterday she would have told the world that they were together, and today she's glad she didn't, thinking of the embarrassment it would have caused her.

He shot her a look as though offended. "We're adults."

"I know, but still, I don't want people talking."

"If you read the newspaper lately, it's no longer a secret. Admit it—we've had some good times."

"Well, I don't want to broadcast it."

"Who's listening?" he asks teasingly and looks around him. "No one."

"Very funny," she tells him, then turns her attention to her students. "Good work. Let's play a game of scrimmage and then class will be over." She divides the class up into two teams, white jerseys and dark-color jerseys. She drops the puck at center ice and backs away from the play.

"So now that we've cleared that up, where do you want to eat?" Ty asks as he watches the kids skate hard for the puck.

"We didn't clear anything up," she says, watching the game. How does she tell him she knows that he was behind her job loss? The man she's fallen in love with has deceived her.

"Okay, we can talk after class . . . go for lunch . . ."

"I don't have time today." Is it better to forget him, forget about what they shared, and pretend that nothing happened between them?

"You're giving me the cold shoulder," he says. "I've never seen you like this before."

"I guess people change," she mutters.

"You don't want to talk to me anymore?"

"I do want to talk to you," she tells him abruptly.

She blows the whistle again. "Another point for the white team," she yells and picks up the puck. She looks over at the people watching the game, and even the maintenance guys are standing around watching. "Looks like you have quite an audience here today," she tells the kids.

"They're watching Caldwell," one kid says as he skates past them.

Eileen thinks to herself, *He's probably right*, but she tries to boost their self-esteem. "No way, they're watching you guys! You're playing a great game," she says, watching their smiling faces. "You have a couple more minutes before the Zamboni comes on the ice," she yells out and then skates backwards to lean against the boards.

"It sounds serious," Ty says.

"It is."

He brings his hand to his heart. "Now the suspense is killing me. I don't know if I can wait."

"Miss Eileen?" a child's voice says.

She glances down at the young girl.

"My mom is here to pick me up. Can I go?"

"Sure," she says and watches her skate off the ice and then waves to her mother. Eileen smiles at the fact that the girl is trying her hardest to succeed, reminding her of her youth and how desperate she was to learn in a class of all boys.

"Okay," Eileen says to the class. "We're out of time. See you all next week. Good work today!" she yells, watching the kids skate to the bench.

She watches the children leave the ice, one at a time, until the last one is sitting on the bench unlacing his skates. Eileen skates off to the bench, grabs her duffel bag, and takes her shoes out of the pouch so she can put them on. Ty sits beside her and does the same thing.

"Ty Caldwell?" one parent asks, and Ty looks up from unlacing his skates. "Can I get your autograph?" he asks. "I'm a big fan. . . ."

Eileen ignores their conversation and continues to untie her laces. She hears another person talking to Ty, and within seconds a swarm of people is talking to him and getting him to sign pieces of paper or their children's jerseys. Some even take pictures.

Eileen shoves her skates into her bag and tosses it over her shoulder. She's not interested in hanging around until everyone has their "Ty Caldwell" fill before starting an argument about why she lost her job.

She walks away from the crowd. Why should she stand around and wait for him?

He didn't care about her career or what makes her happy, so why should she do the same?

As she heads out to the parking lot and clicks off the alarm to her car, she opens the door and throws her bag onto the passenger seat.

"Elle!" Ty shouts, running across the parking lot. "Elle, wait!" His white T-shirt blows like a flag as he sprints in her direction. His hands are waving in the air trying to get her attention, his other hand carrying his backpack and hockey stick. "Please, Elle, wait!"

What does he want from her? She is the one who is mad at him and wanting to give him a piece of her mind. How can she tell him how disappointed she is? Would he even care? Does he even realize what he's done to her?

Eileen waits for him, leaning against the hot car, feeling the burn on her back. When he nears her, he stops and takes a deep breath.

"We didn't get to finish our conversation," he says, easing his backpack to the cement. He places a hand on his hip in a casual manner, holding his other hand on his hockey stick and taking in a deep breath. "What's bothering you?"

She crosses her arms, her skin moist from the September heat. All Eileen wants to do is go home, have a shower, and forget about Ty Caldwell for good, but the truth is, she can't, or it will be pretty hard to. He's on her mind every day, from the moment she wakes up, picturing his morning smile and heavenly embrace.

She doesn't want him to see her weakness for confronting him, so she tries to look everywhere but at him.

"I know why I was fired from my coaching job," she begins, looking at the skating rink in the background, anywhere but at him, and reading the banner hanging on the building.

"You do?" he asks. She can feel his eyes searching for hers, so she makes eye contact.

"Yes, I do," she says. "What I don't understand is, why? I think I'm pretty good at what I do—"

"You are."

"I like to think I'm good at teaching the sport. I've studied the game, I've played since I could walk, and I've played at the highest female level. I consider myself a professional and if I could play in the NHL, I'm sure I would."

"You are a professional. There's no doubt about that."

"It's too bad because I'm a woman, some men think I can't do my job," she says, glancing at him with a sharp eye, and then she breaks her stare and looks at the full parking lot, wondering where he parked. "It's funny because I'm not even competing in the NHL. I thought we've come so far in society. Manon Rheaume played a preseason game in 1992 for Tampa Bay. Sure, it was looked upon as a publicity thing, but still, she can say she played." Eileen takes a breath. "And yet I have all the credentials behind me and it's still not good enough for your team."

Ty lowers his eyes. "How do you know it's because you're a woman?"

"I know Ritchie isn't back at work yet and I was told that he was."

Ty's face is drawn. He holds his hockey stick with one hand, twirling it around with his thumb, nervous, perhaps, or feeling guilty? She wonders what he is thinking.

"The team would rather go without a skating coach than be taught by a woman."

"There's probably more to it. You never know, right? Don't let a few guys ruin your confidence. You know you're good at what you do."

Had she not been told that Ty was part of the decision, she would have thanked him for his compliment. The way he looks at her, she can feel him acknowledge every word and interest himself in the conversation, whatever the topic. He is truly an attentive guy.

"I guess you're right. I shouldn't let a couple of guys on the team ruin me," she says. "I knew it was going to be a bit of a challenge, but I figured since it was for a short time, the guys would be mature enough to accept me. The guys who complained are just big-headed and sexist."

"I don't know about that," Ty says. "A lot of the guys are just used to the same format. I don't think it had anything to do with you as a person."

"Really? It's obviously a personal decision if a couple of guys wanted me off the coaching staff."

Ty stops twirling his hockey stick and holds it as though it's his walking stick. "I can tell you honestly, Elle, it wasn't like that."

"Hmmm. You know more about this than you are willing to tell me?"

"Look, a couple of guys didn't see the reason for having another skating coach. We have Ritchie and we're professionals. Why would we need someone else telling us how to practice?"

"That's a bunch of crap and you know it. Come on, you have a personal trainer. It's not like you need to know how to balance your body on a workout ball. You have a head coach, not to teach you how to play the game but to help you improve by supporting you and encouraging you. You have a trainer to coach you through it because we all know that some days are easier than others."

"Maybe the guys didn't think about it that way."

"No, I'm sure they did. They seem smart enough and care enough about their careers that they would do anything to keep their jobs and to keep their bodies in perfect form in order to play well," she says. "I just don't understand a guy like yourself, who decides to flirt and push me to go out with you when you're the one who wanted me gone."

The color drains from Ty's face and he looks away, gripping his head with one hand, rubbing it as he does when he's in deep thought and is not sure what to say. "I didn't have any say in that. It wasn't me," he manages to say. He is trying his hardest to look at her, but she can't, and doesn't want to, get sucked in by his "I'm so sorry" eyes or "I didn't mean it" look.

"You can't fool me, Ty. I know the truth and I know now I can't trust you. I want nothing to do with you. I don't want to see you again." She gathers her thoughts, staying strong as she rehearsed. She will not cry, she tells herself as she feels her eyes mist.

"You can trust me," he says calmly, finding her eyes, and when he does they take each other in like tasting a glass of wine. "You don't mean it. I can tell you what happened," he says, sucking in a breath. "It's not what you think. First of all, Elle, I need you to know that from the moment I met you at the parking meter I knew I wanted to get to know you, and the more I did, the more I had to see you." He drops his stick to the ground and takes a step closer to her. "It wasn't me. I'm telling you the truth. I will admit I didn't want you on our team in the beginning, but that changed the first time I met you on the ice. Look, I didn't think they were going to get rid of you. Steve likes you, Rick likes you. Hell, the team hasn't said they didn't like you."

"Is that supposed to make me feel better? I'm out of a dream job because you couldn't wait a few weeks, a few months? You couldn't stick up for me when some of the guys complained? You couldn't have told Bret and Joe that it's only for a short time?" she asks, un-hooking her arms and letting them relax on her hips. "I thought you were different. I would never guess that you would do such a thing," she says.

Ty extends his hand on her arm, feathering her skin and then reaching for her empty hand. "Look at me," he pleads. "I didn't do it. I swear. I'd never want to hurt you."

She looks at him, letting him take her hand in his and says, "You did hurt me."

"I'm sorry," he says. "I am really sorry it turned out this way."

"You knew it was going to happen, didn't you?" she asks, holding back tears.

They stand facing each other in silence, and when Eileen doesn't get an answer, she lets go of his hand. "I have to go," she says and opens her car door, gets in, and puts her key into the ignition to start it up.

"It wasn't like that," he says, stuck for words.

Eileen ignores him. It's too late for an apology. She shuts her car door and reaches for her seat belt, wishing she listened to her instincts. Ty couldn't wait for her to finish her job so they could be together.

Where to next? Go home and eat Haagen-Dazs ice cream while taking a bubble bath? Or pour herself a stiff rum and Diet Coke? She had neither rum nor ice cream at home, and she doesn't feel like getting out of her car to buy some with her eyes starting to redden. Instead, she drives around town, wasting time. She has no other place to be.

Chapter 21

Eileen takes the highway home, trying to think of anything but Ty. The thought of him makes her stomach tighten and her heart pound a little harder. She never thought she would feel the need to be comforted by his touch; however, at this moment, he is what she craves most.

She turns into her condo building and parks in her stall. Maybe she'll just lie on the couch and sulk. She could use a little rest anyway, and if she has any energy, she could clean her apartment.

She gets out of her car, alarms it, and takes the elevator up to her floor. This is harder than breaking up with Mario. He might have broken her heart, but Ty crushed her, tore her heart in two, and stomped on it.

She makes her way down the hallway toward her apartment, thinking that she and Ty are done. Done like dinner, done like the end of a good song, done. Why did it have to be this way? Why? How did she get herself into this mess? Maybe it's because she had high hopes with Ty and wanted something more, a connection that could be more than a love affair, a deep yearning to be with "the one" who loves you just because. Like what her parents had: understanding, trust, and meaningful hellos and good-byes that always start or end with a silly pet name.

As she walks closer to her front door, she digs for her keys and is suddenly taken aback at Ty standing at her doorway. Her eyes focus in on him sitting down on the carpet, leaning against her door, his hat still backwards, his arms across his knees. Her heart begins to race.

"What?" She wonders how he got into her building. "What are you doing here?" she asks, unable to take her eyes off him. Her stomach knots at the thought of his betrayal.

Ty stands up to face her and says, "You didn't give me a chance to explain myself."

"I thought you did explain," she answers in a mere whisper. "You told me what you did."

He shakes his head. "No . . . no I didn't," Ty says. "I didn't know what to tell you at first, but as I drove here, I realized that you were right. I was being selfish, I wasn't thinking about anything else but how I could get a date with you. I should have stuck up for you. I knew Bret was jealous about us. I tried hiding it, but the guys bugged me, calling me out, saying I wasn't Slick anymore. But that's not me, that's not who I want to be. I want you, Elle. You changed that for me. I thought I could hide our relationship, especially after, well, you know, the first night together. Then for sure I thought you wanted nothing to do with me, but you still did, right?" he asks hopefully, lowering his head to meet her eyes.

She doesn't answer, but he continues, "I honestly didn't think you would be fired. Upper management rarely listens to Joe. He can be a jerk on and off the ice."

"Well, it doesn't matter!" she says angrily. "It happened. I no longer have that job and I will never get it back." She grips her set of keys as though it's a tension ball, trying to release the frustration, but it's not working. She's only left with indentations in the palms of her hand.

"I had no idea it would come to this," he says, tightening his lips. He steps out of her way, and Eileen inserts her key into the lock and opens the door.

"I'm sure you had some idea or you wouldn't have backed up your teammate's accusations," she says, walking inside, throwing her bag to the floor, and holding on to the door with one hand, keeping it wide open. She's not sure if she wants to invite him in.

He leans into her doorway and she suddenly feels short under his six-foot-one-inch frame.

"I like you, Elle, and I didn't intend to hurt you," he says simply. "You have to believe me."

She's trying hard to think of something to say, but she's overcome by disappointment and hurt. Eileen crosses her arms, admiring his broad shoulders and unshaven face. She takes a step inside and Ty follows her, closing the door behind him.

"I know it sounds crazy coming from a guy who didn't support a working relationship with you, but at the beginning I agreed with them because I wanted to be close to you."

"You got what you wanted," Eileen says. "It was just a night—drinkin' good time, and now that you got what you wanted—"

"Is that all you think I'm after?" he asks, sounding hurt and angry. "You don't get it, do you?" His eyebrows furrow.

"Maybe I don't," she admits. "But I don't want to feel used and that's how I'm feeling, used! I feel like the Warriors used me, you used me, my coworkers used me to get free hockey tickets and autographs, women are asking me to introduce them to players. . . . It didn't stop until I got fired. The treats stopped, everything stopped, and all because I'm not a Warriors employee." She listens to the quietness around her. "Funny how that happens."

Ty softens his eyes, reflecting on her natural beauty. "I'm not using you," he tells her. "Honestly, I'm not. I don't know where you got that crazy idea from. I've never made you feel used, have I?"

"It's not that you make me feel that way, Ty—it's who you are. You're more interested in going to bed with a woman than building a relationship with her. That's not me, that's not who I am, and I can't let you drift into my life thinking that that's all right."

"Nights together never felt like a night-drinkin', whatever you call it. It was something," he says, with a stiff upper lip. "You know, I could easily say that you are using me."

She throws her shoulders back. "Come on, why would I do that?"

"Exactly," he says. "Why would I be using you? If I was, I wouldn't have cared how you felt and I wouldn't have driven to your house to talk to you." For a second she wants him to take her into his arms. She even wishes he'd kiss her. To feel his lips on hers again . . .

"I have something to tell you," he says. "I admitted to Joe and Bret that I was . . . that you and I are together—"

"You didn't!"

He hangs his head. "It was one day after practice. Tempers were flaring, and I said we were together. Joe freaked out, said you could be fired. I stuck up for you and they didn't like it. He told me you had to quit or he'd tell Ted. I ignored him, and that's when I heard you were getting the threats."

"But I got them the first week I was an employee."

"All I know is Joe was furious. He really didn't want you hired in the first place. Ritchie is his friend, and if Ted and management liked what you were doing, it was possible they would have kept you on."

"They wouldn't have. It's Ritchie's job."

"But Gary and Ted get along."

"You think Joe was the one harassing me?"

Ty shrugs. "It's my speculation. He used to be a skating coach. Maybe he was jealous."

Eileen blows out a breath. "It doesn't matter now anyway."

Ty focuses on her long brunette wave that curves past her shoulders. "I'm sorry that it turned out the way it did. I wish I could take back the things I said. I was unfair to you," he says as he brings a hand to his chest. "I'm really sorry it turned out this way."

Eileen steps back and leans against the kitchen wall. He adjusts his hat in place and puts his hands on his hips. His eyes find her gaze as though he's going to confess to something that's been weighing on his mind.

"I know you're going to find this hard to believe, but I have always been in love with you. I have never felt this way before, and I have never told another woman this," he says, his voice pleading and soft. "I swear. I am physically attracted to you, and you drive me absolutely crazy."

Eileen is taken aback by his confession. Her lips pucker, holding back a smile.

"I can't get enough of you. I think of you in the morning, wishing I were waking up with you beside me. I thought of you when I'm at practice, even when you picked on me—"

"I didn't pick on you."

"You did, but I loved it." Ty takes another step closer and shuts the door behind him. "There are a lot of things I love about you."

Eileen's eyes glaze over. Her heart aches with the need to be loved again.

"You're strong on the inside but easy to love. And when you get mad, it only makes me want you more, and I love watching you teach the kids. You're good with children . . . and you don't take crap from anyone." He chuckles and then pauses and tries to be serious again. "I love the times it's been only you and me alone. . . . The times we share are special and when we're out together I can't take my eyes off you. I should have told you sooner."

"When?" she asks gently.

He shrugs. "I don't know. I had to tell you how I feel just in case I didn't have another chance."

"Another chance?" she asks with slight confusion.

"I want to keep seeing you—"

"But?" Eileen cuts him off. "There's always a catch." She braces herself for him to tell her there's someone else, but he still wants to see her. . . . The thought fades when she notices his guilty eyes. He lowers them and brings his hands to his sides.

"I got traded today."

"Oh," Eileen says.

"It happens. I was hoping they'd sign me on again, but I guess they have other plans. It's one of those things, you know? And unfortunately it's part of the job."

"I know it's part of the job, but I had no idea." Eileen's voice rises in fear. At least if she knew there was a chance for him to be traded, it would have changed her outlook about their relationship, but now this, this makes it even harder knowing he's leaving for another city and chances are it will be a plane ride away.

"I'm shocked too. Honestly, I thought I would be here for at least one more year."

"Where are you going?"

"L.A.," he answers.

"When did this happen?" she asks. Did he wait until the very last minute to tell her or did he know for some time?

"This morning."

"Are you happy about it?"

"Yes and no. Don't get me wrong—I'm okay with playing in L.A. I'm not okay with moving away from you."

Eileen lowers her head, frustrated and confused. How could a new relationship that's going so well end so suddenly? It is an end, whether they want to face it or not. How can they continue long-distance?

Eileen holds her hands together. "That's good for you, right? I mean, moving to a new team can be a good thing, right?" she asks, trying to be positive and hopeful for his future.

"I guess," he says. "I should have expected it."

"Good things happen when you least expect it," she manages to say.

Ty reaches for her hand. He steps closer and their fingers interlock.

"Call me crazy, but we could continue with us. We don't have to give up just because I'm moving. . . ."

Eileen looks up at him to meet his eyes. "How?" There are suddenly tears in her eyes. "How is that possible?"

They share a brief moment of silence.

"It's not supposed to be this way," she says. *Always losing the ones you love . . .*

Spontaneously, he smiles and says, "Move to L.A. with me."

"I can't!" she shouts.

"Move with me!" he urges, smiling, tugging her hands.

She presses her lips together. "Is this a spur-of-the-moment feeling?" She knows it sounds disrespectful, but she has to know the truth. Can she picture herself living in L.A. with Ty? Would they be moving too fast? Probably. They've only known each other not quite two months. Can they really move in with each other?

"No, I've thought about this before," he says. "I just wish this wasn't happening now."

"You know, those feelings can lead to disappointment," she says, remembering her past experience.

"Why are you being like this? I'm asking you because I believe in us."

She breathes in, trying to control her emotions. Why does Ty do this to her? She has always been strong, yet a part of her feels weak whenever he shares his feelings with her.

"I appreciate you offering," she says, trying to choose the right words. "But how do you know it will work?" She's trying to be realistic. Is he worth it?

"I told you, I believe in us."

"We've hardly been together two months. How do you know?"

"My gut tells me," he says. "I just know."

"This would be a huge step," she says.

"Well, you don't have to move in the same week as me. In fact, I still have to find a place, but we can set a date when you're able to move."

She tilts her head back so that she can see his eyes. They're warm and comforting, inviting yet playful. How does she tell him she can't move with him without sounding unappreciative and uncaring?

"I can't. I'm sorry," she whispers as though ashamed. "How would that work for us? I have my skating school business. . . . I don't know . . . and I don't know why this is so difficult."

He pulls away. "Because this doesn't feel right for you," he says, his voice cracking.

She looks at him with a sense of loss. Maybe it's better now than later when their relationship is serious. "No, that's not it at all," she tells him.

"Then why is the decision so difficult?" He keeps his hands secure on his hips, like he's anchoring himself for an argument.

She can feel his tension in his voice. Maybe it's nerves; maybe it's uncertainty.

"Because . . . because," she stammers, "I can go with you and everything will seem fine, but how long will it last?"

"I don't understand," he says, shaking his head.

"I knew from the start where this would lead," she admits.

"You can't stop how you feel, can you?"

"No, you're right." Eileen puts her head in her hands, frustrated and torn. It's just another person she cares about being taken away from her. Can she live with herself knowing they had a chance and she was the one who blew it? She finally has someone who truly cares about her and it's over as fast as it started.

"I guess I know the answer then," Ty says.

Tears fill her eyes. She wants him to hug her and love her more. Being with him is like a fairy tale and her heart is still in dreamland.

With disappointment, Ty finally says, "You don't have to tell me an answer right now. You can sleep on it if you'd like."

Maybe that's a good idea. She wouldn't sound so cold and uptight if she agreed to that.

Ty takes a step back. "I have to go. I've got to go home and pack."

She closes her eyes for a second, trying not to cry. Why does it have to end this way? Why is she letting him go when she doesn't have to? Ty is asking her to live with him, to take a chance, a chance that might never happen again in her lifetime.

"Think of it this way, Elle. This would be our own adventure. We would be moving to a new city we both have never lived in," he says. "It'll be fun, exciting for both of us."

Eileen forces a smile. Would she be happy? What about her job and her friends?

"We'll talk tomorrow, but I won't ask you again if you are coming with me. I'd hate to pressure you into something you don't feel strongly about."

She takes a second to think about it again. If she goes, where would she work? She would be living in another country—can she do that? But if it is just temporary, then why not? She still has her house here. She could hire a replacement for her skating classes.

"There's a lot to think about," she finally says, letting it all digest.

"I know, and it's asking a lot, too, but I know we can make it," he says, reaching for her and pulling her close to him. "We make a good team. So, think about it and let me know what it's going to be. The suspense is going to kill me."

Chapter 22

"I'm happy you're doing better," Eileen says. She sits across from her uncle at his kitchen table, drinking a glass of cranberry juice. "You look well."

"I feel good," Gary says. "I went out for a walk this morning. I was a little slow, but at least I'm up and moving around." He holds still, his whole body stiff as he reaches for his glass. "You know, Elle, you can come talk to me about anything, anytime. You and Nick are like my kids."

"I know."

"I miss having Keaton around," he says. "He said he read about you in the *National Post*."

"Is that right? I didn't think my life was that interesting," she says and then smiles at her uncle.

"A woman in the NHL is interesting," he says. "It's a big accomplishment, even after the fact. You should be proud of yourself. . . . I know your parents would have been real proud."

"Thanks." She swallows hard, picturing their faces.

"I spoke to Ted and Rick, and they seem to think Joe had a lot to do with letting you go."

"I figured so. He made it clear from the beginning he didn't want me there."

"That's no excuse. He shouldn't have done what he did."

"My car is fixed. I don't get threats. Things are looking up," she says, smiling at her uncle and noticing his resemblance to her dad. "It was a good experience. Thank you for putting in a good word. Coaching was fun and I have no regrets taking the job."

"You're like my daughter," he tells her again, sipping his juice. "You know, Elle, you should go after Joe for what he did. He should pay for your loss."

She thinks about her losses. It's Ty she has lost, more than losing a job and her reputation. She has lost a potential relationship with a man she loves.

"He won't admit it," Eileen says. "Besides, apparently Ty knew I was going to get fired and he never told me." Her eyes fill up, but she tries hard to hold back her tears. She stands up to take a tissue from the box on the counter and dabs her eyes. "I just want to move on from all of this."

"Ty wouldn't hurt you. I know for sure he didn't believe them. Joe can be inconsiderate at times. He and Bret are friends; Ty didn't have anything to do with it. I can promise you that."

"Are you sure?"

He smiles, still sitting stiff and upright. "Positive."

She thinks about this. "It just seems so . . . fixed. Ty wanted to go out with me and I told him I couldn't, we couldn't make it public, it's unprofessional . . ."

Gary tilts his head, taking in her concern. "All I can say is if you didn't work with the Warriors, you wouldn't have met Ty."

"No, I wouldn't have."

"How's it going between you and Ty?"

"Okay, I guess." Eileen wipes a long strand of hair away from her face and tucks it behind her ear.

"He told me it's going pretty well."

"When did you talk to Ty?" she asks with growing suspicion.

"I talk to all the guys. But Ty came to talk to me and asked what I thought of him dating you."

"Really?"

"He wanted to make sure I was okay with it."

"I'm not marrying him!" She laughs.

"He likes you a lot. You know, Ty surprised me. He has a lot of respect. He's a good guy. I thought it was nice of him, treating me like your father. . . ." He looks away. "I don't normally consider one of the guys for my kids," he says and glances at Elle. "He's a good fit for you."

Elle can't help but grin slightly, trying not to show her emotions, even to her uncle, afraid of putting her heart out there and having it broken for everyone to see.

"You know, he got traded," she says. "I have a dilemma. Ty was traded to L.A."

"I know. What are you going to do?"

"I don't know, really. He asked me to move with him," she says. "I care for Ty a lot, but isn't it too soon? We hardly know each other, but if I don't go, it would be over between us."

"You have nothing to lose, do you?"

"But L.A.?"

"I think you should follow your heart."

"And chase Ty down?"

"He cares about you. I can see how he talks about you."

"I know. . . . I care about him."

"Then you should go with him."

"Hmmm. When does he leave?"

"That all depends on when he's due to start with the team. I'm not exactly sure. My guess is right away."

"I don't know how to make up my mind. Can I leave everything behind and start somewhere new?"

"Of course you can! Maybe not right away, but you are a smart woman. You'll figure it out."

Eileen says good-bye to her uncle, jumps into her car, and drives off, feeling desperate to see Ty. What will she say to him? What is her plan? Can they carry on a long-distance relationship? Would he want to?

She grips her steering wheel, thinking she was getting used to him making cocky remarks and telling her how she turns him on with her quick wit. He isn't the typical guy she's used to. He isn't like other guys she's met or gone out with, and he definitely isn't Mario.

Eileen focuses on the road, convincing herself that she needs to know where they stand with each other. Is she going to be a pit stop when he comes to town, or is she more than that? If she gives up everything here, what does she have there? What does she want from him? That is a question that is hard to answer because there are lots of wants in her life, like a man who would be there for her and protect her when she needed reassuring. Eileen wants to one day get married and have children and teach her kids how to skate just like her dad taught her.

Eileen parks her car in visitor parking. Is this the right thing to do? Show up unannounced and expect him to take her in his arms and tell her that she's the only one he wants? Why does Ty make her feel wanted and important when she has nothing to give?

Eileen alarms her car and walks apprehensively to the front door, fidgeting with her keys until she decides to throw them into the purse Brooke made for her. How did she and Ty get this far? From the beginning, she thought the relationship wouldn't amount to anything—how could it? They have their own lives to live, even if the attraction is obvious. And now she can't imagine being away from him.

"Here to see Mr. Caldwell?" the concierge asks Elle when she gets to the lobby doors.

She looks up at him in surprise. "Yes . . . yes, I am. Unless he's already gone. I might have missed him, since he's busy packing and moving. . . ."

"I'll let him know that you're here. I'm sorry—I can't remember your name."

"Eileen," she tells him, recalling she never did introduce herself to him.

The gray-haired man turns around and picks up the outside phone. "You know what? I'm sorry. I shouldn't be here," she says, shaking her head. "He's busy. I'll call him . . ." she stammers and saunters back to her car.

"Miss!" he yells. "Mr. Caldwell is home."

She turns around. "Thanks. I'll talk to him later."

What is she doing here? What is she going to say that hasn't been said? Seeing Ty will only make her hurt more, knowing she won't see him again. How long can she go without seeing him?

Eileen unlocks her car door. She sits in the driver seat, unsure of what to do. She is numb with disappointment. Why couldn't she make up her mind? Why is this so difficult for her? She knew he'd get traded eventually; it was always a risk getting involved with him.

"Elle!" a voice shouts as she closes her car door, and a hand stops her, forcing the door open. Elle looks up and her eyes meet Ty's as though she just felt the first signs of spring. He inhales deeply, catching a breath.

"Hi," he says. "What's going on?"

Eileen doesn't answer. Her eyes soften and she glances at the ground, trying to find the words that will help her explain her actions.

"I'm so confused," she admits. Her misty eyes look up at him, and he takes her hand in his to pull her out of the car. She folds her arms to her chest, telling herself she can't cry. This is the last of Ty Caldwell, she realizes.

"I didn't think you cared," he says.

"I do."

His hair is messy. He's wearing his favorite hat backwards, flip-flops, an old T-shirt, and board shorts. His healthy skin glows, and his facial expression shows a deeper sensation in his eyes.

"Are you here to tell me you're not coming with me?" he asks.

She presses her lips together. "I can't," she says in a mere whisper.

"Why not?"

"I have jobs," she says as though he needs reminding.

He sighs. "Come on, this is the perfect time to quit. You can open your own hockey school in L.A."

"Where would I live? Realistically I would have to find a place. It would be a new life, Ty, and I can't just move with nothing." Her body aches; her eyes close. The realization is clear.

"But you wouldn't have nothing," he says. "You would have me." He grabs for her hands.

"Ty," she says, looking at him as though trying to knock some sense into him.

"You're on the road a lot. How is that possible?" She squeezes his hand.

Silence hugs the moment, and their eyes drift everywhere but at each other, hoping to find answers in the sky, down the road, on the rosebush in the parking lot. . . .

"Can we go upstairs and talk?" he whispers.

She doesn't know what that would accomplish; however, she follows him up to his place. They barely say a word until they're in his suite.

"You move quickly," she says when she walks through the door, noting the stack of boxes.

"I'll be in L.A. before my furniture."

"Looks that way," she says and walks into the open kitchen that is adjacent to the entranceway.

"I can't even offer you a seat—the couch is covered up with moving blankets. I do have a kitchen stool; it's in the other room."

"Don't worry about it, I don't mind standing. Besides, I won't be here long. I just wanted to clear something up," she says, bracing her hands together.

Ty stands with his hands on his hips like he is posing for a clothing ad.

"I don't want to come between you and your job, so I think it's best to just pretend nothing happened and we go our separate ways."

Ty moves closer to her and searches her eyes. "What? That's impossible for me. My feelings for you are stronger than ever."

"How can that be? We've only been together for a short time."

"I think we have something and I don't want to ignore what we have. I'm sorry that I have to move cities, but that doesn't mean we can't continue with us." He points to her and then himself.

"How? Really, Ty, how is that possible?" She can feel the fear and disappointment rise in her chest.

Finally, Eileen meets a guy she cares enough about, and he is leaving her. What happens now? Is it foolish to think she will ever find happiness with someone else? Is this the way her life is supposed to be played out? Being single, belonging to those singles clubs that go out every Friday night dancing together and then it evolves into dinner and then vacationing together on a singles' cruise? Eileen wants more than that. She wants a man home every night, a house that is well lived in, a hallway dedicated to family pictures, and children sitting at the kitchen table doing their homework after school. Would she ever live that life? It seems so foreign to think about.

As she sits pondering her thoughts, Ty gently asks, "What's stopping you from moving?"

"I have my skating school, and Brooke and Kelly." Is that all she has? She realizes that she doesn't have a lot. Eileen looks up to see his eyes and asks in a loving but sincere tone, "What would I do in L.A.?"

Her life is here, in Vancouver.

"I don't know," he answers honestly, dropping his face to stare at his bare feet. "I thought about that too."

"That's just it. I have my life here," she pleads.

He lifts his head, letting himself fall back against the couch. "Can you hire someone to take your place at the rink and open a new skating school in L.A.?"

"I wish it were that easy. It's a lot of work. It has taken me years to build up my credentials to get this far."

His mouth comes together like he's processing what she's saying.

"Let's be realistic," she says. "We both have our own careers. . . . That's just the way it is, and if we want to work around our schedules, then that's what we'll have to do. Otherwise . . ." She pauses and bows her head so that she doesn't have to look at him when she says, "We know nothing will come of this, not the way it is right now. I mean, we're in different cities, different countries. We'd be kidding ourselves if we think this can work out."

"Kidding ourselves?" Ty asks, falling back against the kitchen counter. His eyebrows lift in confusion. "What are you talking about, Elle? I thought you felt the same way I do."

"I do, I just don't like the way this is going," she admits. "You know . . . me . . . you . . . this whole thought of *us*," Eileen says with caution. Could they really consider themselves a couple? They've been together for such a short time, so what were they? Just two people, attracted to each other? "Would it really work?"

"Damn it, Elle! Of course it can! Why can't it? Why don't you believe in us?"

She walks past him, going to the window for a change of scenery. "Because . . . you know how it's going, and how can we sustain what we have?"

"It takes two people who are dedicated to making it the way they both want it."

"We're not talking marriage," she says softly.

He puts his hands on his hips. "I know. . . . Of course we're not. We're talking about moving in together so that we can see each other more," he says. "This can work, I know it can . . . unless you don't want it to."

"No! I want it to work, but we aren't twenty years old with nothing," she reminds him. "We're both established in our careers, and I'm not giving that up for a chance that this could or couldn't work. It's a gamble. A huge gamble for me." This is when she misses her mom, times like these when she needs advice. What would her mom say if she were alive?

"Look, I was leery about us dating—you know that. I was afraid that it would turn out this way, and now look where it's gotten us."

"You have to take chances, Elle. Had you not taken the job with the Warriors, we wouldn't have met."

"You're right and I don't know where this will lead, but I can't move with you. This is probably a good time for us to go our separate ways," she says, guarded in her tone of voice. She tries not to choke on the words when she continues, "It would be best for both of us, don't you think?" She eyes his messy do and two-day-old facial hair. "You have your life, I have mine. We're that odd couple. One wants one thing; the other person wants something entirely different." She tries to find a reasonable excuse, but she's not sure she has one.

Ty shakes his head. "I don't agree with you."

"No?"

"No, I don't. I thought things were good between us. I thought this is what you wanted," he says, pacing, rubbing his forehead, try-ing to figure out this situation they got themselves into. "This is what I want. Is breaking up really what you want?" He takes her hand and rubs the top of her hand with his thumb. The soothing, coaxing rhythm of his touch makes it harder to move on.

"It doesn't have anything to do with what I want. It's how it is, and how it's going to be when we're both living in different countries," she says, softly. "You have a busy career and are never around any-way during hockey season, and what am I going to do, keep doing what I'm doing and hope that I'll see you the next time you're in town? I don't want that. Besides, people change," she says, having a flashback of how much Mario has changed. "We'll hardly see each other."

For a moment, silence hushes their thoughts. He looks away as though ashamed. Neither one of them could have predicted their feel-ings and how much they both wanted to be together, but they are stubborn and neither one wants to give in.

"Come with me," he says, pulling her into him. "I mean it, move to L.A. with me," he begs, putting his arm around her. Their bodies are fully embraced.

"And live, where? In a city where I don't know anyone?" she cries into his chest.

"Think of it as a mini-adventure, a new city, a new job, a new life. . . ."

"That's a lot to ask of someone."

"That depends on how they feel."

Eileen looks up to meet his eyes. "It would be different if I had nothing to lose." Did she though? "Besides, as soon as your plane lands, you'll forget about us and move on."

"You think so?" he asks sternly.

"That's how it is," she says, trying to convince herself.

"You're wrong." He holds her firmly.

"Okay, then, what happens if you're only there for a year? Then what happens?"

"We pack up and move again. There's no foundation, you know that."

"You are on the road a lot. When would we see each other? You would have your place, I would have mine."

"You know, Elle, even if I wasn't traded, I'd still consider what we have."

She closes her eyes, trying to stop the tears.

"I just know we're meant to be together," he says. "Are you scared?"

"Of what?"

"Of me cheating, doing what Mario did to you?" he asks softly.

She closes her eyes again. This time she can't help the tears that are welling up, blurring her vision. But it's not why she's crying. She's crying because she realizes that she's going to lose another person in her life that she loves.

Eileen feels his hand on her back, rubbing it as though soothing her worries. "I'm not Mario, and I would never do what he did, I promise. You have my word." His voice is calm and reassuring.

A rush of tender emotions comes over her. She believes him.

Ty pecks her on the forehead and then brushes his nose against her earlobe, and he takes her head in his hands and kisses her deeply. His hands roll down her arms. He strokes her hair. "I love you," Ty says, bringing her chin up so he can see her eyes. "I've never felt this way about anyone before." His voice fades into a whisper; he clears his throat as though trying not to choke up.

Eileen fears more than anything that they will go their separate ways and he will find someone else to fulfill him.

"Where does this lead us?" she whispers, breaking away from him, searching his eyes for clarity. "Visit whenever you are in Vancouver? But even then they are very short visits, since the flight is less than three hours. I'm sure you'll go home the same night."

"You can visit me."

"How often? You only play here maybe three times a season."

"When I'm playing at home, you can spend the weekend."

"I suppose."

As much as she doesn't care about venturing off to see different places, the thought of spending time with Ty makes it seem exciting and fun.

She smiles at him, enjoying the thought, imagining what it would be like hanging out at the best tourist destinations and waking up beside him every morning.

"I guess I should leave so that you can finish up," she says, taking a small step backwards.

"I want you to consider us, consider what we have. You don't have to give me an answer now. It's a lot to take in, I understand." He glances at his watch and then looks at her. "I'm expecting a call from my agent. Darrel should be calling with the details. I'll be able to tell you where I'm staying."

He takes her hands in his. "We'll see each other before you know it."

"I hope so."

"I know so," he says gently as he stares into her eyes. "I guess this is it."

"I guess so," Eileen says, not wanting to let go of his hands.

"I want you to promise you'll visit me," he says.

"I will."

"And I'll call you when I know where I'll be."

Eileen relaxes her shoulders, tilts her head slightly to one side, and gazes at him, lost in a moment of doubt.

"When I find a place—hopefully it won't take me long—I'll call you to let you know where I am," he says, following her to the door. "I'll give you Darrel's phone number, just in case, for some reason, we can't connect and you need to reach me."

"Okay," she says, pursing her lips, afraid she'll cry. "I'm not good with good-byes."

"Neither am I," he says. "But it's not really a good-bye. Is it? We'll see each other soon and we can talk everyday if you want to."

She nods.

"It's not the same," he says. "But it will help pass the time until we see each other again. Why don't we plan on you visiting at the end of the month? It will be hot as hell, but they have air conditioning." He grins, showing off his dimple. She's going to miss those endearing looks.

"That might work," she says, not wanting to make any promises.

He leans his head back and combs his fingers through his hair.

"This is hard, Elle." He lets out a big breath. "I'll admit, I've never felt this way before." He walks in close and takes her in his arms and holds her in a lasting hug. "I'm really going to miss you," he says.

"I'll miss you too," she says.

"I miss you already," he says in a rush.

"Just a few weeks. And when we see each other again, you might change your mind. You might get sick of me," she teases.

"Never," he says. "I can't get enough of you. I'm counting the days until your visit."

"I already am, two weeks and one day."

"How do you figure?"

"Just a wild guess," she says with a smile, trying to sound pleased with her decision. Ty leans in and kisses her on her forehead, "I love you," he says.

Eileen can't wipe the grin off her face. "I love you too," she tells him.

Ty embraces her and kisses her hard on the mouth. It is exciting, yet emotional. Elle lets him kiss her neck and run his hand through her hair in a relaxed motion. Why did he make her feel so good? He is romantic and gentle, and knows how to make her happy. She wants him even more.

She lets him touch her freely, and as his hand slips down the side of her body, Eileen inhales. Tears prick her eyes as she realizes how much he cares for her and how safe she is in his arms.

Why did he have to be so damn good? He makes her feel beautiful and wanted. No one else makes her feel the way Ty Caldwell does. She didn't want to get this far with him, but she couldn't help it. There is a force that pulls her close and she lets herself fall into his arms.

Eileen smiles, looking into his eyes as though seeing love for the first time. She is really in love with him. Is she letting Ty Caldwell go? How easy would it be for her to move? It's not like she cares about her job anyway. She remembers what Mario said about his fiancée: *When the right person comes along, you can't let them go.* She has enough in savings to pay her own way. Then, without another thought, she blurts out, "I'm coming with you!"

His eyebrows furrow as though he didn't hear her right.

"I'm coming with you," she repeats. "Maybe not now, right at this moment, but I'll move with you once you get settled."

"What about your job?"

"I'll see what I can do about hiring a replacement if I have to."

"You're really okay with that? Your job is what you are most proud of."

"It's a job. I can't replace us." She exhales, holding back from tearing up.

Ty takes her into his arms, and her head nestles his chest. "We're going to have the time of our lives. I promise you." He squeezes her.

Eileen looks up at him; she has never felt so sure and complete as she does that moment. Living without Ty, she knows, would be the biggest mistake of her life and she's set to start a new life with the man she loves.

Dear Reader:

I started playing ice hockey when I was around ten. Growing up, I envied the girls who played with the boys and the women who played at the highest level. Their determination to be the best in the sport they loved resonated with me for years as I, too, only dreamed of being that good.

I still play ice hockey. I love the game and the excitement it brings to a city. I love a strong heroine, and I wanted to write about a female athlete who could play with the guys and be recognized for her talent.

In Canada, we pride ourselves on our ice hockey teams and their athletes are celebrities, so what better way than to add sex appeal between the hero and heroine? It was a story I was excited to write. There are many female athletes who play professional hockey, yet only a select few are heard of. I wanted my heroine to be feminine, yet hold her own and be a celebrity in her own right.

Once I wrote *His Game, Her Rules*, I couldn't say good-bye to the Warriors. There were other characters that I needed to write about. I began to think about other strong female characters that would be a part of the team. I imagined other players and the lives they could potentially live. Look for the next installment, *Cold as Ice*, coming in December 2014.

Thank you for reading my story. It's always fun writing about something you're passionate about. I hope you enjoyed reading my book as much as I enjoyed writing it. You can visit me online at www.charlenegroome.com.

Happy reading,
Charlene Groome

Please turn the page for an exciting sneak peek of

Charlene Groome's

next Warriors novel,

COLD AS ICE,

coming in December 2014!

Carla Sinclair skims through her notes as the buzzer rings, indicating the end of the second period. The Dome is a loud and exciting place for Warriors fans. Eighteen thousand people erupt, cheering them on. Tonight they're playing against Carolina, a team that isn't doing so well, which makes Vancouver's winning streak even longer.

Devin Miller, the Carolina defenseman who was on the ice for two of the four goals scored against his team, screened his goalie when Vancouver scored the first goal, and the second time he didn't cover his man, which left the net wide open.

Tragic. He's the best defenseman in the league.

Carla shakes her head. *Some defenseman!*

The Carolina players head off the ice and strut down the hallway, drawing their banter closer. She throws her notebook into her bag, drops it to the ground, and grabs her microphone from Randy, the cameraman. She arranged to meet with Devin in the corridor, where other interviews will be taking place.

Carla stands straighter, lifts the microphone under her chin, and wipes her other hand down the length of her pencil skirt. She waits and watches for Devin to walk around the corner. Her mind races with potential questions.

Carla sucks in a breath when a red and white jersey comes around the corner. He comes into view without a helmet or gloves on, no hockey stick in hand. A giant in skates—six-foot-two and two hundred pounds of muscle—Devin is even taller than she imagined. As he approaches, she realizes her five-foot-six-inch height—thanks to heels—only reaches his chest.

"Hi." Carla flashes him her TV smile. Her stomach flits with butterflies and she warms all over. Why is she suddenly nervous? She's used to speaking to male athletes, especially those as attractive as Devin. "You can have this." She hands him a face towel displaying Channel Five's logo.

He dabs his face, proceeding to run the towel over his short, black hair and down the back of his neck.

For a moment, she pictures him drying off after a shower as the water droplets slide over his tightly sculpted muscles. What would his hard body feel like against hers? "You, uh, can wear it." She blinks to return to reality and remembers to close her mouth.

His face is clean shaven and from what she can see, his teeth are all intact.

"Y-you can wear it around your neck while we interview."

"Thanks." He gives her a sturdy glance that weakens her knees.

She turns to face Gary, the cameraman. "Ready?"

He gives her a nod, and she begins by bringing the microphone into position and making a quick introduction.

"The last two goals were unexpected." She pauses, looking up to meet Devin's cinnamon eyes. "Can you run us through what happened with the first one?"

Devin wipes his face again with the end of the towel and puts a hand on his padded hip. "One of those things." He looks down. "I saw Keller with the puck. He faked a shot. . . . I tried to block it, but I was too far out and he managed to score on the other side." He sniffs, wiping the bridge of his nose. "The net was open."

"And the second goal?"

He shakes his head and takes a few seconds to answer. "Yeah, well, one of those things . . . the puck was loose, and we couldn't get control of it." He wipes his face again, holding the towel at his collarbone.

"I want to talk to you about your contract. You'll be an unrestricted free agent." She pauses to think of her question without the distraction of his wet lips. "With the end of the season approaching, are you planning on staying with Carolina or is a trade something you're interested in?"

He looks at the rubber floor and shakes his head. "I don't know." He chuckles, wiping the sweat from the corner of his mouth.

She waits for him to expand on his answer. Those lips of his are widening as he laughs again. He rubs an eyebrow and looks at her patiently. Carla is sucked into his gaze, again. She has to get him talking. There's one more minute left to kill before signing off. Carla wiggles her moist fingertips on the microphone, trying to air them. Her face heats. She gulps. Three seconds of silence wasted. Devin is looking at her now, urging her on with a stretch of his eyebrow. Her pulse intensifies as she scrambles to think of something to say. Anything. She doesn't want to look like a fool in front of Devin, or her audience, but she fears the damage is already done.

"Well?" She keeps the microphone up to his face.

"I don't know."

She inhales, giving herself a chance to ramble out something, anything, so she's not standing in front of him like the worst sports reporter he's ever come across, but Devin is the big deal right now and probably knows it. She swallows to moisten her throat. "Have you been approached by any teams?" She wants to break the story first.

Devin wipes his face with the end of the towel, revealing an eagle tattoo on his forearm. "I can't talk about it."

"I'm sure you can tell us if a trade is possible."

"I'll talk about the game, but not my contract."

She can't let him get away without hinting about his future. She has to know. Wants to know about the best defenseman in the NHL. "I heard a rumor you may be traded to Vancouver. Is there any truth to that?"

He shakes his head. "You're unbelievable, Carla." He laughs. "What more can I say? I told you I'm not talking."

"I'm sure you can tell me something." She stares into his dreamy eyes.

"No." He licks his bottom lip. "Are we done?" He steps away. "You're pretty good, Carla. You're pretty good." He hangs his head as he walks back toward the dressing room.

Carla puckers her lips and drops the microphone to her side. *I looked like an idiot.*

Devin disappears around the corner.

He's never gonna want me to interview him again. She pouts and blows out a breath while looking at her cameraman in dismay.

www.ingramcontent.com/pod-product-compliance
Lightning Source LLC
Chambersburg PA
CBHW021243260626
47155CB00004BA/1292